The Sheepfold

The Sheepfold

A Living Memorial to the Living God

Fran Lundquist

ACW Press
Eugene, Oregon 97405

The Sheepfold
Copyright ©2003 Fran Lundquist
All rights reserved

Cover Design by Alpha Advertising
Interior design by Pine Hill Graphics

Packaged by ACW Press
5501 N. 7th Ave., #502
Phoenix, Arizona 85013
www.acwpress.com
The views expressed or implied in this work do not necessarily reflect those of ACW Press. Ultimate design, content, and editorial accuracy of this work is the responsibility of the author(s).

Publisher's Cataloging-in-Publication Data
(Provided by Cassidy Cataloguing Services, Inc.)

Lundquist, Fran.

   The Sheepfold : a living memorial to the living God / Fran
   Lundquist. -- 1st ed. -- Eugene, OR : ACW Press, 2003.

      p. ; cm.

      ISBN: 1-932124-07-1

      1. Women's shelters--California. 2. Women--Services for--
   California. 3. Abused women--Services for--California. 4. Abused
   children--Services for--California. 5. Shelters for the homeless--
   California. 6. Lundquist, Fran. I. Title.

HV1446.C2 L86 2003
362.83--dc21   0306

Printed in the United States of America.

IN MEMORIUM

This story of my life and God's use of it to establish The Sheepfold is written as a living memorial unto God. I dedicate it with tears to the memory of my beloved son, Robert Craig Lundquist, who found his life too painful to live, but did not live in vain.

Whenever there was a great move of God among His people, to deliver them from their enemies, to save them from destruction, to give them victory over oppression, or to bring them to their Promised Land, He always required that a memorial be made. It was to be a reminder of the miracles He had done, so the people would trust Him and remain faithful. It was also to be a symbol to those who came after; so that God would be glorified, and given honor and reverence for His eternal love and mercy.

It is my earnest prayer that this book will be that kind of a memorial.

...and God said, "I Am that I Am: this is my Name forever, and this is my memorial unto all generations."
Ex. 3:14a,15b

"And the Lord said unto Moses, 'Write this for a memorial in a book'..." Ex. 17:14a

"Thy Name, O Lord, endures forever; and thy memorial, O Lord, throughout all generations." Psa. 135:13

FOREWORD

Dear Fran,

In my experience as a police officer for thirty-six years, I have listened to many people tell their stories, often ones of great losses and hurts. Police officers are trained to be able to "do their job," which means to remain composed and to be able to take notes and concentrate on the objective of the interview, regardless of how emotional the situation is or how much they hurt with the person doing the telling. During our interview today, that was difficult for me, and I doubt that the "normal" person would be able to do it.

I also began to see the reality of the verse that says, "God turns cursing into blessing." If you had not experienced the past that you describe, God probably could not have used you in the mighty way that He has. The love and compassion that emanates from you comes out of that past, coupled with God's healing power, and it is what attracts people to your ministry. Even over the radio, the anointing that is on you comes across! What a mighty and loving God we serve.

I have felt in my spirit for some time that your story must be told because it is going to bring healing to, and change the lives of, many people. As I read your words this evening, I was assured that what was being said was from the Holy Spirit, and that God will be glorified for it.

I know that it is very hard for you to go through this, but I also know that it is God's will and that He will bless you, as well as others, when it is done.

You are a very special woman Fran, and I love you very much. It is a great honor for me to just be a part of this ministry, and to be associated with you. I never leave a board meeting, or set down the phone after talking to you, that I am not uplifted and encouraged. That is the effect you have. Your honesty, sincerity, and dedication to God always come through.

Love,

Lee DeVore
Police Chief
Twin Falls, Idaho Police Department
Vice President, The Sheepfold
Formerly Captain
Fullerton, CA Police Department

INTRODUCTION

Coming from a background full of despair and grief, God has guided me on an incredible journey to bring me to this place in my life.

I decided to write this book, not to tell you of things that I have achieved, but to share the wondrous miracles that I have witnessed firsthand, and to give God all the praise and the glory for what has come to pass.

This is my story. It is a true story. It happened to me. My life happened in clearly defined chapters. That is the way I have chosen to present it, starting at the beginning in order for it to be a testimony of hope to those who feel weak or broken-hearted. May it be a present-day example of God's faithfulness to keep His promise given to each of us in 2 Corinthians 12:9, *"My grace is sufficient for you: for my strength is made perfect [complete, fulfilled] in your weakness."*

At the risk of criticism, I have shared the causes of my brokenness in great detail to lay the foundation necessary to reveal the glorious, overcoming victory of God in my life, and the resulting ministry that He called me to. That ministry, The Sheepfold, stands as a living memorial to Him today. This is the story of how it came into being. It is proof that God heals brokenness, and uses the very things that make us weak to show Himself strong.

Thousands and thousands of books have been written about God, yet millions of people still live in darkness. Every book that gives Him glory and reveals His faithfulness to His promises is like a shining star in the midnight blackness of unbelief and blasphemy that has much of the world in its stranglehold.

As the story now unfolds, it is my prayer that this humble sharing of my life will be one of those stars, and that its light will be an encouragement to others to reach for the success in life that is guaranteed by the faithfulness and unconditional love of God.

—*Fran Lundquist*

The

FIRST

Chapter

As the unwanted child of a rebellious teenage mother, I was passed around to anyone who would take me off her hands. This neglect exposed me to abuse and abandonment that left me with wounds, bruises, and scars of the soul that altered my personality and made me unable to function properly in relationships.

The abandonment left me with a deeply rooted fear of being lost and alone. The vast emptiness of not being wanted caused me to search desperately all of my life for security and acceptance in relationships. The desperation took me into situations that often ended in embarrassment and pain.

The warping of a personality can form a mold that will shape its destiny. God's plan is that every child should have a loving mother and father to nurture and provide for it. My father's heart and life were broken when he came home one day to find his house empty and his wife and two baby daughters gone. My sister was two, and I was one year old. My mother was not ready to settle down and be a wife and mother. She refused to come back to him, and later divorced him. He began drinking heavily and ended up on skid row. I don't know how long he was there, but later in life he recovered and remarried. He was never involved in my life. I only saw him once or twice growing up. I didn't see him again until he was in his eighties, dying, and his wife needed help.

My childhood became a series of prolonged visits with a variety of people since my mother's need for fun and attention was never fulfilled. The seeds of fear of abandonment were planted deeply and they bore fruit in a lifetime of feeling lost and alone. She was my only security, and I never knew if she was coming back to get me or not.

She threatened not to come back if I said or did the wrong thing while she was gone. Whenever I was left with other people, often strangers to me, for hours, days, or weeks, I always thought it was because I had done something bad. Every night before I went to sleep I would lie in bed and review all the bad things I could have possibly said or done that would make mother not want me, until I found the one I thought it *must* be, and then I would punish myself and hate myself. In my childish way I vowed to never do or say that again. Then I would cry myself to sleep. In my soul I was calling out, "Please come back and get me—please don't leave me here—I'm so scared—I promise I won't be bad again."

When I knew I was going to be left somewhere again, I would cry and beg her to please not leave me. It was only met with coldness. There was no comforting—no words of assurance I could hang onto—no promise to come back to get me—just the look which said, "I might come back and I might not—you just behave yourself, young lady."

When she did return, on the way home I would suddenly be asked in an angry voice, "Why did you do that?" or "Why did you say that?" which really meant, *Why did you tell that.* But, I was not told what "it" was that I had said or done. I was only told, "You know perfectly well what you did (or said). You only did that to embarrass me." There was slapping, spanking or hair-pulling if it was what I "did," and mouth-washing with soap if it was what I had "said." I didn't find out what it was that I had done until we were with other people; then my faults were told in front of them.

My mother was a pretty woman with a feminine aura that attracted men to her like a magnet. But there was nothing attractive about the person I knew as "mother," who only showed herself when no one else was around. Her glittering eyes and sharp critical tongue so decimated my personality that all I wanted to do was hide so no one could see how bad I was. I tried to destroy that child within me that its own mother couldn't love.

Part of my shamed self-hatred was because of what happened when I was left with one of mother's friends whose boyfriend was a sailor. When I was alone with him he violated my young innocence by holding me between his legs so I couldn't get loose and forcing me to perform sexual acts upon him. He told me if I ever told anyone he would tell my mother what a bad girl I was. That terrified me even to think what my mother would say or do.

To this day I can't bear to be held down. Instant age regression occurs if I ask someone to stop doing something that upsets me and they won't stop. Knowing my mother was not going to protect me from dangerous, emotionally destructive situations kept me in an extremely insecure and hypervigilant state. I would watch every movement of anyone near me, and listen intently for any word or innuendo that might put me in danger.

One night I woke up screaming in fear. It was so loud that a neighbor, Mrs. Eisley, came running over. My bed was on the screen porch at the back of the house.

She took me in her arms and held me until I stopped crying. I don't remember anyone else in my childhood ever doing that.

Mother must have been inside the house with a boyfriend. She was married for the second time and her husband was a fireman who stayed at the fire station some nights each week.

She never came out to the porch, so when I was quieted down, Mrs. Eisley took me in the house. There was a man's hat on the arm of the couch near mother's bedroom door. Men wore hats in those days. Mrs. Eisley put me back to bed on the screen porch and stayed until I fell asleep.

She must have said something to my mother the next day because I was severely punished for waking the neighbor and having her come over.

In my adult years I have never been able to remember anything about the inside of that house, not rooms, furniture, nothing—except that hat on the arm of the couch.

I was always afraid of my mother. I would tremble when I was alone with her. I never knew where she was, or if she was watching me. She would sneak up and look in windows at me, or hide and watch what I was doing. It frightened me to look up and see her eyes staring at me. I began hiding from her, anywhere, in the closet, in the orange grove, anywhere.

The neglect and abuse were painful, but it was the stinging criticism that broke my spirit. The result was a fearful insecurity that made me withdraw from everyone. I learned early to be worried about saying or doing the wrong thing to adults that brought punishment without explanation. My whole attitude and perspective on life, growing up and as an adult, was through the eyes of an emotionally wounded child who never felt like she said or did the right thing.

The agony of trying to adjust to different people's rules about eating, sleeping, hygiene, participating in their family life and not doing anything wrong, formed a pattern of trying to be good. I began imitating the ways of others to the repression of

my own personality. Matters worsened when another molestation occurred when I was about seven. My mother found out
about it when I accidentally told. The trauma of her anger
toward me caused my fear of saying and doing the wrong thing
to rise to a level that severely hindered my ability to communicate. The inability to express myself verbally without the fear of
saying something wrong manifested itself at that early age and
remained with me my whole life.

I have a little framed certificate in my bedroom today that
really touched my heart when I came across it. It showed me
that I had been dedicated to God when I was nine months old.
This makes me feel like I have always belonged to Him and
blesses me every time I look at it.

The earliest spiritual memory I have is a very special one.
I remember walking down a narrow aisle between rows of little
green toddler chairs. I kept looking down as I walked. I can still
see my feet in little white socks and black shoes with a strap
across that buttoned on the side. I remember I always felt
excited and happy to see my teacher.

My destination was the seat on the end of the front row,
because it was closest to the teacher. I felt a love from her that
I was starving for. I know now that it was the love of Jesus that
she shared and I never forgot it. It was an awakening to love. I
felt happy. When bad things happened, I would hide and talk
to the Person the teacher told us about. She said He was in me,
so I knew He was in my hiding place with me, and I felt happy.

Another strong spiritual influence that has always stayed
in my memory and made me feel close to God occurred in a
church service when I was eight years old. As the communion
tray was passed, the bread and the little cup fascinated me. I
now know it was a sense of the holiness of God. I was not
allowed to touch anything as it passed, but the power of the
preacher's words struck a responsive chord in my young soul
that continued to respond to the Word of God all the days of
my life. It gave me the same feelings I had when I hid and

talked to the Person inside of me. I didn't know who it was, but knowing He was there inside took away the hurt for awhile.

One more such memory was when I was in the fourth grade. A lovely Castilian Spanish family lived on our street. Their son was in my class at school. The grandmother still clung to the ways of her native country. She wore a long black dress and had a fan-shaped comb holding her hair. She was a gentle, godly woman.

Every morning she walked us to school. She would stop at the corner across from the school and lay one hand on Frankie's head and the other hand on mine, and then she would pray, in Spanish.

I didn't know what she said, but I loved it. Frankie said she was asking God for a blessing on us. And then she would kiss each of us on the cheek and watch us cross the street. I loved her.

At home, I withdrew more and more into the maelstrom of confusion inside of me. In my need to escape the shame, I started *becoming* the heroine in books and movies. My uncle owned a movie theatre and mother used that for a baby-sitter. The movies in those days were magnificently staged with elaborate costumes. It was the Ginger Rogers, Fred Astaire, and Shirley Temple era. I had found my escape from myself. Inside me I could become someone else—someone cute and beautiful that always said enchanting things, and always acted gracefully. Someone everyone loved.

I began withdrawing by refusing to participate in social gatherings. The sharp reprimands that invariably followed such gatherings were unbearable. I chose to remain in the car when we went visiting. But, because the people embarrassed my mother by coming out to the car to try to persuade me to come inside, she would be furious with me when we got home.

These may not sound like things that would be destructive to a child, but I was extremely sensitive to every critical word or harsh attitude from anyone. I was so disturbed that by the time

I was ten I had serious emotional problems. At school, my sister often repeated something embarrassing about my size or made fun of me in front of the other children. They would all laugh and run away from me, leaving me feeling sick and miserable. I learned how to hide, but I never learned how to remove the consuming turmoil of emotions. I felt awful, and knew there must be something very wrong with me that made me act and talk awkwardly. I was so self-conscious I could seldom enjoy myself. I knew I wasn't like other girls whose mothers loved them and talked nicely to them and did nice things for them.

My closest friend was Fido, our dog. I loved that dog with all my heart. He kept me company and let me hold him and love him. One day Judy from next door playfully tried to take Fido's bone away from him and he snapped at her. He didn't bite her, but it scared her. Judy ran home crying and told her mother that Fido tried to bite her. Her mother called my mother and told her what Judy had said. Mother wasn't there to see what happened, and she wouldn't believe me that it was because Judy tried to take his bone.

Because she didn't want Judy's mother to be mad at her, she put Fido in the car right then and drove him to the pound to be put to sleep. I begged her and begged her not to do it and I ran along behind the car, crying as she drove off. I hurt so badly! I couldn't get over it. I had lost my best friend. To this day, I have never wanted to own another dog.

Not long after that mother had what they called a nervous breakdown. When she recovered, she left her second husband, and took my sister and me to Idaho to live with a different boyfriend. This was another one she was seeing while she was still married. She would dress us up on Sundays and take us to his house. We had to play outside.

When we moved to Idaho with him, we lived in a motel room behind the service station that they ran together. There was no bathroom in the room so we had to use the public restroom in the service station. It had a shower in it.

After a few months, they had a terrible fight and he beat her up. Mother left him and we went to live in a residential hotel in Pocatello, Idaho. As soon as she started waiting tables again, the nights alone for me started again. She had found another boyfriend. After a few months in the hotel we moved back to California.

Mother was gone a lot at night working as a waitress, or out on dates with boyfriends. She would sleep during the day, then leave in the early afternoon for the rest of the evening. Home was always an apartment, a motel room, or a residential hotel; most of the time the three of us slept in the same bedroom.

Mother's work at night left my sister and me alone constantly. I always faced an undercurrent of deep resentment from my sister. As a baby, pushing me over in my high chair was a common occurrence. She just seemed to always want me out of her life. Growing up, she and I had to sleep in the same bed. Every night as I was going to sleep, she would whisper in my ear, "Nobody likes you, you big fat cow; you've got mole teeth and your breath stinks." Then she would wait until I was asleep and reach over and pinch me, or painfully rub her toenails up and down my leg until I cried. If my mother happened to be there in bed, she would call out in anger saying, "Stop your whimpering." I lay there every night crying myself to sleep with my mother turned away from me on one side asleep, and my sister turned away on the other side asleep.

Until I was an adult, my sister's words about my mouth brought me shame. For years I covered my mouth with my hand whenever I would talk, which became less and less. And even today, to hear a whispering voice disturbs me.

The constant turnover of schools and friends caused me further withdrawal and greater loneliness. My sister, who was one year older than I, attracted people with her wittiness and outgoing personality. She had blond curly hair and was very pretty, which didn't help matters, because my hair was straight as a string and brown, and I was what they called "stocky."

I took it all very seriously, and believed her when she said that nobody liked me and nobody wanted to be around me, so I spent most of my growing up years trying to hide myself. I just kept to myself, and never tried to compete with my sister for friends. Being so close in age, all of our friends were the same. When a teacher insisted she be held back a year, this put her in the same grade as I was. This destroyed any chance of my forming close friendships with those in our age group.

I finally quit trying. I would find someplace to hide—behind the school building, or up in a tree, or some place dark—too traumatized to cry—hating myself. I didn't know how to fix myself, and there was no one to help me. I wanted to be invisible, so no one could ever look at me. I wanted to disappear, so I wasn't anywhere anymore. My soul had entered a prison. I lived hidden inside of myself—so afraid of saying or doing something wrong. I had a grave sense of not belonging anywhere.

It is very strange. In my mind, as an adult, I can't remember my mother or my sister living in any house with me, but I do remember their words. I never heard a kind or soft word come out of their mouth. Mother's thoughts were always on something that someone had done to wrong her. It could have happened twenty years before, but it was never forgotten. I remember the constant confusion in trying to communicate, which added to my seeming inability to express myself. No matter what statement I made, her response was that it wasn't right, or that it was a different way, or time, or thing. A typical example of our conversations would be:

"What kind of sandwich do you want, Fran, tuna or ham?"

"I'd like tuna."

"The ham is fresh, I just got it; or I could make egg salad."

"The ham is fine."

"I can make egg salad."

"Make what you want to, Mother."

"Well, I just want to make what you want."

"I don't care what we have, Mother."

"You always get so moody."

"I don't want any lunch, after all."

"I'll fix it for you anyway."

Apple or pumpkin; coffee or tea; go or stay; you never did; you always do; why did you; why can't you be... I never did achieve communication with my mother or my sister. Things got worse as we grew older.

In the ninth grade I worked after school and on weekends in a small real estate office in the same building as our apartment. Trench coats were very popular among the schoolgirls in Pasadena those days. I saved my money until I could buy one. I was so proud of it. One Saturday while I was working, my sister went to the beach with her boyfriend. He had a hot rod car. Those cars had no hood on them. When I got home from work, I was going to wear my coat to the library but it was gone. My heart sank. When my sister came home later that night I asked her for my coat. She said they had needed something to put over her boyfriend's car motor at the beach so the salt air wouldn't hurt it so they had used my coat. It was covered with grease and had four holes burned into it from battery acid.

I climbed out on the roof and sat there for hours feeling utterly hopeless. There seemed to be no way to stop her. If I bought a new thing for school, or washed and ironed something the night before, she would get up before I woke up, put it on and wear it to school. I was never able to stand against her. I was too afraid of her. That helplessness left me with overwhelming feelings of hopelessness and aloneness.

My mother and her new boyfriend, who was soon to be her third husband, went to the Black Cat bar down the street every night. When they came home, Mother would be so *tired* she would go to bed. He would sit beside her on the bed, patting her, whispering to her, bringing her whatever she wanted. I hated being there in the apartment with them. I hated the little murmurings in the bedroom. I hated her sexuality. I hated the shady innuendoes in every conversation.

There were always little betrayals that eroded my trust. Late one night they brought me home a sandwich and woke me up to eat it. They said it was roast beef, and I was very hungry. After I ate it, they told me it was cow's tongue. I nearly threw up, as they sat there and laughed. Oh, how I hated them. Strong words, wrong words to say about your mother, my pent-up emotions were so strong that no other words could express them.

When I was afraid or disgusted, I would go to the library down the street until it closed, or to the bus bench across the street, or sit outside on the roof, or on a wall or in a tree. But as I hid in those places, God was there with me. It seemed like someone was listening and comforting me. It seemed like I could talk to God there—and then I didn't feel so alone. It seemed like He was there and He heard me crying. I was no longer crying alone. God always seemed to be with me and I could talk to Him without fear of saying the wrong thing.

In the ninth grade I was invited to a young people's church meeting in a home. It was a joyous experience! The leader was a kind, fatherly man who seemed to see something of value in me. He was an encouraging, uplifting man of God. He helped me by teaching me how to read my Bible. I didn't want to ever leave him, but before long, when I started the tenth grade, we moved again.

In the new location there was a little church down the street. Mother worked late nights as a waitress. I used to go stand outside the church and watch the people because I was lonely. On Friday nights they had family potlucks. One night someone saw me and invited me in. One of the families asked me to sit at their table and included me in sharing their dinner. We all played volleyball. Then everyone gathered and sang together, fathers, mothers and children, all singing about Jesus and God. I tried to imagine what it would be like to have a family like that. It affected me deeply. Everyone was happy, laughing, and liking each other. I went every Friday night until we moved again. I did a lot of baby-sitting so that I could earn my own money. I was always big for my age, and of course, quiet. The parents took this for maturity, so I got a lot of babysitting jobs. I would take my little Bible with me, and even though I didn't understand a lot of it, I loved reading it. I have always been thankful for those times. I used to dream about becoming a nun. Even though I was not Catholic, and I didn't know exactly what being a nun meant, I thought they were very holy people.

In my last year of high school I met a boy. It was the first time I had ever dated. We both experienced our first love—that one you never forget in a lifetime. My mother was against the relationship from the beginning and suspected us of wrong-doing. If we sat outside the apartment in his car and talked, she would sneak up and throw open my car door to see what we were doing. She checked my underwear, which was a shameful, disgusting thing to me. She could not have known the sweetness and the purity of our first love. I have never known anything like it since.

At first I did not suspect that she was the instigator of a sudden visit from my wealthy aunt who I barely knew. My aunt invited me to come and live with her. The plan was for me to be a baby-sitter for her three children, and work at my uncle's theatre while I went to junior college to get the last few credits I needed for college. Then they would put me through college. Her promise of new clothing, a car to drive, and payment of all college expenses was more than I could resist.

My boyfriend agreed it would be a wonderful opportunity for me even though we had talked of marriage. We both knew we were a little too young yet for that. So we naively agreed that he would drive down to see me every week and we could continue our relationship just as it was. As the weeks passed, it became more and more difficult for him to come every weekend. He had started working in a gas station and they wanted him on weekends.

Soon, the inevitable happened. A lovely blond girl moved into the house next door to him. His visits became fewer and fewer. A few months later they were married. The heartbreak was almost more than I could bear. All of the emotional inse-curities, abandonment, and feelings of loss, which had been briefly held at bay because someone finally loved me, now crashed in on me and there was no one I could share them with. His mother and I had become close friends and shared a deep affection for each other. I thought that at last I had a mother. But, of course, her loyalties had to be with her son and her new daughter-in-law. She and I communicated once in a while, but soon that ended too. It was then that I formed the habit of sitting alone in the dark every night listening to music.

During my stay with my aunt and uncle, I continued to go to church by myself. God's influence was growing stronger in my life. Every Sunday morning I walked to church and then went to work as an usherette in my uncle's movie theatre.

The pastor of the church taught about being baptized if you loved and believed in Jesus. He announced there would be a baptismal service the following Sunday for those who wanted to follow the Lord's command. My heart's response was imme-diate. I knew I wanted to be baptized in water so that I could show Jesus I loved Him. Family and friends were helping the other candidates prepare on the morning of the baptisms. Although I experienced the familiar pain of aloneness, I was glad I was alone because it made me more aware of the holiness of the moment. There was nothing to distract my thoughts from Jesus. It felt like I entered another dimension to a place I had never been. That feeling was even stronger after the bap-tism as I changed into my street clothes and walked to work.

To this day I remember the feeling I had as I walked along the street. I was a sight with my dripping wet hair and my wet clothes. I was totally unaware of anyone or anything around me.

Along the way to work, I passed a large building that looked like a cathedral. The most heavenly music was coming from that church. I stopped and felt a sense of holiness and rapture that held me spellbound. I felt like my feet weren't touching the sidewalk. And I knew my spirit was experiencing the presence of God. That awareness of His presence has remained with me in varying degrees throughout my lifetime.

The only sour note was when my mother came down the next week and I told her I had been baptized. She yelled at me, "What do you mean you were baptized? I had you baptized as a baby!" The reason for her anger was because it would make her look like she had not been a good mother in front of my aunt if I had never been baptized.

My aunt and uncle had long-standing marital problems. My uncle often came home drunk after working late at his movie theatre and would come into my room and approach my bed. My aunt would hear and come and get him. This continued until finally she fixed a room for me on the back side of the garage that had high windows and a sturdy door with a dead bolt and a chain lock. But then he would pound on the door and call for me to let him in, waking everyone in the house.

A blatant indiscretion with the cashier of his theatre brought about the final break-up of the marriage. A divorce followed and I was no longer able to stay with my aunt. The plans for my future were not going to happen. But, I did complete a year of junior college and I did learn how to drive while I was with her. I was heartbroken when she told me that I had to leave her house. I had little hope for the future. During the last years of her life my aunt and I lived in the same small town. She became my best friend and I loved her dearly.

My mother had married for the third time and was not glad to have me return. I had to find a job right away to support myself. I was almost nineteen by now, and my hopes for a college education were gone. I did not have knowledge of the college process, no one in our family had ever gone, and I did not have the emotional stability to undertake putting myself through college. I was still bound tightly by fear and loneliness.

I found a job running a check-sorting machine in a Bank of America branch. After working there a few months, mother told me she and her husband were moving to Nevada and they did not have room for me.

I was at an age when I should have been mature enough to face the world, but I wasn't. I didn't want to live with my mother and her husband, but I didn't want to be alone either. I still equated "alone" with "abandonment." Emotionally I was unequipped to be on my own, even though the law said I was now an adult.

I rented an upstairs room in an old, dark boarding house run by a friend of my mother. My job at the bank required that I stay later than the other employees in order to prepare the bundled checks for the courier. That meant taking a long bus ride after dark to the street where I lived, then walking to the house. Big trees and shrubs surrounded the dark brown house. At night the wind rubbed and thumped the branches against the house. I was full of fear, fear of living alone, fear of walking down the street at night, fear of who was in the boarding house with me, fear I would do something wrong at the bank—the list was very long.

An old trunk held all my possessions and was my only furniture in the room besides the bed. I was told I had kitchen privileges but I was so backward I didn't know what that meant. I was gripped with that same old fear of doing the wrong thing, and so afraid of the landlady that I never went near the kitchen the whole time I was there. I didn't eat there and never went downstairs. There was an outdoor stairway to my room.

I lived on snacks and just sort of existed but was desperately unhappy inside. I covered up my pain and severe loneliness that seemed to be there all my life. I started going to a Nazarene church with a girl from the bank that was studying to be a missionary. I began studying with her and thought that I, too, would become a missionary.

There was a young man who was assigned to do late-night clearing with me. We were the last two employees to leave the bank. After two or three months he began offering me a ride home. Then as we became better acquainted he began to share his lunch with me. He learned of my boarding house situation and began taking me to his family home for dinner before taking me home.

There were seven adult family members all living in his family home. After he dropped me off, I would sit on my bed and dream of how enjoyable it would be to have a close-knit family like his. I was like a child with its nose pressed against a candy-store window. I wanted in. I wanted to belong somewhere, anywhere. His family liked me, and they were good to me. I was overwhelmed with a desire to be part of a family. I married the young bank teller to be in his family.

I knew I did not have the love or affection for him that I had for my first love. But, because of the desperate loneliness and my desire to remain part of his family, I married him. Thus began the second chapter of my life.

Before we leave this one, there is something I would like to add: Being afraid of the only two people who were my family saved me from doing many of the things that troubled young people often do. I didn't have to go through the trauma of recovery from drugs or alcohol, and all that goes with that lifestyle. I was too afraid to do anything like that. But, I did have to go through a lifetime of seeking mental and emotional healing, having become verbally inarticulate in social situations, especially with anyone in authority—all of which led to a reclusive life style.

It is not easy or pleasant to share these tangled and tormented things of my soul, but it is necessary in order to reveal the incredible mercy and healing power of God as the story unfolds in the chapters ahead. No human can open the locked prison doors of their soul; only God by the working of His Holy Spirit can reach into those humanly inaccessible places. David understood this when he wrote in Psalm 142:7, *"Bring my soul out of prison that I may praise thy Name."*

I have studied God's commandment to "honor thy father and thy mother." To honor them according to the Bible is to provide for them when needed, and be available to them for their care. I did that with my mother all of her life. I was the person my mother relied on whenever she needed help, especially in her later years. I never spoke a disrespectful or unkind word to her, and when she died at the age of ninety-two in a pitiful state of mental illness and paranoia, I was the only one with her. There was no funeral for there was no one who would come. She had driven everyone away.

There is now total forgiveness and understanding in my heart. Her own childhood was one of rejection and harshness. Her mother left her when she was ten. She was raised by her father. He was very hard on her as the oldest girl. She never learned how to give or receive true love and affection. Her security was in men because of being raised by her father. Her promiscuity was not from a sinful heart, but was from a heart searching for love in the only way it seemed to be able to find it. I neither judge nor condemn her, especially since experiencing motherhood myself.

And, about my sister, although I reacted to our childhood with shyness and becoming an introvert, my sister reacted to it with boldness and being an extrovert. That which was witty and cute in her as a child became coarse and wild by the age of sixteen. She was pregnant and married at seventeen. She became a lifetime alcoholic and was married four times before she died of cancer.

The
SECOND
Chapter

My husband's parents came from a stern and stoic background of life on a cold, small farm in Sweden. Due to their early years of hard work and long hours working in solitude, they did not learn to physically or verbally express affection to each other.

Later when they had children, they loved them but it was not in their nature or upbringing to verbally demonstrate that love. The father never learned English well and scarcely ever spoke.

Having grown up in this atmosphere, my husband had the same lack of affectionate expression. I thought that after we were married that would change and that he would become more openly affectionate. However, that was not the case. In our twenty-five-year relationship there were never the little caresses or words of endearment that keep a love relationship alive.

I began early in the marriage to mask that empty void within me that longed for love. I covered that emptiness with humor or light heartedness around other people, believing, but not yet accepting, it would be this way for the rest of my life.

Acceptance of the lack of tenderness and affection was very difficult. I couldn't understand why when I asked him to please stop doing something that upset me, he would not only keep doing it, but wouldn't answer me. Learning to live with the silence was more difficult to accept, in a way, than the lack of affection or consideration for my feelings. I never got used to asking a question or making a request, and being completely ignored as if I weren't there. Trying to discuss an issue with him was a one-sided waste of time.

The resentment grew to be a deep hurt within me at being treated as unworthy of regard or consideration. Through the years I began to realize that my feelings did not matter to him. I felt like two people. One, on the outside, did all the things required of her and appeared as though everything was normal. But inside was one who knew the agony of being married to someone who killed any affection she had toward him.

Trying to make conversation or ask a question of someone who deliberately doesn't answer is very demeaning and made me feel unloved. I did not know if I could continue to live my life like this. After five years of marriage, I thought I couldn't.

By this time I was afraid of him. His sternness and unresponsiveness only heightened that lifetime fear of doing or saying the wrong thing. I was breaking down mentally and experiencing deep depression. All I wanted was to get away. I wanted it to end. But I was afraid.

The only place I could think of to go was to my mother's. I did not tell him I was going and to this day I don't remember how I got from California to Reno, Nevada, where she lived

I was only there one night before I realized what a mistake I made by going there to seek help. When she found out he didn't know where I was, she secretly called him and arranged for him to take me back. When I saw him drive up and realized mother had once again violated my trust, I was heartsick. In my despair, on the verge of an emotional breakdown, I was too weak to stand against them. I felt so betrayed. In my mind there was no way I could strike out on my own. So I went back.

A few months later, at age twenty-seven, I became pregnant with my first child. I knew then that I would not leave my husband, having learned the devastation that divorce inflicts on children through my own childhood. I was joyful at the prospect of having a precious baby to love. I knew it would help to fill the emptiness I felt.

Because my insecurity always demanded perfection from myself, I was going to be a perfect patient during my pregnancy, so the doctor would think well of me. My sister-in-law knew a doctor, but he was not an obstetrician. This concerned me, but she was a nurse and I felt confident she would help me. And, I was afraid if I didn't go to him, after she had recommended him, she wouldn't help me.

The doctor said maximum weight gain could only be twenty-five pounds. The perfectionist in me determined not to gain an ounce over that. My dieting was so strict that even after a low-calorie meal, I only allowed myself one-half of a graham cracker for dessert. It was an extremely difficult birth in spite of my lack of weight gain. The doctor was unskilled in delivering babies. After two days of hard labor the baby began to experience trauma, so the doctor cut three deep incisions around the birth canal to free the baby. The next day after the delivery he ordered the nurse to insert suppositories in the birth canal to fight infection. The nurse came to do it and said, "There is no way to do this. The area is cut up like chopped meat and I can't find the opening."

The baby was a fine healthy boy until we discovered he had a staph infection from the hospital. The doctor came to the house and gave a large injection of penicillin in that tiny little bottom. It hurt to watch that needle enter his tiny 5-day-old body.

The first night home from the hospital I wanted to have a big dinner to celebrate after the months of strict dieting. I enjoyed every bite, but about three hours later I began vomiting and having severe pain in my upper chest. I was literally writhing on the bed in pain. Finally the pain eased and I fell into an exhausted sleep.

The next night I didn't eat, but the third night the same thing happened. The doctor was called to make a house call. Even though I was jaundiced, he determined it was nervousness due to all the trauma of the delivery. He thought I was too young to have gall stones and too thin.

So, night after night, I sat nursing my infant son, rocking back and forth in agonizing pain, telling myself it was all in my head. There was no one to share my suffering with because my sister-in-law and my husband believed it was all in my head like the doctor said. Their response was, "Snap out of it, you didn't have it any worse than anyone else."

For the next year I went through the excruciating pain of passing gall stones. The doctor had given the wrong diagnosis, but everyone, including me, believed him that it was all in my head.

Many times as I sat nursing my baby, in waves of pain, I would look out the window at the rising sun and cry out to God to help me. I felt overwhelmed as I looked at my baby, and already felt like a failure as a mother. I knew I never wanted to have a child again ever. For the next two months the attacks of pain continued. Then one night my husband insisted that I perform my duties as a wife. My incisions were not healed and I begged him and cried out to him not to force himself on me, but he did. A door closed in my heart that night that never opened again to him, because of his cruelty.

That night I became pregnant again. My greatest fear at that time had come upon me. I did not want to have another birthing experience. My boys would be just thirteen months apart, but there was no escape. As the pregnancy began, however, I began eating a very low-calorie diet again, and unknowingly that caused the terrible gall bladder attacks to come less often, which gave me some relief.

Before this second baby was born we moved to another city. Our house was in a housing tract in a canyon area. There was a large dam at the head of the canyon.

One night in the middle of the night when I was eight and a half months pregnant, expecting the baby any day, the dam at the head of the canyon above us burst open.

Tons of built up silt, debris, and water overflowed into our housing tract. Police and fire equipment had to evacuate us. The roads were impassable, buried two feet deep in mud, so I had to slosh through the mud to a ladder set against a ten-foot wall at the far end of our street.

I was so pregnant that I had to turn sideways to be able to put my feet on the rungs. With a fireman above, and one below, it was a major project getting me up and over. But, we made it to a car waiting on the other side away from the mud.

Another big, beautiful boy was born to me. But, once again the delivery was extremely difficult. I had decided at the outset of the pregnancy that I would find a good obstetrics doctor on my own. My former doctor had never come to see me in the hospital as I recuperated from the first baby. I would see the other mothers in the ward be attentively visited and checked and given instruction on what to do, and felt so bad because mine never came. I remembered this new doctor had visited the lady next to me every day and he was so kind and told her how to take care of herself and the baby. I had determined then that if ever I got pregnant again, I would call him. Little did I know I would be making that call just three months later. His office was close to the hospital. He was shocked at the way I had been cut up by the doctor who delivered the first baby.

If I had not changed doctors I would not be here writing this today. My second son was a big boy, almost nine pounds, and somehow he got turned when labor started so that he was breeched in the birth canal. This was not discovered until after many hours of intense labor. At that time, they did not have all the modern methods of diagnosing birth-related problems. Because my new doctor was a specialist, he was able to manually turn the baby's body after the breech position was discovered. The baby's head did not have to force the opening of the birth canal, so his face was like a little porcelain angel—perfectly round and beautiful. The delivery nurse took him all around to show the other nurses.

Because of the other infant at home, my stay in the hospital was not as long as I needed. My doctor was very caring and gave me instructions. After I returned home I started eating normally and those dreaded attacks began again, with nausea and greater pain than ever.

One night after an especially bad one, I called my obstetrician, crying, and told him I couldn't take care of two babies and have these attacks. He drove right out to the house even though it was late and in another city. After examination he told me I had been passing gallstones ever since the first baby was born. I went in for Xrays that confirmed his diagnosis. His mother had just passed away from cancer of the gallbladder because of untreated gallstones. Because I had mine for over a year he wanted me to have the gall bladder removed right away to stop any further irritation of the lining. Arrangements were made. Within three weeks I was in the hospital for the surgery.

When the gallbladder was removed, within it were seventy-five to one hundred gallstones of various sizes. He explained it is the tiny ones that cause the problems because they enter the bile duct when fat is being digested, and cause great pain until they have passed through. I kept those stones as proof to show my husband and his family that all that pain was not in my head.

After I was home just one week, my mother, who had come to watch the children while I was in the hospital, went home to her husband in Las Vegas. My husband was at work from 9:00 A.M. to 5:00 P.M. every day with a long drive to and from work. So I found myself alone all day with a thirteen-month-old and a one-month-old, recovering from the surgery. It became necessary to begin lifting the boys, carry heavy baskets of wash, hang diapers out on the line, and to continue cleaning up from the flood. They made big surgical incisions in those days, with lots of stitches, which took a long time to heal. The lifting created adhesions from the surgery.

Those were very difficult days. Then, a little later, when my youngest boy was four months old, he developed a strangulated hernia in the upper intestine. It was very large. The pediatrician told us it was very serious, that if it burst he might die, and he would have to be operated on right away. Shriner's Children's Hospital in Los Angeles was the only place at that time it could be done on such a young baby. My husband stayed with the older boy while the pediatrician drove the baby and me to the hospital in Los Angeles.

It was a frightening experience. The pediatrician said, "Hold the baby very still. If that hernia bursts on the way to the hospital, he will die right here in the car." I prayed all the way and God answered my prayers. Thanks be to God, we made it to the hospital. After painful examinations he was admitted and emergency surgery was performed on him that night.

The house we lived in had been my sister's. When she and her husband divorced, we bought it from her. After the baby's surgery, I desperately needed help. I was hurting from my own surgery still and was exhausted. My sister was an alcoholic and she and a neighbor across the street used to go to the local bars and get drunk when she lived there. During the time she had lived in the house, she had alienated the neighbors by her drunken and disorderly conduct. They had nothing to do with me because of that. One neighbor openly told me she didn't want to be friends because of my sister. My sister came every other day to see her friend across the street, but she never came over to see me. I would stand looking out the window with tears in my eyes watching as the two of them drove off laughing and having a carefree time. I was so scared, crying out inside for someone to help me.

So once again I began a lonely season of life, home alone every day with my babies. We only had one car so my husband drove it to work. We were too far from anywhere to walk. The children couldn't play outside because the front and back yards were still filled with mud and all kinds of debris: old headlights, cans, bottles, and dead animals from the broken dam. We eventually got it cleaned up.

Then my husband received a job offer from a bank in Las Vegas that he felt he couldn't refuse. We enjoyed the change and found the high desert a beautiful place. That many years ago there were more churches than casinos in Las Vegas. It was still a small town. We had relatively happy times in the beginning.

After a year there, our older son, now five, had to have his tonsils removed. That was pretty standard procedure years ago when a child had repeated attacks of high fever and bronchitis. The surgery went fine. But, after we came home, he was playing quietly and suddenly began hemorrhaging in his throat. We rushed him to the hospital where he was given a blood transfusion. We all thought the crisis was over but he had to stay overnight to be watched in the event any bleeding occurred. Later that night we received a phone call to come immediately to the hospital. He had had an allergic reaction to the blood he was given that had shut down his kidneys and he was showing signs of going into a coma. It was touch and go for several days. On my knees in the chapel I cried out to God to save my son. He heard and answered my prayers once more.

It became financially necessary for me to go back to work. At first I worked nights, so I could be with the children during the day. I worked as a baby-sitter for the big Vegas hotels. My hours were very erratic. Sometimes parents wanted their children fed dinner in the hotel room and they would be gone from 7:00 P.M. to 2 or 3:00 A.M. or longer. I often had to sit in the bathroom to read because the light from a lamp kept the children awake. The pay was good, but the work was exhausting.

After a few months I could no longer keep up the schedule. I began working days as church secretary in a local Lutheran church until my youngest son began showing signs of deep problems. It was when he started kindergarten that we realized something was wrong. He is the only child I have heard of that played hooky in kindergarten. He would run away and not go to school.

We did not know it then, but he had a learning disability stemming from the high, extended fever he had when he was five years old. He had suffered a severe case of German measles. He was a solid red mass literally over every part of his body, from the crown of his head to the soles of his feet and even between his toes. In spite of our efforts, his fever remained 106° for over two days. His eyes watered continually. He was so sick and so miserable, I should have driven him to the hospital. But, the doctor had said to just keep sponging him and give him liquids and the medicine he prescribed.

That is one of the deepest regrets of my life that I did not take a stronger stand against authority for my son. But, as that weak, fearful person who was so overawed by anyone in authority—teachers, doctors, pastors, anyone in leadership—I was too fearful to demand that he be taken to the hospital.

The result was brain damage that was manifested in a learning disability. But we did not know that until years later. We interpreted his rebellious actions as self-willed. We knew something was very wrong, and it was frightening. My husband was very hard on him because he didn't understand and we didn't know what was wrong with him. He thought the boy was just being stubborn and wasn't trying to learn.

This memory is one that still causes great heartache today, years later. I can still hear the voices in my memory from when my husband took my son into the bathroom. I could hear him knocking him around and my son protesting and crying. I stood outside the door with tears streaming down my face begging my husband to stop. My pain never goes away. It's too painful to think of a child trying to defend himself for something he couldn't help.

In elementary school his fourth grade teacher set his desk in the hallway where all the children could make fun of him because he disrupted the class by refusing to read. That was over forty years ago and teachers were not instructed in reading and learning disabilities as they are now. Back then, punishment seemed to be the only answer to a child's failure to perform. Even as I write this, the agony stabs my heart again that I didn't stand up for him against that teacher. If I allow myself to dwell on the torment he must have suffered, not knowing what was wrong with him, the pain becomes unbearable.

During this time, I gave birth to our third son. The older boys were ten and eleven. The doctor who delivered the baby was going on vacation right when the baby was due so he decided to induce labor. The day of the procedure I entered the hospital in the morning. I was placed on a gurney and given an injection to begin labor. By that night I was still on the gurney and had not started labor. I was given another shot and spent the rest of the night waiting. It still had not happened by the next morning and I was given another shot. When the next nursing shift came on duty at 3:00 P.M., my nurse was shocked that I was still on the gurney and labor had not started. I had had nothing to eat and had not gotten off the gurney the entire time. My nurse said, "I'm going to fix you an intravenous cocktail so strong that it will guarantee that baby will start being born." And she did.

Right after the baby was born I was unable to come back to reality. All those drugs on an empty stomach had affected my mind. They would not bring me the baby for the first three days because of my condition. They thought I might hurt him because I was out of my head. They kept new mothers in the hospital longer in those days than they do now. After a week they let me take him home.

We had moved to a new home during my pregnancy and I didn't know any neighbors. It was a desperately lonely time for me because my mental condition was very bad. I lived in extreme anxiety. I was fearful of everything and the care of a newborn was overwhelming to me. Depression was so deep no tranquilizer could reach it.

Fear was like a ferocious tiger in my mind. It paced back and forth, trying to escape its cage, and I knew if it ever got out it would devour me. Fainting sensations from fear would overtake me. Prescription drugs only added to my problems, because the drugs from the hospital took a long time to completely leave my system.

During this time the boys were trying to adjust to their new school. This was an especially difficult time for them, especially for the boy with the learning problem. His teacher openly ridiculed him in school. To my deep sorrow, I was in no condition to help him when he needed help the most. I went to parents' day and the teacher ridiculed him there in front of me and the whole class and the other parents, and to my eternal sorrow, I didn't do anything about it! I didn't even defend him. I thought anyone in authority knew best. This has tormented me all my life and I know it caused my son much suffering.

We were only in the new home one year when my husband was transferred to the Reno branch of the bank where he was employed. It did not seem possible that all of our lives were to be uprooted again. But as far as I knew, from what my husband said, we had no choice.

The move was made and Reno was lovely. We rented a big home and again we were happy there in the beginning. I worked very hard fixing up the home and started going to YWCA swimming and exercise classes.

Before long, however, my second son was having the same school problems and he developed a very unattractive, unpleasant facial tic that he repeatedly did with his face and hands. We knew he had some very real problems that were getting worse and worse and we didn't know how to cope with them.

On the bright side, we had learned that he had unusual inventive abilities to build things and create things. He began attending a young boys' group at a local church where his friend went. The two boys became good friends and the father took an interest in my son and helped him with truths of the Bible. This was a good time in his life. I will be forever grateful to this fine Christian man who cared about him.

Refusing to wear his jacket in cold Reno weather, he developed severe ear and bronchial infections. The doctor we went to referred him to a psychiatrist because of the continual embarrassing tic. Tests revealed wild brain waves from the bout with German measles that had affected his brain. But, the doctor was unable to offer much help. Again this was many years ago when less was known about brain function. Teachers did not know how to reach him. His discipline problems alienated him in school. Even my husband's family ridiculed him, and my mother never had a kind or loving word for him.

In trying to make life better for him, and for all of us, I soon made a well-intentioned decision that had tragic consequences.

The

THIRD

Chapter

To this day, I do not know why I made a decision to adopt a child. At the time, I thought it would help our family as well as the child. My husband left the decision entirely up to me.

There was a ten-year gap in age between our older boys and the youngest. Idealistically, I thought a cute little girl would easily fit into that space—someone we could all love, who would be a playmate for the youngest child, and would be a blessing to all of us.

It was a fateful decision that would change the rest of our lives forever. Living in a big house with plenty of room, the more I thought about it, the more it seemed like the Christian thing to do, knowing there were children forced to live in state-run agencies because they had no home.

I decided to test the water a little bit and see if this was even something feasible. To my surprise, when I called the State of Nevada Social Services they were eager to place their wards in private homes. They told me they had a little girl in the age bracket that I wanted but she had a sister who was two years older and they would not separate them. The girls had been badly abused before they were taken from their parents, and the further trauma of separation from each other would be too cruel.

My husband was not against the adoption because it would be my job to raise all the children. In his birth family the mother did all the caring of the children, and this was his mind-set also. The girls were three and five. We agreed to adopt both girls without seeing anything other than one photo. They were in the northern part of Nevada. Because of the distance across the state we never met them until they were brought to our door by a social worker.

I knew it was more than I could handle from the first day. They had severe emotional problems from having suffered extreme neglect and abuse all of their short lives. My fears for the future success of the adoption were heightened in the first few minutes of the first day when the three-year-old walked over to my happy little one-year-old sitting on his favorite toy. She pushed him over onto the floor, took it away from him and sat on it, refusing to give it back.

I thought and prayed, "Dear God, how can I send them back?" I was caught on the horns of a dilemma of my own making. When I told my husband I thought we should give the girls back, he said, "If you give them back you will never forgive yourself." So, I kept them.

There were twelve children in the girls' birth family. The mother was dying of a fatal disease and could not care for the children. When their father's old car broke down for the last time, the older children could not get to school. After missing school for some time, the school official came to the house to find out why.

When the unbelievable filth and poverty the children were living in were reported, the state took all the children away. The ten oldest went to separate foster homes, but they let the two youngest be together.

I was shocked at the stories the five-year-old told me about their life in the backwoods of Elko, Nevada in an old house with no doors and broken out windows.

She told of crawling under the stove when she was hungry to get a raw potato out of a box to eat, and eating green algae from the river. I noticed small, unidentifiable scars on her body from neglected wounds and injuries.

In winter the only warmth they had was to go out in the sunshine. They were cold all the time. The five girls slept on the same mattress to try and get warm because there were no blankets. I understood the reality of this when I would go in to the girls' room after they were asleep to be sure they were tucked in, and find the older girl shivering and shaking under her blankets, even though she was fast asleep and warm.

My heart ached when she told of the bugs crawling on their bed and in the mattress. They had no sheets. There was no running water in the house. There was no bathroom or indoor plumbing. The outhouse was far from the house, and the winter snows are heavy in Elko. They didn't have any shoes to wear most of the time.

Abused children are extremely self-centered. They have had to be for survival. They need immediate gratification and their desire for attention is insatiable. Never having known love, any kind of attention to them appears to be love. Their limitless demands for attention exhausted me and my patience.

Within a short time they found out they got a lot of my attention when they were mean to my little boy who was just a toddler. They shut him in his room and wouldn't let him out until he was crying in fear. If I went to the grocery store, even though my husband was home, they would tell my son that I was not coming back; that I had gone away and left him like their mother had. I would come home to a hysterical little boy who would not let go of my skirt for hours. They began to be mean to him in every way they could. As the months went by, he developed emotional problems that carried over into his adult life in the form of anxiety attacks.

By the time he was two I was sleeping on the floor by his crib every night because he had two or three nightmares every night, waking up screaming. As he grew a little older, I still had to go in and lie by his bed because he woke up terrified. I spent more time on the floor than I did in my bed. When he was older and had the nightmare, we often went in to the kitchen to have a cup of hot chocolate and talk, to calm his fears. Although it was a painful time back then, now sometimes we jokingly say, "Is this a hot chocolate problem?"

In the midst of adjusting to caring for five children, four of whom were displaying obvious emotional and behavioral problems, my husband came home one night after being away at a banking convention, and told me he had been fired. He would never tell me why, but he was acting very strangely that night and saying bizarre things that made no sense. My life was so overwhelmed with the responsibilities of the children that I had not paid attention to his drinking habits, not recognizing that alcohol had become a problem in his life.

The next morning he told me the bank president had abruptly fired him at the convention because of something he had done, and told him he would no longer be able to work in any bank in Nevada. That meant we would have to move back to California.

He went ahead of us to find a job while I packed up that big house and tried to keep the children on an even keel about having to make another adjustment to a different school and leaving the friends they had made. The second boy with the reading problem took it especially hard. He was very angry and upset.

My husband had to find a job quickly in order to support our now five children. He found a job in a bank that had a

6,000 square foot home in foreclosure that needed a caretaker on the premises. Because we had no money, we moved in to it. I soon found out who the caretaker was going to be.

By now the older boys were in junior high school and the girls were in elementary school. The junior high school allowed corporal punishment and my second son began receiving it for what they perceived as rebellion. But, in reality he was lost in the classroom, not being able to read, and not knowing why. He was very disturbed over the treatment he received. Naturally, he hated the school and wanted desperately to return to Reno. We all did.

After a few months, the bank sold the house and we had to uproot and move again, this time to a small home in a nearby city. Because of the obvious demands from the younger children's problems, family life as the older boys had known it no longer existed for them. Their needs were often unspoken and neglected. I tried to make home pleasant. I tried to keep a sense of humor but, as I saw my family beginning to disintegrate, my spirit was heavy.

One evening, after a very long and difficult day, I was standing at the stove fixing dinner. The children had been unusually contrary that day and I felt as if I could not go on. I was praying in my thoughts and suddenly it was like warm oil was poured all over me. It was a very strange experience but not frightening. I knew it was from the Lord. It was a very comforting and strengthening experience. I felt touched and encouraged by the Holy Spirit.

My second son was now fourteen and this move along with everything else was just too much for him to cope with. He began to get into serious trouble. He began using drugs and alcohol. I was unsuccessful in getting help from the school. As always, they felt it was a discipline problem.

He began to act out his problems. He broke into the candy machine at school and the police brought him home. He drove a car that belonged to a friend's father and damaged it. He began stealing cars for joy rides. The police were at our door many times.

Yet, in the midst of all his problems, he had a certain kind of joy of life. His inventiveness kept him from all-out wrongdoing. He had a lot of creative ability. He built a workbench without any plans to follow so he would have a place to build his motorized model airplanes. I took him to model airplane meets and practically begged the men there to take him under their wing and help him fly his planes, but no one would. He also laid the forms and poured a beautiful curved cement walk around the back of the house all by himself, without instructions.

I took him to live at Teen Challenge to see if they could help him with the drug problem. He accepted Jesus as his Savior while he was there. After about six months he ran away and came home.

After a poor start in public high school, I was able to find a special school for boys who were unable to function in the public school system. It was important to do this for the sake of the older boy also. Because of their close ages, they would be attending the same high school and the younger boy would surely have brought embarrassment to the older one if he continued to vandalize school property.

The special school was run by a former Los Angeles policeman. He made it very clear that he did not want any kind of parental involvement. He was angry at me for allowing my son to be in this condition. His words burned into my heart when he said, "You had your turn and you missed it, and now leave him alone." I took him to the school every day and picked him up because the distance was too far for buses. I couldn't seem to communicate with him. His relationship with all the family became more estranged as the days passed.

Long times of separation began when he turned sixteen. He worked up north during the summer on a farm owned by a friend of my husband. With the money he earned he bought an old motorcycle and fixed it up. He was also able to buy an old yellow Ford Mustang, and kept busy restoring it.

When he was seventeen, he agreed to join the Navy, at the urging of his father, who thought the strict discipline would straighten him out. This required written parental permission because of his age.

My husband had served in the Navy in WWII and felt that joining would mature our son and make a man of him. I believe that was part, or perhaps all, of my son's reason for wanting to join, so he could finally do something to please his father.

Fear of his inability to learn in a structured classroom gnawed at my heart. I was deeply troubled. I didn't know much about the Navy, but I knew that strict discipline was enforced. I didn't know until later how heavily it would be enforced. Had I known, I would never have agreed to sign the paper.

A foreboding sense of tragedy entered my heart as soon as I laid down that pen. I knew in my heart of hearts that he was not emotionally stable enough to handle boot camp. This was during the Vietnam War.

After his first six weeks in boot camp, my son came home on leave on the morning of December 31, 1973. He was very thin and quiet. As we talked he asked me, "Why are people so cruel to each other?" He was very serious. At first I did not relate his question to the training officers in the Navy because we were just talking about general things.

Even when he asked me, "Mom, does the soul go to heaven when a person dies?" I did not understand the penetrating depth of his question. I paused and looked at him. "Why do you ask?" He just shrugged. "Oh, I just wanted to know." I gave the best theological answer that I could. Through the years I have asked myself a thousand times how could I have been so incredibly stupid and insensitive. Every time I think of it, the knife turns in the wound.

Since it was New Year's Eve, he said he wanted to see his old friends and spend time with them. The older son was going out somewhere also. After the other children were asleep, I decided to do my ironing.

Shortly after midnight two plain clothes police officers came to the door. They identified themselves as detectives so I invited them in, thinking that my son may have gotten in trouble. I offered them coffee and apologized for the clothes hanging around.

"Are you Mr. and Mrs. Lundquist?"

It got very quiet in the room, and then he said, "I'm very sorry, but your son is dead.

"He ran a hose from the exhaust pipe into his car, closed all the windows and doors, and left the motor running." The detective paused and cleared his throat, visibly moved. "He killed himself. I'm sorry, very sorry."

The shock of his words completely blocked them out of my mind. I remember pleasantly thanking the officers for coming by and wishing them a Happy New Year as if it had been a social call. I remember wondering why they had come, thinking they had never told us the reason for their coming. Their words didn't register even though they had said where his body was and that we would have to go to the county morgue to claim it. Someone would have to identify it. And we should do that right away.

I couldn't ask my husband why they had come because when they left he went into our bedroom and did not come out for the rest of the night. I went back to my ironing. An hour or so later, even though I still felt nothing—as though my head and body were disconnected—I seemed to know there were things I was supposed to be doing.

I called a compassionate Christian couple who were friends from our church. It was 2:30 in the morning but they came right over. When they asked about the details, I told them someone would have to go to the coroner's office at the morgue and identify him. Still without tears the state of shock continued. The man undertook the unpleasant, disturbing task of going to the morgue, identifying the body and gathering my son's clothes and property. I wouldn't have known where to go and my husband still would not come out of the room. The children were awake by now after hearing the voices. I don't remember anything after that until the day of the funeral.

I didn't go to see him at the funeral home because I wanted to remember him as he had been the last time I saw him alive. But his older brother did go to see him. He told me that when he was sitting there beside the casket looking at his brother, he had a vision. He saw Bobby, dressed in his jeans and a T-shirt like he always wore, standing beside a person in a radiant white robe. It was Jesus.

They were standing above the sun and before they turned and walked away, Bobby smiled at him, and waved goodbye. When he told me that, I knew from that day on that my son is saved and is in heaven with Jesus.

I have heard preachers come on TV and radio and say that if someone commits suicide, they cannot go to heaven. That thought is too painful for a parent to bear. That is why my older son's vision is such a blessing to me.

I believe in every fiber of my being that the Lord understood the agony, fear, and confusion in Bobby's tortured mind, and by His grace and mercy He enfolded him in His love and gave him the peace and rest that he could not find here on earth. He felt trapped with no other way out, and if I understood that, how much more his loving Savior understood.

I wanted to remember Bobby the way I had seen him alive, but not going to see him at the funeral home was a great mistake. By not seeing him dead, I had no closure. I had not yet faced the massive pain that was waiting for me, but when the storms of agony did come, the vision sustained me. I believed the scripture, *"My son shall not return to me, but I shall go to him."* 2 Samuel 12:23

It was a naval ceremony at the gravesite. I still had not cried, even when they played Taps and presented me with the three-cornered, folded flag from his coffin before it was lowered. My husband never put his arm around me or even held my hand, not even on the night we were told, or from that time on. That closed a door in my heart that was never to open again.

On the day of the funeral I tried to comfort Bobby's girl-friend. She was sobbing and brokenhearted. Looking back I'm sure she must have thought I did not love my son because I had not cried at the funeral service or at the gravesite.

When people came to the house after the funeral, I received them as a hostess, accepting their expressions of sympathy still without tears. I still had no feeling at all. It was not until two weeks after the funeral when I was home alone one evening that the protective cushion of shock that had kept me together lifted.

I had gone into the garage to put a load of laundry in the washing machine. I happened to glance at the workbench that my son had built, and that was when it struck me like being hit by a truck. I doubled over in pain like nothing I had ever felt. I cried out to God over and over—weeping in convulsions like I had never known. As the convulsions finally began to slow down, I grabbed a bat that was lying on the workbench and began hitting the bench in a frenzy of grief.

From that time on, the tears were always right behind my eyes and fell unbidden without notice any time of the day or night. They fill my eyes even as I write this.

It is a pain that will not end until I am with him again. The agony of knowing the opportunities I had to help him and failing to recognize them, or act on them, is torment. To allow myself to feel the abandonment and the suffering he felt is more than I could bear and keep my sanity.

His death further confirmed my sense of failure as a person and as a mother. I wrote the following note years ago at the time of his death:

> "It seemed like I never really had a quiet time to mourn my precious son who could not bear to live another day.
> I pray the Lord to tell Bobby I love him. I feel that he never knew how much I loved him. I think I corrected him more than I told him I loved him. Yet I love him so much.

*We laughed together a lot. He had a joy of life about
him. He ran the strings with the fireworks on the 4ᵗʰ of
July. He decorated the tree and set up the tape player with
Christmas tapes. He built the workbench we all used. He
built the paneled partition. He built the cement walks—
all without instructions.*

*One of the most painful things for me was seeing his
notebook from classes at boot camp. He tried so hard to
write and spell well. He kept everything so neat.*

*It breaks my heart to think of him trying so hard to be
good and do right, not knowing how to read. Oh! God! I
know how hard it is to try to do things right when you don't
know how."*

All this had a powerful negative impact on the children,
especially the youngest one who was already struggling. The
children in his grammar school knew about his brother and
kept asking him questions that he could not answer. I wrongly
tried to protect him by not telling him that Bobby had killed
himself. The kids knew somehow, but he didn't. It made him
feel excluded from the family instead of protected.

The older son was also experiencing great trauma over the
death of his brother who had been with him all of his life.
When he began having severe headaches and bouts of vomiting we thought it was his emotional reaction to his brother's
death.

The attacks became so severe after a month or two that I
had to take him for various tests to find the cause. Blood tests
and standard medical examination did not reveal any cause
and we were all beginning to feel that it truly was post-trau-
matic stress at the root of the problem. The doctor ordered one
last test, which was more intensive than the others. Standard
Xrays had revealed nothing, but this test was different.

When the doctor saw the new Xray he said, "What in the
world is that?" There was a cloud on the film that extended in

a circle about eight inches wide. They had never seen anything like this. Experts examined the film and determined that the left kidney had been retaining liquid for my son's entire life and it was now filled up like a water balloon.

The tube that would have drained the kidney was pinched off behind an artery instead of being in its proper place in front of it as the other one was. The decision was made that the kidney would have to be removed right away because the toxins were no longer tolerated by his body and he was in danger.

Another doctor was called in for consultation and was able to perform a surgery that would cause the kidney to drain by bringing the drainage tube into the correct place, without removing the kidney. The surgery was a success but it was a very difficult time for my son to have to go through such an extensive and painful surgery like this just after his brother's suicide. Our lives would never be the same, but things settled down somewhat, and took on a semblance of being "normal" for about three months.

The

FOURTH

Chapter

The next defining moment of my life came on a Saturday morning when I left the house to go to the grocery store. This was our usual weekend routine. My husband kept the children while I did the shopping. It was often my only time away and alone.

For some reason, on this morning, the oldest girl came running out the door as I started down the street. She was yelling and running in the street after the car. I stopped the car, turned around and pulled back into the driveway.

As she came running up to the car, I rolled down the window and asked her what was the matter. Seeing her tear-stained face I turned off the motor and went into the house. My daughter followed me into my room. My husband and the other children were out in the backyard. I sat down on my bed, drew her close to me, and asked her what was wrong.

She replied, "Please don't go, please!" I said, "I always go grocery shopping on Saturday. Why don't you want me to leave this morning?" Her answer to that question shook the only foundation that I thought was solid in my life, the permanence of my remaining family. She said, "Because when you are gone, Dad does bad things to us." Shocked, I said, "What bad things?" I expected to hear that he was harsh with them when I wasn't there.

The younger sister had come in from outdoors and found us in my room. She had listened at the door and when she heard what her sister said, she came in the room and said, "He does it to me too, Mom." Then they both began to tell me the ugly story. He would keep one or the other of the girls in the house and lock the other children out while he performed sexual acts upon them. They told of visits made to them in the night. The detail of their description made me sick to hear, but it made it clear that they were telling the truth. It was too graphic to have been made up.

The girls were twelve and fourteen when they told me. They had been only five and seven when my husband began molesting them. Learning this made several things clear. My husband and I had not been intimate for seven years. Now I understood why. He told the older girl that she was more of a wife to him than I was. That knowledge helped me understand why she had always seemed to be contemptuous of me—as though we were in some kind of competition and she had the advantage. She loved my husband as an adult woman loves a man. Coming from their love-starved background, I understood how it could be that they couldn't resist his advances. He promised the older girl trips with him, and bought her gifts that she wanted.

Why they decided to tell me that day I will never know, because they both said they still loved him and I realized then that they saw nothing shocking or ugly about it as I did. They seemed to know it was wrong, but saw it as love and didn't want to lose him. I was so shocked and confused it seemed like

the room was spinning. I tried to assure them of their innocence in God's eyes. I said nothing to him that day. I had to
have time to think of what I must do.

On Monday morning when everyone was gone, I called
the police department anonymously to ask them what I should
do. The officer told me incest was a serious crime in California.
He said it was a felony that carried an automatic twenty-year
prison sentence and that I had to turn him in now! He wanted
my husband's name and at that I hung up—shaken and overwhelmed by the decisions I had to make.

Knowing my primary responsibility was to protect the girls
from any further abuse, I called my aunt. She said her daughter had an attorney who could probably help me. I obtained
the number and made an appointment right away. Urgency
had taken hold of me to have whatever I was going to do
planned before one of the girls told my husband that they had
told me. I did not want to have a confrontation before I was
prepared. I was still as afraid of his anger as I had always been.

When I went to the attorney the next day, he told me that
if I did have my husband arrested, and pressed charges, he
would lose his job and be put in prison, leaving the family with
no means of support. "But," he said, "you can't let the abuse go
on. So, I suggest filing for a divorce. You certainly have grounds.
Have the divorce papers and a restraining order served to him
at the same time. Hopefully, that would protect both you and
the children. However," he warned me, "keep the divorce proceedings quiet until the last moment. Someone with his problems might become violent when he finds out he is losing his
family."

I now had a decision to make. Before I made the final decision, after much prayer and seeking the will of God in this
dilemma, I felt that I must give him a second chance before I
could be completely sure that divorce was inevitable. But, it
had to be under safe circumstances. Before giving him that
second chance, I wanted a restraining order in place in case of

any confrontation. I knew that even though it required beginning divorce proceedings to obtain a restraining order, those preliminary proceedings could be stopped any time. So, the attorney prepared the papers and within two weeks my husband was served with them at work.

The attorney was concerned for our safety and had advised me not to be home the day the papers were served, and for the week after, while my husband was removing his belongings from the house.

I had to plan ahead carefully to coordinate this very difficult time in our lives. I put the girls on the bus for a week at Girl Scout camp, and my youngest son and I went to stay at the Disneyland Hotel for two days, then with the couple who helped us before. I hoped that a couple of days in a fun-filled atmosphere might take the edge off the new trauma that this child had to face. He had lived through so many in his formative years of life. His nightmares still continued on a regular basis.

A few days after we returned to the house, my husband called saying how sorry he was for what he had done—afraid he would lose his job, his friends, and go to jail. He wanted a second chance. This was exactly what I had planned, so I invited him to dinner to see how things would go. The evening seemed to go well enough so I was planning to let him visit again.

But, after he left, the older girl told me that when she was washing the dishes at the sink he had come up behind her and was sexually fondling her.

I could not believe he would do something like that on his first opportunity at reconciliation. I knew by this act, that if the shock of what we had all just gone through and the threat of prison had not changed him, nothing would, and I had to protect the children. So I proceeded with the divorce.

My attorney informed me I could not give the court the real reason for the divorce or the judge would be obligated to have him arrested in the courtroom. By not publicly giving the reason for the divorce, my husband was off the hook legally. He told everyone there was something wrong with me because one day, out of the blue he was served with divorce papers at his work. As a result, he appeared the victim, and I was the one with the problem. I was, however, given custody of the children.

None of his family believed that what he had done was true. My mother and sister didn't believe it was true. I soon noticed that neighbors and even friends at church began to shy away from me. We had appeared the perfect family because we were in church every Sunday. I was the Parish Visitor and my husband was the church treasurer. The rejection of friends and abandonment by family once again produced that deep sense of aloneness.

It became apparent that we could not exist on the child support, so I went back to school to prepare myself for work after twenty-five years. I also needed to prove to myself that I was smart enough to hold a job.

I worked the class schedule around my responsibilities at home. After a year, a very strange thing began to happen. I couldn't understand it then and I still can't. The girls began rebelling strongly against me and seemed to resent me. Then I found out that my husband was in contact with them more than I knew, or was supposed to know.

He had moved back to Nevada, and when the divorce was final, he remarried. He was calling the girls to get them to come and live with him and his wife. That would totally clear his name in the event the truth might come out, and prevent any legal action which might be taken. He would be given custody if they lived with him.

The girls began saying they wanted to go and live with him. I was appalled. I couldn't understand it until they told me he said he would buy clothes for them and a car for the older girl.

I refused to let them go, although by now the older girl was old enough to make a choice of parental custody. They began to make my life a nightmare. Having new clothes and shoes and money are great temptations for girls their age, especially because of the poverty of their early years. They were angry and resentful because I would not let them go.

It became so bad that finally I took the older girl to Social Services to see about foster care because I could no longer control her and the situation was totally out of hand. But, when I saw the filthy condition of the house they were going to place her in, guilt wouldn't let me do it. The psychiatrist that the case worker had sent us to told me, after evaluating her, "You know she hates you, don't you?"

One night about 8:00, I was in my bedroom talking on the phone to a friend. Suddenly I heard the older girl screaming at me outside of my window. She was standing in the middle of the street. She was furious with me because she had gotten her driver's permit and wanted to take my car to the mountains with friends.

I had told her no—if anything happened to the car I could not afford to fix it. My denial infuriated her. She was yelling that she wanted to go live with "dad." I didn't worry about the neighbors anymore. So many police cars and problems had gone on at our house, the neighbors all shunned us except one next door.

I asked my friend on the phone if she could hear the screaming. She replied that she certainly could. I told her, "I can't live this way any more." She said, "Call your attorney." I reminded her that it was after 8:00 and his office would be closed. She said firmly, "Call him anyway!" So I did.

I could hardly believe my ears when he answered the phone. I said, "Listen!" Then I held the receiver up to the window screen. He listened a few moments, then said, "What is that!" I told him, "It's my oldest daughter standing out in the street screaming at me through my bedroom window because she wants to go live with my husband and his wife. Her desire for the material things he can give her and her sister has outweighed the effects of his abuse to them, and I can't live this way anymore."

When I asked my attorney, "What can I do? We can't go on this way," he replied, "It's been two years. Your husband has remarried. There are probably no more problems. You might as well let the girls go to live with them. He will file for custody because that will clear his name if the truth ever came out."

When I told the older girl she could go live with them, she was delighted. As soon as the younger girl found out, she wanted to go also. I knew I would have the same confrontations if I didn't let her go, so I decided to let her go also.

There was a deep hurt as I watched their absolute joy and excitement as they got ready to leave. Their eagerness to leave me after the years of working with their problems and adjusting our entire family to their needs at the expense of the needs of my natural children was painful for me to watch.

Within days my husband drove up in his new car, with his new wife beside him in her fur coat, and the girls ran out the front door and jumped in the car, scarcely even saying goodbye.

By now, my oldest son had begun working and going to school. He had his own apartment and was no longer with us. His pain and anger at the loss of any kind of close family life and the loss of his dreams of college kept him at a distance for several years. We scarcely saw each other during the next ten years. His emotional scars from his trauma-filled childhood never did completely heal. But now, twenty-five years later, we are very close. This closeness has brought healing to both of us.

With him gone, and the girls gone, that left just my youngest son with me in the home. Because of the way they had all left, I began to break down emotionally. I went into a time of deep apathy and sorrow. It was the beginning of the holiday season. I wasn't able to function. I made the mistake of calling my mother. I was hoping for a word of comfort, but there was no response. I couldn't talk and hung up.

My mother called my sister and told her my condition. My sister came over. I thought that she had come out of love, but she had come only because my mother had called her and told her to. She told me she was going to take my son and me with her to San Clemente. Because of being in limbo, and being so hungry for somebody who would reach out, I went. She had a half gallon wine bottle in the car and had been drinking on the way over and continued to drink all the way to her home. I just stared out the window and didn't say a word. I couldn't deal with reality. She and my son talked the whole time.

When I had gotten into bed that night she came in, around midnight. She stood over my bed and bent over me in a menacing attitude with her fists clenched, and said, "Has anyone ever really beaten you up?" I tried to talk with her quietly but she verbally let out a lot of hatred, saying I was demon-possessed. She told me that the next day she was going to call her psychiatrist to take me to the mental hospital and commit me, because I was crazy and I had demons that I had received attending church. Then she said, "I have a gun under my pillow and my bed faces the door. If you try to sneak out of the door tonight I'll kill you." I lay there a long time, shaken and trembling with fear of her. I was shocked out of my former stupor. When I thought it was quiet enough, having realized that she hadn't thought of the telephone, I sneaked the phone under the covers. I was shaking so hard I almost could not dial. How I remembered the number and dialed it in the dark, I'll never know. I called the couple that had come to help when my son died. They lived several miles away. I told them to come and get me right away. How I gave them directions to get there, I have no idea. I remembered the name of the street, but I didn't even know the house numbers. I just tried to describe the stairs at the front of the house. I crept around the bedroom gathering up my things without turning on the light, and I sneaked in where my son was sleeping and whispered to him, "Wake up; you can't say a word and don't make any noise." I tried to explain it to him without scaring him too badly. He was about twelve at that time, and bless his heart, he did exactly as I said. He and I started sneaking down the hallway past the open door of my sister's room. We were terrified.

Just as we got to the front door, a friend who had been staying with her opened the door from the outside and came in. I grabbed my son because I knew my sister had heard the door open. We ran down the stairs and out to the sidewalk. The couple from Placentia pulled up the exact second that we reached the bottom of the stairs. It was a miracle! Only God could have brought them all that way in such a short amount of time. They weren't even sure where the house was, and were going along slowly looking for it when we came running down and leaped into the car. I had no further contact with my sister until many years later, when she was dying of cancer. The years of drinking and dissipation had contributed to her early death.

When my son and I returned home that night, I realized that this terrifying experience had snapped me out of my inability to function. I became involved in my son's activities as a Little League mom, and a city basketball league mom. We enjoyed our companionship, but our peaceful time together did not last long.

The girls began calling him, telling him he needed to come up there where all the good stuff was. He was unable to resist the fun things they were talking about, and he was weary of all the questions from his classmates at school about what happened in our family. One day he finally asked me the dreaded question, "Mom, can I go and live with Dad?"

In spite of my best efforts at being the outgoing, energetic mom that an active twelve-year-old boy needed, I was emotionally wiped out and almost fifty. He was a good boy and a good sport about everything, but there was a sadness about him. Being the only other person left from what had been a family of seven, he was not a very happy boy.

I wanted his happiness more than anything. The guilt of my failures drained me of any confidence that I could make him happy, so I said he could go. The words caught in my throat and I could not even think what life would be like after he left.

School was not in session so they came to get him the following weekend. I helped him get packed with tears in my eyes that I could not let him see. I wanted him to feel this was going to be a time of fun and new experience in a different environment. I said my good-byes to my precious son inside the house, and watched out the window as he walked toward the car. Words cannot express the depths of my despair as I watched the happy, smiling faces of my ex-husband and his wife and the girls, as my son put his things in the trunk of the car and got in and they all drove away.

The

FIFTH

Chapter

I was alone. There was a chilling heaviness inside of me. The day my youngest son left, I got in the car and drove, and drove. I don't remember where. I felt devoid of life or feeling.

After four days of trying to evade the issue, I knew I had to go back into that empty house. I sat in the driveway a long time. As I entered the house and closed the door behind me, the awful stillness foretold the quiet emptiness of the days ahead of me.

I automatically started walking slowly down the familiar hallway leading to the bedrooms. Memories from the thousands of trips I had made up and down that hallway began to flood my mind. The mournful cry in the middle of the night, "Mom, I'm sick," that sent my tired feet flying to care for the needs of one of my children or the "hot chocolate" trips with the child who had a nightmare.

To me the bedroom doors now stood as silent sentinels of my failure as a wife and mother. As I walked by each door I thought of the occupant of that room. First there was my oldest son, who was so quiet, obedient, intelligent, kind, and hard working—now separated from me. Then my second son, with the all too familiar stab at my heart, his trauma, his suffering, his trying so hard, not knowing what was wrong with him; and finally his death. Next my youngest son, his struggles, his unmet needs, his fears and anxiety attacks, his cleverness in entertaining us and his quick wit. And finally, the girls; and the abuse they suffered in their early years, their insatiable needs, their inability to love me.

It was hard to open the door to the bedroom my ex-husband and I had shared—with his empty closet, his empty dresser, his bed removed. As I stood there in that barren room that had never known love, my single bed in the corner seemed to symbolize what my life had become.

I was alone and abandoned, two words that I had been afraid of since earliest childhood. My entire family was gone. I had no reason to get up in the morning. There were no meals to prepare, no lunches to fix, no laundry or ironing to do, no shopping, no haircuts, nothing, nothing, nothing. I had no purpose for living. My life had come to an end.

I lay down in bed that first dreadful night, with my Bible lying open on my chest, hoping in some way the words would permeate my body and enter my heart. The tears continued until exhaustion took over.

The next morning when I woke, I just sat on the edge of the bed in a stupor with my Bible in my hands. Then, as the ever present tears began to flow again, I fell to the floor with my face in the open pages of my Bible. I lay that way for hours, seemingly unable to get up. I seemed to feel closer to the Lord there.

Toward evening I pulled myself up and went to sit in a big chair in the living room. I sat there staring at the wall listening to soft classical music hour after hour to fill the silence. Music had always been my solace during lonely hours. Once again it soothed my aching soul. The phone never rang. It was a time of desperate aloneness and shame. This was my pattern for many days. I don't remember eating, but I must have eaten. Gradually the length of time spent on the floor began to lessen, but it was a long time before I stopped spending time there altogether and sat only in the chair all day, unable to concentrate on anything.

In her book *Honestly*, Sheila Walsh wrote so beautifully of the Lord:

> *"I never knew you lived so close to the floor, but every time*
> *I am bowed down, crushed by the weight of grief, I feel*
> *your hand upon my head, your breath upon my cheek,*
> *your tears upon my neck. You never tell me to pull myself*
> *together, to stem the flow of many tears. You simply stay*
> *by my side for as long as it takes, so close to the floor."*

That is the way it was for me on the floor.

After a few weeks, God began to comfort me. I could not have known it then, but the comfort He comforted me with at that time was the beginning of the fulfillment of II Corinthians 1:3,4 in my life.

> *"Blessed be God, the Father of our Lord Jesus Christ, the*
> *Father of mercies, and the God of all comfort; Who com-*
> *forts us in all our tribulation, that we may be able to*
> *comfort them which are in any trouble, by the comfort*
> *wherewith we ourselves are comforted by God."*

One night I was sitting in the living room, without feeling, without purpose, overwhelmed by failure in life. I slowly became aware of the presence of someone standing by me. My eyes had been closed. As I opened them and looked where I felt the presence, I saw nothing. But, somehow I knew it was a heavenly being and that it was standing close to me. I seemed to see the shadow of a white figure with my spiritual eyes, and not my physical eyes. Because I was seated and it was standing, I only saw a long skirt or robe. I was too overwhelmed to look higher.

There was a gentle force coming from that divine presence that seemed to surround me. At first I didn't know what it was, then it began to enfold me in a love like I had never known. I was enfolded and enraptured by it. It had the power within it to lift my spirit and my soul into a spiritual realm that I had never entered before. It was pure, absolute love. I couldn't move, I couldn't speak, the love became so intense that I wanted to respond some way, but I didn't know how.

I didn't know how to receive love like that. What does one do when immersed in the pure love of God? It was a profound spiritual experience. I don't know how long it lasted but when it was over, I felt strengthened. I felt life flow back into me. There was no way I could know it then, but this experience was an anointing for a ministry He was calling me to in my life.

My floor days were over. I stayed up during the day and went to a church the following Sunday. It was a different church than we had attended as a family before the divorce.

In the days that followed, an amazing thing began happening. In church, whenever I touched people to pray for them, they fell down. This was something new to me. At one evening service another strange thing happened—I couldn't open my eyes for almost half an hour, no matter how hard I tried. I didn't know the spiritual significance of that experience, but I knew it was God.

I knew I was going to have to go back to work, so I enrolled at Fullerton Junior College to finish my A.A. degree. This probably would not have been necessary, but the true underlying motive was that I had to prove to myself that I was not stupid.

Due to my inability to express myself well, I needed confidence to face the public. I did not know how the college-age kids would accept a classmate who was nearly fifty, but they were very *kind* to me and accepted me openly.

It was a great encouragement to me to be able to carry and pass with As and Bs such subjects as Anatomy and Physiology, Advanced Algebra, Astronomy, Psychology, and Political Science. All except for Physics—after eleven days I was totally overwhelmed and dropped the class.

Now that I was functioning again I was going to have to go back to work. At that time the only work experience I had was some secretarial and six years in banking twenty-five years ago. I seemed to have an aptitude for learning, but no skills. I applied at the local Bank of America and God gave me favor with the operations officer. She said normally she would not hire someone my age with so little experience, but she was touched by the circumstances that had forced me to go back to work. I was hired as a clearings clerk, which was a fancy name for operating a machine that required manual entry of every check and deposit that came in that day—the same work I had done years ago. It was physically demanding and tiring, but I was grateful for the job. Later on I became a teller again, as in my earlier years.

The operations officer and I developed a rapport. She was a member of the local Optimist Sorority. They gave scholarships to help women who have had to struggle through difficult circumstances, but have gone to work determined to improve their lives. The Sorority was very kind in giving me their Optimist "Award for Achievement After Sorrow"!

In all the years of my life I had never lost my deep love for the Lord. And, except for the "floor time," I had never stopped reading and studying His Word. I quoted verses to myself continually, especially those regarding peace of mind.

2 Corinthians 10:5 was my stabilizer when memories tried to overwhelm.

"*Casting down imaginations [reasoning and thoughts], and every high thing that exalts itself against the knowledge of God, and bringing into captivity every thought to the obedience of Christ.*"

Because the painful memories tried to control my thoughts, in spite of my efforts to subdue them, I had to find a way that I could *choose* not to think about them.

I knew that verse was the answer, but I didn't know how to bring the thoughts into the obedience of Christ.

As I was attempting to do this one day, sitting at my kitchen table, I clearly imagined Jesus standing with His hands outstretched to me, palms up, waiting for me to put those painful memories in His hands.

I tried thinking of them one by one and mentally putting each one in His hands. That was too scattered. I needed somehow to bundle them up.

In my mind I spread a piece of brown wrapping paper on the table in front of me. Then, deliberately, one by one, I placed on that paper all of the haunting thoughts, discomforting emotions, tormenting words, and disturbing pictures in my memory that I wanted to be free of.

I took a lot of time with this. When I was finished, I mentally folded the paper, tied it with a string, and placed the package in His hands.

If I chose to spend time thinking about any of those things again, I would have to go to Him, ask for the package back, take it out of His hands and open it.

I consciously focused my thoughts on God in the long hours alone, and before long, I began to think of other women who were alone. Because the Holy Spirit was giving me deeper understanding in the Word of God, I began writing Bible studies for women.

There was a small group of us who sat together in church. We were all women who were alone. We wanted to get together for fellowship during the week. It seemed a natural progression from that for me to start a home Bible study. They were excited and so was I.

The anointing of God continued to manifest itself in the teaching and personal ministry. The group soon grew in number. The gifts of the Holy Spirit were in operation and all of our lives were changed and enriched.

The desire to minister to women who were alone continued until it seemed to have become a divine compulsion. In bed at night, my thoughts and prayers always turned to them out there in the night somewhere. Maybe they were homeless and abandoned. Maybe they were on the street. Maybe they had children, with no place for them to sleep and no food for them.

Now, I no longer cried for myself at night, I cried for them as if I were experiencing their pain.

Going to work every day at the bank, often encountering the unattractive side of people where their money was concerned, I found it increasingly difficult to be serving the public in the secular world. I wanted to be serving God. My thoughts and my heart were concerned with spiritual things, not monetary things.

At church I heard that Western Medical Center needed chaplains to visit the sick in their hospital. I asked my pastor about it to see if he thought I was spiritually qualified to do that. He encouraged me to do it by all means.

The director of the chaplain program at the hospital was the head of a department there called Someone Cares. Besides the recruiting and coordinating of chaplains, this department did many other one-on-one services of compassion for patients in all areas of the hospital.

The chaplain ministry was rewarding, but as I learned more about the work of the Someone Cares department, I wanted to be doing something meaningful like that in people's lives.

I called the director of Someone Cares one day at work. I told her if she ever needed someone in that department, I would like to do it. Her response was immediate. She said, "It just so happens that the hospital administrator told me just today that I could hire another person in this department."

I gave my resignation notice at the bank and began my season of work at Someone Cares. One phase of our department was decedent affairs. This involved comforting families, obtaining releases for autopsies, and taking family members to the hospital morgue to view their loved one.

One day when I entered the autopsy room, a body was still on the table. A knife of pain pierced my heart as I thought of my dead son lying on a table like this.

But, strange as it sounds, seeing these dead bodies proved to me that the human spirit and soul go in to eternal life and the flesh truly is just clay. That is exactly what it looks like and what it feels like when the spirit and soul have left it. This was an assurance to me that the spirit and soul of my son were alive, even though his body was dead.

As I continued my work there, I was still leading the Bible studies, and the desire to help women and children who were homeless was still very much alive and continuing to grow stronger.

After a year in my Someone Cares work, my youngest son called and was very upset. He did not like living with his father and stepmother and was very unhappy. And because he was very tall and athletic, his basketball coach was putting excessive pressure on him to excel in training, with unrealistic expectations from him on the basketball court. The pressures were causing severe anxiety attacks.

He wanted to come home and live with me because he was getting into some bad habits with some of his friends. He wanted to stop that and go to a Christian high school down here. His father had not requested custody of him, only the girls, so I told him he could come back. He had been gone three years by now. He gave away all of his un-Christian albums and magazines, and came with only his Bible and his clothes, wanting to make a new start.

After he came I began having trouble at work. The only Christian high school was too far to take the bus, so he had to be driven. By the time I got to work, because of the traffic, I was often late.

By now I had come to realize that the desire to help homeless and abused women and children had become a calling on my life. I knew that I was going to do something about it. I heard myself saying things like, "Someday I'm going to have a house where women can go with their children when they don't have any place to sleep at night." This had to be from the Lord, because at that time, the plight of the homeless was seldom recognized and not publicized to the extent that it is today. But God knew the day was coming when homelessness among women and children would be a major problem in our nation.

The

SIXTH

Chapter

B y this time I had finally sold what had been our family home. For a long time after the divorce I had hung on to it as my only security. But the constant reminders brought back by the surroundings began to wear on my emotions. After the legal division of the equity with my ex-husband, I put my half in the bank. I never felt it was mine somehow, so I never withdrew any of it. This proved to be part of God's plan for my life that was soon to be revealed.

In 1978 I attended a church retreat in the mountains. A woman named Daisy Osborn was our speaker. She was a missionary to Africa with a powerful anointing from God. Her words captured and held me as she exhorted us to do whatever it was we were going to do for God now.

Her words could not have hit me any harder if she had called my name when she said, "If God has been calling you to do something, but you're not sure how He wants you to do it, when you go home from here, take a pen and paper, kneel down beside your bed, ask God what He wants you to do, write it down and DO IT!"

Those words went off in my spirit! I could hardly wait to go home and do exactly what she had said. Somehow, I knew this was the beginning.

When I returned home, I locked the door, took the phone off the hook, took my pen and paper, knelt down by my bed, and waited! When He spoke to me by His Holy Spirit, it was not an audible voice, it was a voice in my mind. It was as clear as if it had been audible and I began to write.

He told me to take the money from the sale of the family home, put it as a down payment on a large home that would be a shelter for homeless women and their children, and that I was not to engage in any fund raising. I was to trust Him to make the mortgage payments, and there would be more shelters.

I stood to my feet feeling like a modern Joan of Arc waving the paper like a banner. I was excited and ready to begin. But first I had to find a house. This was in early 1979. I was still working, which made it impossible for me to go house hunting during the day. I needed a real estate agent but I doubted I could find one who would take me seriously when I told him the circumstances: I wanted him to find me a big five-bedroom home to be used for a shelter, for $20,000 down (the money I hadn't touched after the sale of the family home); I couldn't qualify for any financing because I'd never had any credit; I had no collateral for a loan; and God was going to make the house payments.

With the agents I talked to, I hardly got past line one. Then as the word began to spread in church that I was looking for a home to start a shelter, a young real estate agent named Bill Cho approached me and said he would like to help me. He began researching and visiting his listings without success until one day two months later he called me on a Saturday saying, "I think I've found the house for you!"

There was a house that had been listed on the market for a long time by the owners, but agents were never able to show it because the tenants would not let them in. Bill had tried two or three times to get in to see it, without success. Then on the day he called me, he had gone to the house early to see about getting in to see it. To his surprise, a young man answered the door and let him in.

The young tenant explained that his father and mother had gone to Mexico to visit relatives. He was a little developmentally disabled. If he had been told not to let anyone in he must have forgotten it. After Bill looked around he called me to come right away before the parents came back. He felt it could be what I was looking for.

I was excited! As I drove through the rain, I was praising God and asking Him to let this be the house. As I drove up I liked the old-fashioned style of it. It was set in the older section of town, where many such historical homes had been carefully preserved.

At one time this one had been carefully preserved too, but when I saw it, it was a mess. It had been raining hard that day. There were two big, muddy German shepherd dogs that kept running in and out through the sliding screen door. Literally through the door, because the sliding screen door was closed. There were old cars up on blocks in the yard and thick black grease was everywhere. The carpets were black where the grease had been tramped in on dirty shoes. The dogs ran freely through the house, sopping wet, chasing each other.

Bill began pointing out basics that would make the house work as a shelter. The first condition was met. There were five bedrooms. Four were upstairs and one at the foot of the stairs. I had to trust his judgment because all I could see was the incredible amount of work it would take to make the place livable. But, as he pointed out, the grease and dirt and debris in all the rooms was cosmetic stuff. The basic structures underneath were solid. It's funny how we remember little things. I thought how cute the wall oven was because it had a little round window on the door. That somehow made me like the house and know that I wanted it.

But the thing that made me like it the most was what Bill told me as we sat in the car and talked after seeing the house. He said, "The second condition is also met. Because of the lowered price, due to the home's condition, $20,000 would be the required down payment. And, the third condition is met because the owners are willing to carry the mortgage, so you don't have to qualify for financing, which would have been impossible."

That left only one condition to be met. That was to trust God for the mortgage payments. I smiled knowing that was the surest condition of all that would be met, because above all things, I knew God is faithful.

We went into escrow immediately. This led to some very interesting and unusual circumstances. The escrow officer was a wonderful lady that I will never forget. She said, "I have never had an escrow like this before and I can't believe I'm doing it. The property has been sub-leased because the tenant owes money to the Mafia, we will have to evict them, get the financial papers of the tenant straightened out before the owners can receive their money, and the purchaser has no income to make house payments."

But this lady worked hard for us because she was so thrilled about the venture we were undertaking to shelter homeless women and children. By the grace of God, escrow closed on July 29, 1979. I was the owner of a big five-bedroom house. The next mortgage payment would be due September 1.

The die was cast. The decision was made. The step had been taken. To turn back was not an option. I quit my job and for two weeks the women from our Bible study and other people from the church worked very hard with me to clean the house enough so I could move in. We all felt so much love for the homeless women and children who would be coming to live in the house that we wanted everything to be as lovely as possible. There was joy in our hearts, thinking of the women and children who would be living there, as we mopped and scoured, painted and papered, scrubbed grease from the carpets, and declared war on the fleas.

As others heard about the ministry we were preparing for, donations of all kinds began coming in. When the house was ready, people helped me move in the furniture from my apartment.

When I turned off the light and climbed into bed that first night, all alone in that big two-story house, that's when the full realization hit me.

My conscience took that opportunity to be heard. "What have you done? What have you done?! Do you realize you owe $137,000 and you have no money! They can put you in jail if you can't pay it!"

Then my faith would lift a rather feeble voice in response. This roller coaster continued off and on during the night. But, in the morning, when the sun came up, my faith rose with it. It was no longer feeble. It seemed to have entered into a new dimension.

From that day I began to realize I was different. I was experiencing a strength and confidence for ministry that I did not have before. It overrode my fleshly fears and insecurities. God had given me this spiritual gift of faith listed in 1 Corinthians 12:9. What a tremendous gift it was! It was a taste of heaven on earth. Not only did it carry me through the beginning years, it has carried me through every year since. It has never lessened or vacillated and has never left me. How I treasure that gift. No one can take it from me and time cannot erode it.

Thus began the exciting, demanding, rewarding, stretching, satisfying, loving, heart wrenching, divine, emotional, exhausting, heart warming, sorrowful, uplifting, courageous, draining, maturing, fulfilling, glorious adventure that became my life.

There were eight people in those early beginnings that were willing to serve as volunteer corporate officers and board members. They were instrumental and used of God to help with the initial phases of establishing a non-profit corporation and applying for federal and state tax-exempt status, which was granted in October, 1979.

I would like to honor them even after all these years by mentioning them here. The officers were Bill and Tenette Cho, and Tony and Rita Palmieri. The board members were Ben and Diane Carrington, Roy and Bev Shebeck, and Bill and Verie Whitaker. Bill Cho is the agent who found the house and believed in the vision.

I am eternally grateful to these wonderful friends who believed in the vision and had a deep love and desire to help desperate mothers and children.

Rita, who was to be corporate secretary, and I, met with the attorney who was to draw up the incorporation papers. In order to have a corporation, we had to have a name that no one else had. I had the name already picked out; in fact I had already accepted two checks made out to that name. It never even occurred to me that I would have to choose something else. But, when the attorney checked with the state to be sure I could have that name, Faith House, they told him it belonged to someone else.

When he told me I would have to pick a different name I couldn't believe it. It seemed like a major setback to my naive, new-ministry sensibilities.

I sat stunned for a few minutes, looking out the window wondering why the name I had chosen was taken, (emphasis on the "I") when I had been so confident it was right. Finally, I sighed and silently said, "What shall we call it, Lord?" The words, "The Sheepfold" dropped into my mind. I disposed of the thought, thinking it could not have been from the Lord because I didn't like it at all.

The attorney told us that we would need to come up with a name before the end of the appointment in order to proceed with the incorporation. Rita sat leafing through her Bible while the attorney and I went on with other matters of by-laws and articles.

When the appointment was drawing to a close, the attorney asked, "Have you decided on a name?" Rita looked up from her Bible and said, "I believe it should be called The Sheepfold, from John chapter 10." In my astonishment, all I could do was nod my head in agreement.

Ever since that day I have thanked God for the perfect name He chose. A sheepfold is referred to in the Bible as an enclosure made of stones or brush where the shepherds bring their sheep and lambs at night to protect them from being attacked by wild animals. The shepherds lay across the door to sleep in order to protect the sheep and keep the predators out.

Jesus portrayed Himself in Scripture as the door of the sheep. *"I am the door, by Me if anyone enters in, that person shall be saved, protected and nourished."* John 10:9

Jesus said, *"Verily, verily I say unto you, he that enters not by the door into the sheepfold, but climbs up some other way, the same is a thief and a robber. But He that enters in by the door is the shepherd of the sheep."* John 10:1,2

"I am the good Shepherd and know my sheep and am known of mine. I lay down my life for the sheep." John 10:14,15

So many Scriptures fit that name for this ministry to homeless women who often come to us pregnant and with children we call little lambs.

"He shall feed His flock like a Shepherd; He shall gather the lambs with His arm, and carry them in His bosom, and shall gently lead those that are with young." Isaiah 40:11

On my birthday, September 2, 1979, we held an open house for all of our friends and church members to dedicate the house for the ministry of providing safe refuge, love and daily care to homeless women and children in Jesus' name. The pastor's words and prayer were an inspiration for us all and truly set the atmosphere of the house.

I wore a dress with pockets that day, unaware of what a happy circumstance that would be. During the afternoon people began quietly slipping money into my pockets for the ministry, and for my birthday. I had my first house payment.

One week later I received a phone call from the pastor of my church telling me a homeless woman with a child had called him seeking shelter, and asking if I was ready to take her in. I assured him I was. He told me she was in another city and asked if I would be able to go pick her up. I assured him I would. He gave me her name and phone number. I called her for directions, got into my little blue Honda Civic, and away I went—a woman on a mission! I was excited!

On the way there I was checking myself to see how I felt actually starting the ministry. I was amazed at my peace of mind, my confidence, my joy and excitement, and my feeling of absolute faith that could only come from knowing that I was in the perfect will of God for my life. Just three years before, I thought my life was over, and here I was at 53 starting a brand new life with meaning and purpose.

She was waiting when I arrived, surrounded by plastic bags filled with her only possessions. She was very nervous and unsure where I was taking her. Her name was Linda Mayberry and her little boy's name was Chris. He was six years old.

Little Chris gave me something to remember him by on the way back to the shelter. He was so nervous; he put his little face between the bucket seats to talk to us from the back seat. His mom and I were in the front. We were almost home when Chris suddenly said, "I don't feel good." Next thing we knew he threw up all over us, the gear shift, and the dashboard. I remember thinking, "My ministry has been launched and christened, but not with champagne." There have been many such christenings since then.

As we drove in the driveway of the home, I felt this was the beginning of what would be the most challenging, yet fulfilling, adventure of my life—and I was right!

It was with great pleasure and satisfaction that I took Linda and Chris up to their room. Everything looked so fresh and homey. Clean sheets and soft blankets awaited their tired bodies. Linda had been physically abused and little Chris was sick.

I set about providing every form of tender loving care that I had dreamed of doing since accepting the call of God to begin a ministry to women and children who were on the street or would be if someone did not help them.

Linda had a history of abuse that brought tears to my eyes. She was the only woman in the shelter, so we spent much time together. I spent hours guiding her in Bible study and prayer. My single desire was to make her feel loved and cherished, not just by me, but by God. She committed her heart and her life to Jesus Christ, and little Chris accepted Jesus as his Savior.

Within four weeks another call had come. One of our church members had been beaten and thrown out of her house by her husband, who was also a member. She had no children, which did not fit the criteria for the shelter but I could never have said no to such a need. Valerie was a lively, intelligent lady who loved Jesus. It was my first encounter with true domestic violence. Her experience showed me that it can happen in any family. We remained close for years after she left the shelter. She always called me her second mom.

It was she who told me the value of a monthly newsletter. In spite of my shyness to do so, it was at her insistence, and with her help, that I wrote the first newsletter, sitting in my little closet under the stairs after the women and children were in bed. I have written one every month for twenty-three years since then, and still continue to do so.

The calls for help began coming more often as word began to spread that a shelter such as ours now existed. At that time, there was a little known, but growing problem with homelessness, especially among women and children. People found it hard to believe that there were actually women and children on the streets who were homeless, abandoned, and abused.

Police departments and other agencies began giving out The Sheepfold number to any woman needing shelter. Calls were coming in at all hours of the day and night. Many a night after I had fallen in bed exhausted, a call came for help. I would get up, pull my clothes on, like a fireman answering the fire bell, and away I would go. (Fortunately, my bedroom was on the ground floor so I didn't have to slide down a pole.)

I went fearlessly down dark alleys, into run-down motels, hotels, parks, bus stops, anywhere, anytime, to pick up a woman in need.

I remember one night going out at 2:30 in the morning to a very dark, forbidding motel. Most of the lights were out. The bulbs were mostly broken or burned out. I went down a dingy passageway and finally found the room.

The abuser who had just beaten her up was standing there in the room. He looked about ten feet tall to me. But, I was on a mission. He just stood there with his arms crossed, glaring at us. So I just started putting her things into a suitcase, asking her what she wanted to take.

The baby was in great need of a diaper change, so I laid it down and changed it. Then I took the children and the suitcase out to the car in front and began putting them in. The abuser was still standing in the same place, in the same position, without moving, without saying a word. It was as though an angel had used spiritual cryogenics on him.

When the mother came out and got into the car, I put the stick shift of that little Honda Civic in first gear and took off with screeching tires.

The phrase "Fools rush in where angels fear to tread" kept running through my head, and I pictured the angels waiting at the curb while I rushed in.

Unfortunately, the woman herself turned out to be an abusive mother. I began to suspect something was wrong in the children's behavior. I met the woman's mother and she hinted at it as though she wanted me to do something about it. The day I looked out the window where the little boy was in his bathing suit playing in the sprinklers and saw her begin to beat him viciously with the rubber garden hose was the day I did something about it.

After I ran out and stopped her, I called Child Protective Services to report her. They told me she had six prior reported incidents, so this time they would take the children away. I was totally devastated—I had never witnessed a mother brutalizing her child before.

The woman's mother called me later and thanked me for reporting her daughter to the authorities. She had known abuse was happening to the children, but was afraid of her daughter.

There are hundreds of stories of abuse to children that have been told to me through the years, and the anguish of my mind and spirit is fresh with every story.

The

SEVENTH

Chapter

Cooking, housecleaning, laundry, organization, and sharing
the love of Jesus with people—nothing in this list would
appear as qualification for a God-ordained ministry. But,
those abilities were exactly what were required for the ministry
that God called me to.

I found that every experience I ever had was needed in
ministering to hurting, frightened women and children. Even
the reclusiveness and loneliness of my early years, and after my
family left, had trained me to be able to stand alone as the one
in authority. This was important because there were sometimes
strong-willed, angry women who came to the shelter. They felt
cheated by the world, and by God. They felt somebody owed
them something and rebelled against any kind of authority or
rules.

Most of them had looked for love in the wrong places and had not found it. They gave themselves to whoever seemed to care about them. Their need for love was desperate and often started at a young age. Pregnancies and school dropouts were common. Back then, abortion was not a legal option and was seldom a consideration. So having two or three children by different fathers by the age of nineteen or twenty was not uncommon in the women who came.

There were women and children of all ages, and every kind of need. Some were pregnant and had the baby while they were with us. I remember a lot of nights sitting for hours in the uncomfortable waiting room chairs, at the local emergency room, waiting for the delivery of one of our "little lambs."

The whole house always took part in the celebration when mother and baby came home. Everyone took turns holding the baby, feeding it, loving it. We had a little shower for the mom with a special dinner and cake. The Sheepfold supplied all the infant clothing and supplies that were needed, because the moms had no money to buy them.

There were difficult decisions to be made in those early days. One was the length of time a woman should stay. At first I tried six weeks. But, that required the children to be registered in school. They would just get settled in, feeling adjusted, only to be uprooted again, upsetting all of us. It caused those whose time was up to feel they were being kicked out when there seemed to be no reason to go. Those times were very hard on me and remembering them is painful.

One woman sat on her suitcase at the end of the driveway for a long time yelling obscenities at me and The Sheepfold. I finally had to call a Sheepfold board member to come and take her to a motel.

Another woman absolutely refused to leave. I spent two days trying to convince her that her time was up and she had to leave. Explaining that she knew this day was coming.

She became so obnoxious and disturbing to everyone in the house that I had to call the police to come and remove her.

There was another single lady who had serious mental problems. One night I was awakened at 2:30 A.M. and heard a strange noise upstairs. I went quietly up the stairs and noticed water seeping under the bathroom door. I opened the door, and the lady was sitting in the bathtub, fully clothed, with the water running, flowing over the edge of the tub.

When I asked her what she was doing, she didn't know. I turned off the water and tried to get her to get out of the tub. She absolutely refused. By that time the other residents were awake. I had no idea what to do. One of the women said to call the psychiatric unit at the county hospital near us and they would send someone to get her.

I had never done anything like that before. They came to get her and she was angry! They took her away for a seventy-two hour hold and evaluation. The next day I packed her things, unsure of what to do with them. My answer arrived exactly three days later when the lady came marching in with a great big man behind her. She accused me of stealing and demanded her things.

She tried very hard to provoke a physical encounter, but the Lord (and seeing the big man behind her) gave me wisdom and love for her. He never spoke and they left without incident. Her sister and mother came to see me a few days later. Their attitude was not pleasant. They tried to question the legality of what I had done. I don't know what she had told them, but when I explained what had happened and the upset it caused the other residents, they understood. I couldn't help but wonder why *they* didn't help her more to keep her from being on the street. They probably had run out of places to send her.

After these incidents and seeing the pain from being uprooted, I decided to reduce the length of stay to two weeks. That way, I thought, the children would not have to be enrolled in school, the women would understand it was a temporary stay and not get so settled in. It would force them to seek jobs more quickly and begin right away to seek more permanent housing.

This really attracted "bag ladies" that lived on the street by choice. I guess the word spread that there was a place they could come and be given good meals, a warm bed, and clothes for a couple of weeks, without much required of them. Do a few chores if their back was all right (and very few were), listen to a Bible study every day, go to church a couple of times, then go back on the street where they wanted to be.

Many of them had problems too severe for me to deal with. It didn't take long for me to realize I was in over my head and needed to get before the Lord on my face again.

As soon as I did that, the dust began to clear, the chaos began to cease, and it was a new beginning. I had been taking in single women, pregnant women, elderly women, and bag ladies, as well as some women with children.

The Lord showed me that I was not following what He had called me to do, which was to provide safe refuge, food, clothes, daily care, and the Word of God to homeless, abused women *with* children—period. In the first months I had more women than children. That was how far off the mark I had gotten because calls had been coming from the police requesting shelter for homeless women who were afraid of being raped or robbed on the street at night. Then agencies for the homeless, the mentally ill, single women, and unwed pregnant teenagers began calling. Well-meaning citizens were also calling because they had found homeless women on the street and had been given my number by the police department. Because I couldn't say no to anyone needing help, it was not long before I had chaos in my lovely home, and I was exhausted mentally, physically and spiritually by the end of the first six months.

I was doing all the cooking, cleaning, shopping, Bible studies, going out to pick up new residents, keeping records, handling phone calls, and ministering to the women and children. My day started very early to prepare breakfast and get everyone up and ended very late getting everyone down.

I had allowed myself to cross over the boundaries that He had set that would have protected me and the women and children. Establishing those boundaries made it like a true sheepfold—a place of rest and quiet where the sheep and lambs were safe.

As I sought the Lord for answers, He showed me that I was to keep the women and children for six months. I was to set a daily schedule, write the rules so they could have a copy to refer to and sign, assign their cleaning duties by their room number, establish a system so they could save their money, from welfare or working, toward the down payment on an apartment, require their focus and involvement in the daily Bible studies, and have them do personal Bible studies during quiet time in the afternoon.

Things were more peaceful after that. But I soon came to realize how deeply these precious women had been wounded and mistreated from childhood. I saw that I had been expecting behaviors they were incapable of producing. They lacked such things as self-discipline, neatness, good hygiene, and mothering skills. They were totally unfamiliar with an ordered lifestyle, and most had never adhered to any kind of a time schedule. To my surprise, I learned that some of them had never made a bed and did not know how to change the sheets.

One of my earliest struggles involved requiring bath time as a daily routine. The list of rules kept growing. Hygiene had to be taught and enforced in every detail. The use of deodorant, proper care of their teeth, wearing modest clothing, hair washing on a regular basis, instruction on proper procedures for feminine hygiene products, proper disposal of diapers and required wearing of shoes at all times for the women and the children were just a few of the things that had to be taught and written down. I gave cleaning assignments, bath times, hair washing and laundry days by room number.

An early discovery that I made was that many of these women were homeless because of their refusal to subject themselves to any kind of authority. They wanted to be free to do whatever they wanted, when they wanted to. Following a schedule was torture for some.

A rule had to be made restricting the smoking of cigarettes to after meals, *after the dishes were done*, in the designated area outside of the house, and only for fifteen minutes. There was a lot of complaining about that one. I tried to restrict smoking altogether, but it was such a crutch for them they would sneak down to the corner to smoke where all the neighbors could see them. Another rule was that anyone who ever smoked any-where in the house would be asked to leave immediately. The fire hazards were too great and smoking did not reflect the Christian values we were teaching. Those who used their money for cigarettes were not supplied with coins for the pay phone in the house. They were used to taking help from oth-ers, but not used to taking responsibility for their choices.

One of the happiest memories for me at the beginning of The Sheepfold was dinnertime when we all gathered around the dining room table for our meals.

I worked especially hard to always make good meals, and as I sat there looking at the faces along the sides of the table, and the little children in their high chairs, I would feel a warm rush of love for them all. I felt great satisfaction at being able to provide good food for them and know there were warm, clean beds waiting for them upstairs, providing safe refuge under The Sheepfold roof.

There were times, because of the lack of facilities or train-ing where they were, that the women and children had come in from sleeping in the park or on the streets with their hair mat-ted, making the air heavy with the smell of unwashed bodies. They often had never been taught cleanliness or table manners. Even when I was not able to eat anything because of the sights and smells, my spirit did not want to be any place else. My heart swells with love for these precious women and children when-ever I am with them, in whatever condition they are.

Even though I was right where I wanted to be, where I knew God had called me to be, it was still hard to comprehend the reality of the fact that I was actually sitting there, in the house God had provided, living the fulfillment of the vision of a shelter for homeless women and children.

This sense of oneness with God, knowing I was in His perfect will, is what gave me the faith to minister to the hundreds of women and children that I lived with, sharing their daily lives, their past experiences, their emotional traumas, and witnessing their restoration to wholeness through the mercy, grace, and never failing power of the Word of God to change their hearts and their future.

Jeremiah 29:11 became a standard we all clung to: *"For I know the thoughts that I think toward you, says the Lord, thoughts of peace, and not of evil, to give you a future and a hope."*

There was a tremendous need for a mother figure in the lives of the women who came. There was a common thread of wounding in childhood in their backgrounds of neglect, sexual and physical abuse, rejection, and lack of love in relationships. Many of them felt resentment when I enforced authority in the house. They felt they were being told what to do, and they rebelled against that authority over them, as if they were being treated like children again.

Almost every woman who has come to The Sheepfold has had what I would call an "orphan heart." I well remember those feelings in my own life, which helped me to identify and understand their reactions and their emotions. They may know who their mother and father are, but when they needed them—there was no one there. Emotional abandonment creates insecurity so deep that only Jesus can fill the void. He said: *"I will never leave you or forsake you. So we may boldly say, 'The Lord is my helper, and I will not fear what man shall do unto me.'"* Hebrews 13:5, 6

I soon found that although they all had a common need for shelter and daily care, this was the only thing they had in common. Every woman and every child was totally different from

the other. Each had a different background, different education, different spiritual experiences and beliefs, and different
relationships.

People used to ask me what the reasons were for women
and children to be in this situation. In answering their questions, I began to see the following parallels:

- They had been wounded in childhood.
- They had been forsaken or violated through violence,
  drugs, or desertion of responsibilities by their provider.
- Their own actions had burned out their families or
  friends.
- They had never accepted Jesus as their Savior, or they
  had at one time, but walked away.
- Because of their desperate need for love and affection
  resulting in emotional instabilities, they gave themselves
  to men who had problems, with or without the benefit
  of marriage—usually ending in pregnancies.

God created women to be a helpmate. A woman is emotionally displaced when robbed of the opportunity to play her
intended role. And when she has no knowledge of the wonderful grace of God, she is open to devilish deceptions.

Knowing firsthand the vulnerability of a woman left alone,
I emphasized the importance of learning about the fatherhood
of God and making Jesus the Lord of their life. I taught the
ability of Jesus to lead, guide, comfort, strengthen, cherish, and
love them more than any human being ever could—thereby
filling that emptiness in their soul.

This was done in a homelike atmosphere of fellowship
with a peer group that understood each other's pain. I knew
that when they understood they were a vital and permanent
part of the Body of Christ, their loneliness would disappear
and they would be able to stand alone in the days ahead. I
knew that learning of God's eternal love for them and the

forgiveness that the blood of Jesus purchased for them, would overcome the scars of rejection, abuse, and abandonment.

There was no TV or secular radio playing in the house. An atmosphere of praise was maintained through the Bible teachings and praise music plus pauses during the day to pray for each other's needs.

Because it was an atmosphere that allowed the Holy Spirit free access to souls, 90-95 percent of the women and children who stayed here either received Jesus as their Savior for the first time, or recommitted their lives to Him.

The percentage of salvations has not changed in all the succeeding years, and to see a soul saved is as thrilling to me today as it was back then. The change is dramatic. Faces with drawn, nervous, and frightened expressions are transformed to radiant joy.

One resident said the moment she stepped across the threshold into the shelter, she was instantly delivered from a "four pack-a-day" cigarette habit.

The peace of the Lord was tangible everywhere in the house and the power of the Holy Spirit was at work in all of our lives.

The

E I G H T H

Chapter

There were many adjustments for all of us in the shelter to make in our relationships with each other. There is nothing like living together day and night to bring out the differences in personalities and the frictions that can result without the oil of forgiveness.

The women who came were from widely differing backgrounds, sometimes involving drugs, alcohol, prison, uncontrolled satisfying of the flesh, rebellion against authority, physical abuse or abandonment, but they were all hurt—deep hurts that the world cannot heal. Only the touch of Jesus can soothe those deep places within the soul, and only the Word of God can pierce to their depths. We learned together that only as we were willing to allow the Holy Spirit to work in us, to *choose* to love each other, and to allow the Word to have first place in our thoughts and lives by applying Scriptures to our problem, were we able to live in peace and harmony.

> *"For the Word of God is alive, and powerful, and sharper*
> *than any two edged sword, piercing even to the dividing*
> *asunder of soul and spirit, and of the joints and marrow,*
> *and is a discerner of the thoughts and intentions of the*
> *heart."* Hebrews 4:12

When they were able to understand why their thinking was wrong, and to identify their true motives for the things they had done, their hearts began to open to the Lord, and those terrible wounds of the soul began to heal, bringing freedom to love God with all their heart, mind, soul and strength—as Jesus commanded us to do..

It was beautiful to see strangers from different walks of life blend into a family where suspicion and resentment were replaced by peace and love. As we shared ourselves and ministered to each other, yokes of emotional bondage were destroyed.

We met during the day and night for Bible study, prayer, and sharing. I wish I could tell you of all the things God did in the lives of the women and children who came here. Each person was different when they left because God's Word does not return to Him void, and He watches over His Word to perform it.

> *"For as the rain comes down, and the snow from heaven,*
> *and returns not there, but waters the earth, and makes it*
> *bring forth and bud, that it may give seed to the sower*
> *and bread to the eater; So shall my word be that goes*
> *forth out of my mouth; it shall not return unto me void,*
> *but it shall accomplish that which I please, and it shall*
> *prosper in the thing whereto I sent it."* Isaiah 55: 10,11

Just in the very first group who stayed at the shelter, one girl, a pregnant teenager, repented of living in sin and received Jesus.

A woman who learned that God loves everyone accepted the fullness of His love and was born again. Another turned away from drugs, found work, and became a witness for Jesus wherever she went. A mother was reunited with her stolen child. Another woman was delivered from demonic oppression; and an abusive mom was set free from the bondage of child abuse.

This was just one little group that was to be followed by thousands of such women and their children.

When the time came for our first holidays together, I had no idea what an emotional experience it would be. I wanted to make Thanksgiving and Christmas fun, with good food and special treats. I decorated everything and set the table with my best dishes. I wasn't prepared for the sorrow and sadness in the eyes and faces of the women when the day arrived.

It never occurred to me that they would be longing to be with their own families, or were reliving the pain of the broken relationships.

The atmosphere was so oppressive on Thanksgiving that I called them all together. One mother didn't even want to come to dinner and stayed in her room; another was crying because she wanted her family back.

When I got them all together, I shared with them that our thankfulness was not based on whether they had a husband, or a home of their own, or family members that loved them; it was based on the promise of God that we were all partakers of the salvation of Jesus Christ that gave them healing, wholeness, soundness of mind, deliverance from their enemies, rescue from a life of sin, and best of all, eternal life in the presence of God—and none of those things depended on their relatives.

Christmas went better. The children were carried away with excitement. We couldn't put the presents under the tree until Christmas morning because they would have opened them the minute they appeared. On Christmas Eve, I gave everyone a candle, even the little ones. They were so precious. Their little faces had a look of awesome wonder as we lit the candles they held so carefully and sang simple Christmas songs. There was no music. There were no strong voices, or even good singers. But, the presence of the Holy Spirit was there as these abused women and fatherless children sang with reverence to the God who loves them so much and told Him they loved Him in simple, child-like prayers. That picture is etched in the treasure house of my heart where my precious memories are permanently stored. It brings a smile to my lips every Christmas.

The next holiday was Easter. It was a good day sharing from the Bible the power and meaning of the resurrection of Jesus. We all attended church and came home to a lovely big ham dinner. We all went to bed feeling physically and spiritually well fed.

About midnight I woke up. Something had awakened me but I didn't know what it was. I lay there in my room for a few minutes listening. I didn't hear anything, but I felt prompted to get up.

I walked into the kitchen, which opened into a big family room. As I looked around, I saw the shadow of a large figure sitting on the couch in the family room in the dark. Startled, I turned on the overhead light. There sat Virginia, all 300 pounds of her. In each hand she had a huge chunk of ham. She was eating from one hand then the other. Grease was running down her arms, dripping off her elbows. I could not believe my eyes.

After taking the ham from her, helping her clean up, and sending her upstairs to bed, my disgust turned into pity as I went back to bed myself. Virginia was not an attractive woman in body or speech. Food had become her only comfort. She no longer cared what she looked or smelled like. I had to force her to take a bath every day—wash her hair once a week, and for goodness sake to use deodorant. Everyone knew when she didn't.

As I thought about the things that had brought her to that point in her life, a deep sorrow came upon me for what she must have suffered emotionally. In her voracious appetite was the only place she could find some consolation for what her life had become. She was on SSI, which is permanent disability. Her mind could no longer bear the reality of her life.

She left shortly after that, to go where there were no restrictions to her eating all day, back to the streets. I've never forgotten her, and each time I remember her I pray for her. God loves her—if she could only have received it. To see the traumas of life rob a person of their God-given talents, and reduce them to a non-productive, self-indulgent victim is to see a terrible waste of human potential.

Among the most degraded and devalued women are those who were battered and abused by the men they thought would love them. I will never forget a woman like this who came to the shelter.

I received a call at 2:00 in the morning from the police department asking if I would take in a woman who had just been beaten, and her two children, a boy eight and a girl four. The officer had found them walking the streets. Her husband had come home drunk and started beating her. When he passed out, she and the children ran out of there with just the clothes on their backs.

By the time I got dressed they were at the door. They were a pitiful sight. As I looked at the cane the mother supported herself with, she seemed to understand my question. "Auto accident two years ago."

The police left. We sat at the dining room table. The two tired, disheveled children leaned against their mom. She was exhausted and frightened. I fixed us all a cup of hot chocolate, which always seemed to be my antidote for late-night problems. I think it helped me more than it did them.

As we sipped our chocolate I told her about the shelter. She hastened to explain that she had no money. I assured her that none was needed because Jesus had provided this safe refuge for her and He never takes money for anything He does. It's always free.

I told her it was a Christian home and we have Bible studies every day. Smoking, drinking, or foul language is not allowed. She raised her head and I could see her eye was beginning to swell shut. While I got her some ice for it, she told me she just wanted to find a safe place for her babies. Nobody had ever told her about God before, so she thought she could listen to that.

When she asked if she would have to believe in something she didn't want to, I smiled and told her, "God always gives everyone the freedom to make their own choice about Him, so all we ask is that you be open to listening to His Word."

The boy squared his shoulders a little and said, "Are you going to take care of my mother?" I was touched by his attempt to be the *man* of the family. "I'm going to take care of all of you," I replied.

Tired and dirty, what they all needed was a bath, a hair washing, warm food, and a good night's sleep. I decided to forego the first three needs and just get them tucked into their soft warm beds for the rest of the night. Everything else could wait for tomorrow.

I found some suitable night wear for each of them and showed them their room. Leaving them with the promise of a wake-up call for breakfast, I went downstairs to my room and sank into bed for the few remaining hours. I was exhausted and exhilarated at being able to minister to this precious little family in the Name of Jesus.

The next day after a good breakfast, baths and hair washes, I noticed the boy sitting at the kitchen table, leaning on his elbows. I pulled up a chair and said, "Isn't God good to provide all this for us?"

He shrugged noncommittally, "I don't know much about God, but I don't think He cares about me and Angie and Mama."

The smile faded from my face, and I looked at him with concern. "I know it's really hard for you and your family right now, but God *does* love you. In fact, He loved you and me so much, that He permitted His very own Son to die for us. But He never pushes His way into our life unless we invite Him in. That's why The Sheepfold is here. We want families just like yours to have a place to come when you need it because it's the best way we know to show you how much God cares about you. We want to give you a chance to get to know Him."

He sat looking at the table, clenching and unclenching his small fists.

"If He cares about us so much, why doesn't He keep my mom from getting hurt all the time?"

I sighed and prayed for wisdom. This young boy had already been scarred by life. I wanted to choose my words carefully. "That's a very good question, and a lot of grown-ups ask the same thing. You see, God lets us make our own choices. We can choose to follow His ways or our ways. When we choose our own way, we get into a lot of trouble. God doesn't *make* us do anything we don't want to do, He *invites* us to follow Him. If we choose to do that, we can avoid a lot of problems. I don't think your mom and dad have done that yet."

He gritted his teeth. "He's not my dad," he said, emphasizing each syllable.

"You know, I remember how lonely I was when I was about your age, I was sure nobody loved me, and all I wanted to do was sit up in my favorite walnut tree and look at books." His curiosity was piqued, and I continued.

"My mom and dad split up when I was real little, so I never really knew my father. Then, things were hard for my mother, so we moved around a lot. Once, we got to live in the same house for three years, and I thought that was great, but, mostly, we lived in different places. It was pretty hard to make new friends all the time. I was always afraid I would make a mistake, and somebody would get mad at me."

"You used to move a lot too?" he asked. He readily identified with the feeling of loneliness. His mother, Charlotte, had told me that she had lost count of the number of places where they had lived.

I nodded. "But, one day, I learned that I didn't have to be lonely ever again, because Jesus promised He would always be with me. Ever since then, even when I'm alone, or when I feel like nobody loves me or cares what happens to me, I remind myself of that promise. And I know that it's true, because God put it in His Word, the Bible."

"Were you a kid just like me when you heard that?"

"Yes, anybody can accept Jesus into their life, no matter how old they are. Every day, we have Bible studies here, and we teach about Jesus, but you can tell Him right now that you want to get to know Him."

He looked doubtful. "I don't know, I'll think about it." He pushed back his chair and shoved his hair out of his eyes as he got up.

Before they left the shelter to start a new life, the whole family had received Jesus into their hearts as their Savior and Lord.

This is by far the greatest value of the ministry of The Sheepfold; not just to supply food, shelter and clothing, but to show by the revelation of God's Word through the power of the Holy Spirit, the overcoming, victorious life that belongs to every believer.

Those early days passed swiftly. There were happy days and sad days; easy days and hard days; there was tragedy and there was joy.

Because I was dealing with lives in crisis, we ran the gamut of human emotions and the spirit-breaking bondage of broken relationships that had seemed to hold the promise of love.

Kim was lost inside herself. After a broken marriage, she wildly sought love in sexual promiscuity, in wild bouts with alcohol and drugs, and had warrants out for ignored DUI traffic tickets that didn't go away.

In order to stay at The Sheepfold, I told her she had to turn herself in the next morning. That night before she went, I shared the gospel and the love of God with her and told her He wanted to help her tomorrow in court.

God wrought a miracle in the courtroom—because Kim had a place to improve her life and change for the better at The Sheepfold. The judge significantly reduced her jail time to a few weeks and then she was free to begin a new life in Jesus. The courtroom miracle that God had done transformed Kim. She studied His Word constantly in order to help other girls who were caught in the trap of sin and rebellion. She clung to this promise of God, and He performed it in her life:

"Because he cleaves to Me in love, I will deliver him; I will protect him, because he knows My Name. When he calls Me, I will answer him, I will be with him in trouble, I will rescue him. With long life will I satisfy him, and show him my salvation." Psalm 91:14-16

When Lily's time was up, because she was required to save everything she earned while she was with us, for the first time in her life she had enough money to move into her own apartment with her three children. It was almost impossible for a woman alone to save enough, or have the right credit references, to move into an apartment. Usually security deposit and first month's rent were required up front to even move in. But the Lord made a way for Lily to move in for just the first month's rent and no security deposit.

Debbie's child was kidnapped by its father. Through the donated legal services of a friend of The Sheepfold, we were able to finally locate the baby and go and pick her up.

These are just glimpses of a few of the lives that were touched and changed even in the very early days of the ministry. Changed because there was a place for them to live and be nurtured and grounded in the love of God through His Word, giving them the strength and resources to pick up the reins of their lives and start again.

At this early time in the ministry, when my spiritual knees were still a little wobbly, I had an opportunity to be tested and see God show Himself faithful, proving to me once again that with Him, nothing is impossible.

It was one year into the ministry. It was the last day of the month and the mortgage payment on the house was due the next day. I had gone to the post office box that morning, and after adding the donations that had come in that morning with those of the rest of the month, I was $300 short of the mortgage payment.

My heart was heavy during the day. I thought that since God hadn't provided the money, it was all over. Later that same day I had to file a form that was due to the federal government. I filled it out with a heavy heart knowing it would be my last one. It had a deadline so I returned to the post office in the late afternoon to mail it.

I entered the post office, dropped the envelope in the proper slot and returned to my car. As I put the key in the ignition, there was a prompting in my mind to go back in and open the mailbox. I had learned to recognize when the Holy Spirit was speaking to me by now, so I very patiently and sweetly explained to Him that I had already gotten the mail and there was not enough for the house payment.

Then the prompting came again—"Go back in and open the mailbox." Just to prove my point, I went back in and opened the box.

Lying in the bottom of the box was a letter I had evidently missed. I took it out and looked at the return address. It was from a donor who had faithfully given $25 a month since I had started the ministry.

With tears in my eyes, I kissed the envelope. "Thank you, dear friend, but it's too little, too late."

I put the envelope in my purse, unopened, knowing its contents. I returned to the car and once again was in the act of putting the key in the ignition when the prompting came again saying, "Open it." Again I gently explained, telling the history of the giving of this donor as I applied the key to the ignition. "Open it!!" There was a command this time that required obedience. So, to show what a faithful servant I was, I removed the envelope from my purse, opened it, and took out a check for $325.

It was an exciting, heart-rending, faith-building, magnificent first year.

The

NINTH

Chapter

Mary desperately needed to be free of the memories that haunted her and hindered her ability to live a normal life. Her father and her brothers had sexually abused her. When she became pregnant, her mother, who was living in sexual adultery, put her out of the house to take care of herself.

Mary's youngest brother hung himself in juvenile hall, and the boyfriend she turned to for comfort deserted her in a squalid motel room while she was carrying his baby.

She was deeply wounded by the abandonments in her life, especially that of her mother. She felt that nobody loved her—not even God. She was never going to find true joy or happiness in this life until she became free of the bondages of her past.

She had never been taught spiritual things. She began to understand that from his successful temptation of the first man and woman on earth, the devil has planned wicked schemes to steal, kill, and destroy the people of God. He is the sworn enemy of everything God created.

There are four weapons in his arsenal that he uses to try to defeat us, and they all start in our mind: temptations of the flesh; condemnation for past sins and failures; disobedience to the will and commandments of God; and wrong thoughts of doubt, unbelief, and lack of faith in God's Word and His promises to those who believe in Jesus.

> *"For this purpose the Son of God was manifested, that*
> *He might destroy the works of the devil."* 1 John 3:8

As Mary began to read Scriptures and study what God said, she began to be set free, and after three months, those memories that had held her in bondage began to leave her mind and the words of 2 Corinthians 10:3-5 became a reality in her life: *"For though we walk in the flesh, we do not war after the flesh: for the weapons of our warfare are not carnal* [of the flesh] *but mighty through God to the pulling down of strongholds* [in our mind]; *casting down imaginations and every high thing that exalts itself against the knowledge of God, bringing into captivity every thought to the obedience of Christ* [His death and resurrection that set us free]."

If there is anything more exciting than serving God, I cannot imagine what it could be. To see Him change people from the inside out, give hope to the hopeless, restore a sense of value to those who feel worthless, and change circumstances that seemed impossible to escape from, far exceeds any thrill the world could offer.

The cries for help from frightened women, the seemingly insatiable needs to be met, and the open wounds of broken and bleeding hearts would overwhelm the natural ability to relieve their pain, but the supernatural power of God has proven itself able to calm every fear, meet every need, and comfort and heal every wounded heart.

I have great respect for these mothers when I hear their stories of courage in the face of adversity; and learn their backgrounds, which produced woundedness in childhood in almost every case; and understand the overwhelming obstacles they face in meeting the needs of their children alone; and see the battle they enter when they start with nothing except their determination to improve their lives and make a better future for their children.

Women with children are the highest population of the homeless. What they go through is almost unthinkable, a mother with two, three, or more children of various ages has to be solely responsible for those children twenty-four hours a day, wherever she is, without a break.

She must support them, see that they go to school or she will lose them, provide shelter and medical care, clothe them and take care of every need or problem that arises. Her arms must never be too heavy to hold a tired, crying child. There are no outings or vacations for a homeless mother with children.

One late afternoon when I returned from the grocery store, I found a woman who had been sitting on the patio for over an hour, waiting to see if she could come into the shelter. The pain from her blackened eye was throbbing. She was trying to comfort her whimpering nineteen-month old son, and soothe her three-year-old daughter who had had very little to eat that day.

She had been walking for hours, searching for somewhere to find shelter for the night, and now the sun was beginning to set. Someone knew where our shelter was and told her how to get there. She had left home that morning, after being beaten, and could not return. She had $1 in her pocket and a plastic bag with a few clothes for the children.

As I led her in the door and showed her to her warm, comfortable room and began preparing a hot meal for them, my heart once again rejoiced in the goodness and grace of God for providing all the physical needs, as well as hope for the future, and a new start in life rooted and grounded in His Word and saved unto eternal life by His mercy.

One Saturday night I received a call regarding a young mother and her five children who were in a motel room without any food and no money. She was desperate because she had called local churches and a TV station asking for food and NO ONE WOULD HELP HER! When we got there at 9 P.M., the five children, between the ages of eight months and four years, had not eaten all day. The mother was exhausted. It was hot, the air conditioner did not work, and there were no diapers for the babies, and no milk for them. She had no transportation, the babies were too little to walk, and she had no clothes for them.

Because the shelter was full, and her needs were greater than I could meet, I went before my church the next morning with a plea for help for this woman. Due to their generous and loving response, we were able to feed her, provide clothing, pay her room rent, bring two of her children here to the shelter to give her a rest, and take her to the hospital when an emergency arose. (The three children divided a bottle of baby aspirin between them.) We were able to prepare meals and take them to her, take her to church and most of all restore her hope— hope for the future and hope in God.

One of the greatest blessings I have had in this ministry has been to see the extraordinary compassion and generosity of God's people.

We have witnessed first hand the devastating effects that homelessness has on children. They often come to us exhausted and unkempt. Some are depressed, hostile, and listless while others are hyperactive and have little or no self-control. Many have already been diagnosed with ADD or ADHD syndrome.

They can be desperate for attention, wildly aggressive, or totally withdrawn and won't talk at all. Our house managers recognize these behaviors, and find ways to help the children.

They have not been able to go to school on a regular basis. When they do go to school, the cruel laughter of the other children only furthers their disillusioned perception of themselves. They are quickly branded, and the stigma erodes their self-worth.

All the women who stay at our shelters are homeless when they come to us, and irreconcilable separations have usually taken place between them and the fathers of their children.

But, once in awhile a reconciliation happens after a mother has stayed with us:

> "I just wanted to write a note of thanks to you all. When I first arrived at The Sheepfold, I was scared to death. But the Lord used my stay there to minister to me and teach me that if I put all my trust in Him, that I didn't need to be afraid.
>
> "Since I left, my husband has made a real commitment to Christ and things are working out for us. No matter what comes my way in the future, I've learned a valuable lesson on God's love and provision. Thank you for helping me along to a fresh start. God bless you."
>
> Love, Cathy

Sharon's marriage was also restored because of her stay with us.

> "It was nine years ago when me and my three boys stayed at your shelter, but it left a lasting impression on me.
>
> "I'll never forget the kindness of everyone connected with The Sheepfold.
>
> "Two of my children have graduated from high school and my youngest son will graduate this coming summer.
>
> "I am in court reporting school and hope to graduate in two years.
>
> "My husband is much nicer to us all now, thanks to God's wonderful blessings that I learned from you.

"I give Him praise for our family being together again.
"God bless you for your work!"

Love, S. and Family

Millie didn't think there was any hope for her marriage when she wrote about her life:

"After being married only a year, because of drugs, my life and marriage were destroyed. My husband and I, once strong Christians, began to backslide. The remote area in which we were living had little employment, and my welfare check barely could pay the rent.

"We were evicted from our apartment and for the first time in my life I was left homeless. I would go hungry so my 4-year old could eat. Having no transportation or family to help we'd go from motel to motel until the money ran out. Drugs had taken control over my husband's life and that last night in a motel room he threatened me and beat me. I couldn't stand the suffering any longer. He left because I was calling the police.

"Left alone, pregnant, and a few dollars in my purse, I began worrying where we were to sleep and eat. I cried out for Jesus to help me. I made several phone calls trying to find some kind of shelter. Suddenly I remembered a place called The Sheepfold which the pastor's wife at my church had told me about.

"They took me and my son in. God worked in so many ways to bless us, the week before we even came to The Sheepfold, a woman had come to the shelter and brought brand new baby clothes, baby supplies and equipment.

"The women and children had a shower for me at the shelter, and a volunteer who picks up unsold bakery goods from a local market 'just happened' to bring a lovely decorated cake that day of the shower.

"Nearly all of the things I received were for a baby girl, and sure enough, I had a girl.

"Everything was there waiting for me when we returned from the hospital—including a loving shelter family, and a happy big brother, all eagerly waiting to hold baby Martika in their arms."

We love to hear about happy endings and joyful reunions. Once in awhile we even get to meet their husbands.

After Millie finished her time with us, she came by the shelter to get the rest of her belongings and her husband was with her! He was a strong Christian when they were married but drugs had pulled him down. He was in jail when Millie came to The Sheepfold.

He renewed his commitment to the Lord while in prison and was released completely free without probation.

They have an apartment now and both are serving the Lord. They have renewed their marriage vows. He is on fire for God and will probably become an evangelist. He got a firm foundation in the Bible while in prison, and Millie got a firm foundation while at The Sheepfold.

It is not often we see such a happy ending to a resident's stay, or get a chance to meet their husbands on such a joyous occasion. We pray for more such happy endings.

All children suffer when the family unit is destroyed, but I believe the ones most deeply affected are the teenagers. At a time when they most need guidance and quality role models, they find themselves misfits in their own peer groups, unequipped to make wise decisions for their lives as they approach "legal age" when society expects them to be mature and self-supporting.

Two of the most wounded teenagers came when I took in their mother who had four children, two younger daughters and the two teenage boys. They had lived in the worst kind of filthy and immoral conditions for a child to grow up in. I went there to pick them up and was nauseated at what I saw.

With his head down, hands hanging listlessly between his knees, in an attitude of total dejection and defeat, the older boy said, "What chance have I got? I've got nothing going for me!" He was fifteen, his mom couldn't (or wouldn't) take care of him, his father abused and abandoned him, he was black, trying to make it in a white, affluent society with no one to help him. He was behind in his grade level and had missed a lot of school.

After four months at the shelter, his mom still refused to go to work, or follow the rules better, so I had to ask her to find another place. Meanwhile the children had started school and had a sense of stability and routine in their lives for the first time.

When the fifteen-year-old found out they had to leave, he said, "If I have to go back on the streets, I'll kill myself!" After seeing his bouts with deep depression, lying on his bed with his face to the wall for hours, I knew he would do it. And, after having a son who had killed himself, I took those words very seriously.

I talked to the mother and told her I would keep the boys with me while she tried to get her life together. They were with me a year, attending high school and enjoying the stable Christian environment. They both received Jesus as their Lord and diligently read their Bibles. They never objected to going to church.

They had a wonderful sense of humor, in spite of the suffering they had endured, and kept me and the women and children at the shelter entertained.

There was an amusing incident after they were with me for about six months, and had been coming and going to and from school, while different moms stayed and others left when their time was up.

A neighbor next door to the shelter turned us in to the local police, stating that I was running a house of ill repute here in the shelter.

I did not know it until late one afternoon when a policeman came to the door and identified himself as the Watch Commander of the local police station. He told me the nature of the report and asked many questions.

I had gone to the door with my cooking apron over my dress and a lovely aroma of beef roast filled the air. Everyone was in their room resting, the house was clean and peaceful, and praise music was playing softly in the background.

After a few minutes he said, "There's obviously nothing illegal going on here. The report stated that two young black boys were your pimps and they got women and children to come here."

I kept the boys with me for a year and loved them dearly. They loved to startle people by calling me "Mom." I loved it too. The younger brother contacted me years later and he was holding down a good manufacturing job, was married, and had a baby.

The awakening to homelessness seemed to start in the early '80s when people began to be shocked at finding out there were homeless people sleeping under bushes, in parks, in cars, in abandoned buildings, and on the street. And, an even greater shock, the largest percentage were single moms with children.

The numbers have continued to escalate. God knew the day would come when cities would crack down on sleeping in public places, or in cars, and shelters would be needed desperately.

It has been said to me that the public is tired of hearing the word "homeless," suggesting we should find another word to use in describing the work we do. But, surely, the most basic human right is for a place with walls that they could call "home." Yet, this simplest, basic right is often a hopeless dream for the thousands of mothers and children who are the victims of violence, poverty, divorce, and abandonment.

No, there is no other word for "homeless," because there is no other word that tells what it means to have no place of your own to call "home."

One day as I was scrubbing the floor, I was meditating about the message I wanted to put in the next newsletter. I wanted somehow to bring the gospel of Jesus Christ into focus in the issue of homelessness. As I pondered this, I suddenly realized that there was a time on the earth when Jesus was homeless too!

For the last three years of His earthly life, He had no home. *"The foxes have holes, and the birds of the air have nests, but the Son of Man has nowhere to lay His head,"* was what He said in Matthew 8:20.

When Jesus entered into His public ministry, He no longer had a home of his own to go to at the end of the day. But He was on His way to His eternal Home.

We who are believers in Jesus are all, in a sense, homeless. Our life on earth is temporary. *"It is even a vapor, that appears for a little time, and then vanishes away."* James 4:14. We too, are on our way to our eternal home. *"For we know that if our earthly house of this tabernacle were dissolved, we have a building of God, a house not made with hands, eternal in the heavens."* 2 Corinthians 5:1

"In my Father's house are many mansions," Jesus said, *"If it were not so I would have told you. I go to prepare a place for you. And, if I go and prepare a place for you, I will come again, and receive you unto myself: that where I am, there you may be also."* John 14:2,3

Homelessness has long been a national emergency, and now the "hidden homeless"—families doubled up with relatives and friends, and those living in substandard, makeshift housing such as abandoned buildings, storage sheds, and garages—are increasing in a tidal wave of immigration and job layoffs of an unprecedented magnitude.

The desire to help more and more women and children who needed shelter inspired me to find a second house.

A lovely young woman had come as a volunteer to help in the first shelter. As she assumed the duties and the cooking I had been doing, I seized the opportunity to start another shelter.

Everything had gone so miraculously in getting the first one, I was sure it would be the same with the second. I was very naive in mortgage matters, which I proved by assuming a house with four mortgages on it.

The officers of the corporation and the board members went along with my decision because they had seen the unbelievable things that happened in the acquisition of the first one.

Announcements were made, and work crews came from local churches and our newsletter mailing list. They papered, painted, installed hardware, washed windows, did wiring, and worked from the yard to the attic. The house was three stories high. It was a beautiful old home with wonderful custom woodwork, beveled glass windows, sliding doors, and all the things that make those old homes lovely. I wondered how the price could be so cheap.

I worked for hours in the new house every day, keeping in touch with the first shelter. Then when the volunteer left for the day at the first shelter, I took over there again.

It was exactly two years after we had opened the first shelter that we began taking in women and children in the second shelter. Unfortunately I had not spent enough time in prayer, seeking God's will.

After we settled in and had a smooth-running shelter, with a paid house manager (who had been a former resident), we began having break-ins that took place while everyone was at church or away.

Things began to be stolen out of the garage or off the porch. Our outside storage room was emptied by vandals. The women felt very uncomfortable walking to and from the bus because of the number of men who were loitering in doorways and on corners. I no longer wondered why the price was so cheap.

The house manager finally became uneasy being there in the house at night. So, after a couple of years, I knew the house was unsuitable for a shelter for abused women and children and would have to be sold.

It took quite a while before a buyer could be found because of the unsavory neighborhood. But the improvements we had made helped. It was not a wasted effort because a lot of women and children had been sheltered and ministered to while we had it, that otherwise would not have been.

The house had to be sold for less than I had paid for it. When the escrow closed, there was money owed. I borrowed it from a friend and began making small monthly payments to her for the next five years.

I was humbled and chastened by the experience because it was a lesson in the danger of presumption, presuming what God would do.

He could not put His blessing on it because it was not the right place for us and He knew it. It taught me the most valuable lesson of my life—the vast difference between *believing* He will do a thing, and *knowing* He will do it. Believing can be based on past experience, but knowing can only come from time spent face down before Him, earnestly seeking His will—and waiting until He reveals it.

The

TENTH

Chapter

When Social Services heard about The Sheepfold, we began to get many unusual calls regarding the cases assigned to them. One of the most unforgettable was from a caseworker who was desperate to find a place for a young girl who was homeless and had tried to commit suicide the night before.

He said he had tried everywhere in the county, and someone had told him about The Sheepfold. He said, "Frankly, you are the last hope for her." When he said that, I knew that Jesus would restore hope to this precious girl. It was a knowing that transcended the obvious question—would she attempt suicide again when she was here?

He brought her late that afternoon and what a pitiful sight she was. White-faced, shaking and trembling, completely withdrawn, she sat there staring at the two white bandages on her wrists where she had tried to slash them, but didn't have the strength to cut deep enough.

As the caseworker and I talked, at one point he asked her to look up, and when she did, I was startled at what I saw. Her eyes were deep brown wells of such desolation and despair that I was the one who had to look away. There was something else in those eyes also, there was defiance—the kind of defiance born from innocence having been abused and violated.

After the caseworker left, she listlessly followed me around as I showed her the room she would have, and explained about the Bible studies and some of the house rules. She remained very quiet through dinner, refusing to respond or interact with the other women and children.

The caseworker had given me a poem she had written. It was intended to be her suicide note:

> "I need a helping hand, please help me any way you can.
> I know it's hard for you to see, just how real this is for me.
> I don't understand exactly what's happening, all I know
> is I feel my life ending,
> I feel so hurt, I feel so bad, I want to give up, I feel so dead.
> I'm sorry I caused so much pain; I wish everything could
> be fixed, but it has already come to an end.
> I'm so sorry!"

It was my habit to turn on the tape player by my bed at night to listen to the Word of God or praise music softly playing before I went to sleep. It refreshed me that night when I fell exhausted into bed after that very long day. I finally relaxed enough to turn it off and fall asleep.

I don't know how long I had slept when suddenly, without warning, my bedroom door flew open, and there standing over me, with a dead white face, blazing black eyes, and raised clenched fists, was the young girl.

I knew I faced a real danger, but somehow a peace came over me in spite of my fear, and I quietly said, "Hi, honey, don't you feel good?" A rather inane statement, but as I said it I very slowly reached one hand out to the tape player and turned it on and as the reading of God's Word filled the room softly, under my breath I was saying, "Jesus, Jesus, Jesus," that's all I could think of.

I don't know how long she stood over me in frozen rage. I had had enough exposure to demonic activity to know what I was facing, but an invisible power prevented her from unleashing her fury upon me.

I did nothing but lie there and smile at her gently, murmuring words of God's love and comfort to her. And thus we were frozen in a moment of time that seemed like an hour to me, not knowing what was going to happen.

All of a sudden she fell across me on the bed, sobbing with terrible, wracking sobs like I had never heard. Her sobs were uncontrollable. I knew this was not a time for me to move or say anything. God had opened the wellsprings of her soul and was releasing the poison of neglect and abuse and abandonment that she had endured.

When she finally lay there exhausted, I took her in my arms and held her like a little child. My own tears were flowing as I shared her agony.

As she grew completely quiet, I asked her if she would like to sleep beside my bed the rest of the night. She said she would, so I took out an exercise mat that I kept in the closet (literally) and got a couple of blankets. She curled up like a child and slept all night.

She stayed at the shelter a long time because of her great need for love and restoration. She began to be a great help around the house. She opened her heart to the Lord, and like a blooming rose we discovered a purity and beauty of spirit that was lovely to be around. As she grew in the knowledge of the

Word, and learned to trust and let everyone love her, she changed before our eyes.

Hope for the future and joy in living so changed her life that she returned to school to finish her education, and even competed in AAU meets as a runner.

This is the poem she wrote *after* the Lord touched her and changed her life:

> "You hurt so bad, that you think no one has ever hurt this bad before,
> But there was another One, another day, who hurt this bad and even more.
> He died of a broken heart; it broke for you and me.
> He loved us more than words can say, and more than we can see.
> His death was not from pain He felt, from hanging on that tree,
> No, He died of a broken heart, for you and me.
> Yes, He died because He loves you and me."

I would not have missed the opportunity to be there for her in her hour of need for anything this world has to offer. That was, however, the last night I ever went to bed without locking my bedroom door.

There were many humorous incidents in our everyday lives. One that I shall never forget was the evening when one of the moms accidentally glued her two fingers together with Krazy glue. She panicked. It was her index finger and middle finger. She couldn't bend them and was worried about how she could change her baby's diaper.

Everyone had a suggestion. One even wanted to try and cut them apart with a knife. We tried hot water, nail polish remover and anything we could think of, without avail.

One of the women finally said, "Call the fire department." I said, "Oh, they wouldn't know what to do for something like this." But, everyone insisted, so I called. I explained the situation to the nice fireman and he said they could not give medical advice over the phone so they would have to send the paramedics van. I explained that we were a shelter and did not want to attract any attention of the neighbors. He said he understood.

About fifteen minutes later one of our ladies came in from outside with eyes as big as saucers. "They're coming!" I asked her how she knew. She beckoned me outside and then I knew—the penetrating sound of sirens was unmistakably headed our way.

I ran out in front and here they came. The paramedic's van was there all right, but in front of it was a fire engine, not a regular, run-of-the-mill fire engine. It was the biggest, longest hook and ladder truck I have ever seen, before or since, with the loudest sirens I have ever heard.

I ran out waving hysterically, "Turn 'em off!! Turn 'em off!!" They did, after they were parked at our curb and the neighbor's. Out leaped four firemen prepared for the worst in their yellow hats and yellow slickers.

They looked about for a fire or a victim. I told them to go in the house quickly before all the neighbors came out. Some already were coming and I was running around telling them everything was all right that there was no emergency. One neighbor was just coming around the corner in his pickup truck when he saw the fire engine and the paramedics. He came roaring up to us, slammed on the brakes, in total panic yelling, "It's my wife! It's my wife!"

This all had taken quite awhile outside, because people kept coming. By the time I got in the house, the "victim" was sitting laughing and talking to one of the firemen, and my son was talking to the other three firemen about basketball. There was a bandage around the "victim's" two fingers so I assumed they were through.

Frazzled and out of breath, I asked the firemen if they were finished. They replied that they were. I asked them to please leave so that the fire engine and paramedics' van could be taken away from the front of the house.

After they left, I saw a bandage on the victim's two fingers and I asked her how they got them free. She said, "Oh, they didn't, they just put Noxzema on them and said they would be free by morning."

That was the medical advice they couldn't give over the telephone?!!!

When bedtime came, the "victim" said she had to stay up all night. I asked her why. She said she had to wait for the fingers to separate. By this time, I knew I had to put this day to an end or I was going to lose it. When I told her they could separate while she was sleeping, she seemed surprised.

About that time at the shelter, Helen and her two children came into our lives. After eighteen years of being in bondage to the living death of the heroin needle and alcohol, she made plans for one final attempt at suicide that could not fail. She had all the pills and codeine she needed for it. All that remained was to get a cheap hotel room, some heroin, and some alcohol.

As she stumbled along the street with her daughters, looking for the liquor store, she saw two doors. She tried the first one and it wouldn't open, then a woman's voice said, "It's this door." It was the wife of a pastor.

She found herself walking into a little church. Once inside as the pastor saw her condition, he came over and told her of the saving grace of our Lord Jesus Christ. Jesus touched her that night, and she was delivered from the horrible pit of addiction.

The pastor began calling shelters for Helen and her daughters to stay. He started at 9:00 P.M. that night and could not find anywhere for them to go, so he took them into his own home for the night. This was not an easy thing to do because he had seven children of his own. The next day he began calling again, and by 6:00 P.M. he had exhausted every possibility, except for one phone number, The Sheepfold.

When I received his call, even before he said, "You are my last hope for finding a place." God spoke to my heart to take them in. When I went to get Helen, she was frightened and weeping, not knowing where she was going, or what it would be like. She had not eaten or slept for two weeks, and her body was beginning to experience acute symptoms of withdrawal.

After she came here, the withdrawal battle began, and many times she wanted to surrender to the craving within her to ease the pain with drugs or alcohol, but she fought every step of the way. And the weapon she fought with was "... *the sword of the Spirit, which is the Word of God*" (Eph. 6:17). Even when she was lying there all huddled up, wrapped in her heavy plaid jacket, shivering and aching in every part of her body, nauseated and nearly blinded by headache, she kept the Bible in her hand every minute, and fed herself—spirit, soul and body, on the Word of God.

She stayed with us for a long time until she was well enough to move into her own apartment. Friends of The Sheepfold furnished it and put in a good supply of food. (I helped furnish it too, but I didn't know it until I discovered the vacuum cleaner and several other things were missing after they left. They hadn't learned any better yet. To them stealing was a way of survival).

We continued to pray for her, knowing the temptations she would face without the protective arms of the shelter.

They left right at Christmas time so we made sure they had a tree and presents. Her fifteen-year-old daughter told me they had never had a Christmas. She said, "One year we did have a tree, my mother's sister stole it and brought it home, but it just sat there because there were no ornaments or any-thing to put on it. My mom was always drunk and didn't care about Christmas."

Both daughters accepted Jesus as their Savior while they were here—so that Christmas they had the tree, the gifts and the greatest gift of all, Jesus, the Christ in Christmas.

They all studied the Bible together and went to church together. Helen would give her testimony anywhere she was asked, and in time she wanted to go into prisons, where she had spent some of her life, to bring the message of deliverance to the captives there.

Her story was just one example of the miracle-working power of God's love in one life. There were so many.

After over two years of 24 hours a day, 7 days a week, I needed a break. A friend offered a mountain cabin where I could go. I let the house empty out as the current women and children finished their stay and I did not take anyone else in until after my week of rest.

I did not realize how far away that cabin was. It took well over two hours to get there. It was a big two-story house. The bedrooms were upstairs. Pine cones kept falling on the roof at night and little animals with claws scampered across the roof.

It was terribly lonely. I cried out to the Lord. It seemed whenever I did something, it didn't seem to work out for me like it did for other people. I thought this would be a bright, lovely place, but it was dark and cold and empty.

As I sought the Lord very early the next morning while sitting in the living room looking out the window, He seemed to be speaking to me, so I took my pen and paper and began writing the following words:

"It will appear as though you are standing alone, but you are not. My spiritual forces are at work around you and within you. You have a willing heart and a willing mind. Do not so easily put another in my place of authority. Do not be confused as to your calling. You are to minister my strength to many.

"Never allow yourself to be pressured. I will never pressure you. When tension starts within you, examine the cause; it will not be from me. Doing the works of the ministry at the expense of time with me, and in my Word, is

doing the wrong works. The enemy would bombard you with details. Deal with only those things I tell you and there will always be enough time.

"Anything that robs you of your peace is not of me. My way is filled with love, joy, peace, and righteousness. The way you manage the house—the way you walk with me. Do not limit the Holy Spirit to lofty things. He cares about the grocery list, the rebellion in the women, their treatment of you, whether the food tastes good and the light bills. He had me make clay from my own spit and put it on a man's eyes. I had spit just like you do. Don't make me something unreal, let me be real to you. Ask me about everything as you would a husband and I will complete you and make you whole, lacking nothing, moving boldly and powerfully in the things of the spirit. My Father's nature is imparted unto you. Do not copy the way He works with another, trust the judgment He has given to you for it is divine and to be trusted.

"Greater works shall be done as you keep your eyes upon me. Do not look at what has already been done for that is not the standard to judge the works by. Keep your eyes only on me. We will build together. I will be the cornerstone inside of you. Your inner strength and creativity will be me. Lean not to your own understanding nor depend on your own ability.

"Let this time be a milestone of growth. You have shown great faith to come apart and be alone. Faith overcomes fear—faith is to fear as light is to darkness. My angels are round about you. You cannot be attacked. There will be many things you will do alone by the leading of the Holy Spirit—strange hotel rooms, stranger's houses, business meetings in strange cities, but always I will be with you—together we will work and build.

"There are strange things coming upon the land but you will not be moved. Difficult times shall come, but it will not come near you. Your son shall be saved and all of

*your children. The adoption was of me. You have questioned
many times if it could have been, but it was. I knew the mistakes you would make, but I have made them into blessings.*
  "Now read my Word and I will teach you from it."

The rest of my time there was in the blessed closeness of
His Presence. He seemed so near as I talked to Him. The house
was not lonely anymore.

Upon my return from the mountain, the shelter filled up
fast. More and more referrals were coming everyday. I started
keeping a log of names of agencies and institutions that were
referring homeless women to us and was surprised to find there
were 62 names. These were churches, hospitals, police and
sheriff departments, municipal courts, hot lines, social service
agencies, human services, etc. Not to mention calls from indi-
viduals who had heard of us.

I also kept a log for 48 hours of how many calls there were
for housing. There were 39.

There were only two other shelters in the whole county for
the homeless. We obviously could not take all the women who
were referred, or who called.

I felt emotionally drained whenever I heard the words
from a desperate mother, "I have nowhere to go, my home
right now is this phone booth. I need you to call me back right
away. They'll take my kids and put me in jail. I need a place for
us to live. Please call me, I've got no place to go."

It is not possible to describe the way I felt as I had to say,
with tears running down, "I'm so sorry, I can't help you, I
would let you sleep on the floor if I could, but it's against the
law."

My only comfort was in knowing that Jesus did not help
everybody either. He knew the plight of that mother and her
children and as I prayed for them, I had to trust that He would
rescue them.

By this time three years had passed.

We were setting models of what would work and what wouldn't. I wanted the Holy Spirit to show me how to do it and He did.

One evening there were 20 calls from women begging for help. I knew the time had come to take on a paid staff person to help me. I began praying to God for someone who would be willing to do this kind of work and keep this kind of schedule.

The Lord brought a woman who seemed to have an inborn love for mothers and children of The Sheepfold. She came as a woman needing shelter, but after her initial stay in the program, I hired her to be our first paid staff person. She tells her story in her own words:

"God opened the biggest door of my life on March 16, 1982 when I came to The Sheepfold. He changed my broken life into a beautiful one through being here.

"Only a few short months ago, just five days before my seventeenth wedding anniversary, my husband left me saying he wanted to be free and that the state would take care of me and our two children. No one can possibly understand the emotional impact that has on a woman; the feelings of total despair, pain, and hopelessness. Life just seems to be over.

"That same day the sheriff came and posted an eviction notice on my door. Where were the children and I to go? Having only been in California four months I didn't even know my next door neighbor. I had no friends or relatives and no money. There was no one to turn to.

"But God's plan was already in motion. For four weeks I sought help in every public agency and made hundreds of phone calls. At the end of that time I faced the judge all alone in court and he said 'put her out with all legal means enforced.' That meant I had three days and then I was on the street. My social worker never let me give up hope. She told me to call The Sheepfold.

"The next day I had an interview with Fran at a nearby McDonalds. It was my last hope. There wasn't any other place to go. When Fran came she said I could come to her shelter. I thanked God I was not going to have to be in the street. But being thoroughly exhausted from packing and moving a three bedroom house into storage, and so depressed that my life had come to this, I just wanted to die. I tried to overcome the fear of where I was going. What would it be like? It might be a broken down place just crawling with cockroaches like the missions in New York.

"The next day, when she came to pick us up, I was feeling lifeless. I came with my few suitcases and my daughter to our new home. My son couldn't face the idea of going to a shelter so he stayed with strangers rather than come with me. When we got to The Sheepfold, I could not believe my eyes! What a beautiful, warm home. As I came into the house such a loving feeling surrounded me. What a wonderful experience. Praise God!"

Ada hungrily soaked up the daily Bible studies, and rededicated her life to the Lord. She put her trust in the Word of God and grew in wisdom. She had real compassion for the women and showed a deep love and understanding for them. After watching her progress, I asked her to become the House Manager. She agreed and a new chapter opened up in my life.

The

ELEVENTH

Chapter

For the first time in three years, I rented a little place of my own for myself and my son. It was just around the corner from the original shelter, which was perfect.

After I was settled in it was time to get a little office where I could interview the mothers who were seeking shelter. I had been meeting them in coffee shops, restaurants, in front of markets, on street corners or bus stops, wherever there was a public phone.

I could not interview the women at the shelter itself because once they were inside the house, especially if they came by bus, it was very hard to send them away again. It was also very hard on the ladies living in the shelter to see someone in the situation they had been in. It brought back painful memories.

The ministry was growing very fast as more and more people became interested in it. With that growth came the need for more record keeping and filing, more typing and correspondence, more corporate forms to fill out, and more newsletters to mail, as well as more phone calls and interviews for shelter.

I always remember the day our mailing list increased to 200! That meant we could use bulk mailing—which to me in those early days meant we were in the big time.

From the beginning I began to write down the name, address and ZIP code of every person who showed an interest in the ministry and wanted to receive the newsletter. It didn't matter where I was, or what I was doing, I would grab a scrap of paper, or paper napkin if we were having coffee or lunch, and write down the information immediately.

I treated those names as though they were gold, and that is exactly what they turned out to be. The newsletter became our primary source of income. We did not ask for money, we simply shared what The Sheepfold was doing each month, and told some of the life stories of the women and children in the shelters. Later on we enclosed a return addressed envelope because people who received the newsletter requested it.

When I first started the ministry I converted a little closet in my bedroom, which happened to be under the stairs, into a little "slanty" office. There was a shelf in there with drawers underneath. I took out the drawers, got a tall stool, and I had an office. The only problem was when I jumped up to answer the phone, or heard someone call me, I kept forgetting about the slanting ceiling right over my head, because of the stairs. I must have hit my head at least fifty times. It would seem after three years and a permanent lump that I would have remembered it was there. That little office no longer sufficed.

I found a little 300 square foot office just three blocks away. I set up my card table, a folding chair, my typewriter and had a phone installed. That was it, but it looked beautiful to me.

Having this new office gave me a time and place to begin to formulate and write an organizational structure to cover all areas of responsibility in the ministry.

The office proved invaluable in improving the efficiency of operation in the area of administration. I didn't realize that a shelter ministry has a tremendous amount of detail and paperwork to it, not just ministering.

I developed a form for women to fill out before coming into the shelter. It helped a great deal to know more about their backgrounds and what caused them to be homeless. If a woman was unable to get to the office for an interview, I would still go to meet her where she was.

I set a precedent at that time that has never changed. I did not require that a woman had to be a Christian to come into the shelter, but she had to be open to hearing and learning the Word of God. If a woman would be open to receive the Word, she would be open to receive the gospel, and *"The gospel of Christ is the power of God unto salvation to everyone that believes."* Romans 1:16

Many times because of the brokenness and desperation in the hearts of the women, they accepted Jesus as their Savior during their interview, before even coming to the shelter.

Sometimes during the interview a woman would be very hard and resentful at being asked questions about her life. Single-word answers, given only to please me so she could have a place to stay, gave a clear indication of her deep need for God's love.

I remember Lois. She was like that, hard and non-communicative. "God loves you, Lois," I said. "He loves you so much He wants to bring that love and happiness into your life that you are seeking."

"No, you're wrong," she replied with determination. "God does not love me!"

I pointed to my Bible, "If He doesn't love you then we'll all have to throw our Bibles away," I said.

She looked at me in startled disbelief. I had her attention. "Would you like to accept Jesus as your Savior and become a child of God?"

Her hard shell broke and the tears came. "Nobody ever asked me that before," she said, "...and I have always wanted to do that."

I led her in the prayer of repentance and acceptance and watched her childlike brokenness turn into smiles of joy. I gave her a Bible and explained, "You are not a mere victim of circumstances. Often the things that happen are a result of wrong choices that were made without God. But now you can begin to take responsibility for your own life because Jesus promised He will never leave you or forsake you as others have done."

Most of the women were grateful and appreciative to be received into The Sheepfold, but some women displayed so much anger and hostility in the interview that I could not accept them into the program. I knew if they were that hostile with me, they would be worse in the shelter with the house manager and that would upset the whole house.

Some I could not take because they were members of non-Christian religions and wanted to study from their own books of their religious teachings. On occasion I had to ask someone to leave after finding out she hadn't told me the truth at the interview and had begun to proselyte among the women at the shelter, trying to win them over to her anti-Christian beliefs. One woman was actually going around the neighborhood with her daughters, sharing her religion and passing out materials about it.

The one question that was always a key to the final outcome of the interview was, "Do you have trouble following rules?"

The ones who immediately answered, "No problem," were the ones I knew we would have trouble with. Some women even chose to remain on the street or in their car when told they would have to get up at a certain time, be in the house at a certain time, go to bed at a certain time, and have cleaning assignments and responsibilities in the shelter.

I had received a prophecy a few years before that I would be able to run my fingers over a woman's soul and know her. God did seem to give me that gift. There was a knowing when I looked in the eyes of a woman, what she was like, whether she was lying, and what her true motivations and hurts were.

A major part of The Sheepfold ministry that brought awareness of the work we were doing was daily radio programs.

These began in June 1983, with an invitation by a local talk show host to be on his ninety-minute program. This was followed by an invitation from the manager of KYMS radio, a well-known Christian station in Southern California, to start a daily five-minute program presenting the ministry and the plight of the forsaken women and fatherless children.

Abuse and homelessness were still not well known or understood and people responded with amazement and gratitude that there was a Christian ministry helping mothers and children who were in these situations. We were still a small organization in many ways. But, not in God's eyes.

One of the greatest joys in the new radio experience was meeting Greg Fast. He was the program director of the station at the time. He took my shaking hand, and quivering voice, and led me step by step through the procedures of making a broadcast tape.

He spoon-fed me words to get me started and patiently wrote out suggested questions for me to answer, just to prime the pump of my well of experiences being involved in the lives of desperate women and frightened children.

One day when I walked into the station, he was standing there with a lovely girl whom he introduced as his girlfriend. I liked her immediately. She taught aerobics and looked like the "all-American girl" of that day.

She was excited about the ministry and wanted to do something. Her name was Tami, and in time we both knew she should come and work in The Sheepfold office with me.

That was the beginning of a wonderful time of working together. She was a great help as the office secretary. She and Greg were married, and we three have remained close friends to this day.

Our five-minute spots proved to be very effective. I did live interviews with the women and children as well as tell their stories and share shelter news.

The radio outreach continued as it was until the station no longer did five-minute spots, reducing them to one minute. This was a greater challenge, but proved to be of greater value. With one-minute spots we could broadcast on other stations as well.

The radio ministry continues to be one of the greatest instruments for touching the hearts of thousands of people with the plight of homeless women and children.

Meanwhile wonderful things were continuing to happen in the shelters: women and children were being born again, rededicating their lives to the Lord; being baptized in water in the name of the Father, Son, and Holy Ghost; delivered from alcohol and drug habits; learning the Word of God; and receiving instruction in practical living, child-rearing, budgeting, and common sense.

I may never remember all their names, but I could never forget their faces when they first came; frightened, hurt, resentful, wounded in spirit, questioning, searching, tired, disbelieving, and distrustful. How I loved it when I saw those faces begin to light up with joy and laughter when God's love began to penetrate their shield of sorrow and remove the fear and pain after they had been in the shelter a few days.

Letting them go when their stay here was finished was the hardest part of all. They didn't want to go. They were safe here, and warm, and happy. Memories of their leaving come back to my mind; little Kenny clinging to us crying, "I'm so scared, I'm so scared," remembering what it had been like before. And one-year-old Mark, whose body was the size of a five-month-old because he began life in the womb of a heavily drug addicted mother. His little wizened face was dominated by eyes that spoke of pain and suffering far beyond his one year of life.

Diagnosed as a "failure to thrive" baby, we believed little Mark was going to survive by the grace of God because much prayer and laying on of hands for healing had taken place during his time with us. *"Let the little children come unto Me, for of such is the kingdom of God"* (Mark 10:14). This truly includes the fatherless and abused children.

I began to see more and more the neglect and devastation that happened to children that were abandoned by their father. Like the plight of the woman who called and in a broken, halting voice said, "The electric company is going to turn off my electricity at 5 P.M. today. I don't have any food for my children; I had a stroke a year ago. I have called other places and nobody can help me—can you help me?"

We did help her. The shelters were full, so we couldn't bring them in, but we packed up bags of food, went to the Edison Company and paid her overdue bill so the electricity would not be turned off, and then we went to her house.

We found her to be a forty-year-old divorced woman who had been head nurse at a local hospital until she had the stroke that left the whole right side of her body useless.

The sink and stove were piled high with the dirty dishes of many days. The refrigerator was filled with leftover scraps of dried and moldy food that her children had not been able to eat.

We did the dishes, cleaned the stove and refrigerator, put away the supplies we brought, and prepared everything for their dinner. We asked why no one was helping her. She said her friends came at first but now only one lady came once in awhile.

We left, promising to come or send someone once a week. As we were leaving I looked around the neighborhood. There were houses all around her, but there was no one out on the street and the blinds were drawn. It made my heart sad to know that that woman and her children would have been sitting there in the dark—literally starving—and no one would even have known it. I couldn't help but think whatever happened to God's commandment to love our neighbor as ourselves.

Loss of a father in the family was not always because of abandonment. It also resulted when physical violence or verbal and mental abuse made it impossible for the mother and children to stay with him.

A pregnant woman and her three children, all under the age of four, had to literally run away from her husband because of his violent physical and verbal abuse to her and the children. She came to us by bus from another city. She was nearly deaf, and the two older children had speech impairments and learning disabilities. It took a lot of extra time and special care to help this family. Some of the care was provided by a community agency we found for her that gave help for the speech and hearing impaired. Two of our volunteers had who had some experience in this area were able to give of their time to help us communicate with this family.

Some battered women had to run out of the house with just the clothes on their backs, with the children still in their night clothes, just to escape a violent abuser, husband or boyfriend.

One mother came with her baby, no clothes, and no diapers, just her purse. Another had to start a whole new life with her five boys after seventeen years of physical and verbal abuse to her and the children by her husband. Another came from the hospital with her newborn baby because she could not return to the father of the baby because of abuse, and the hospital would not release her until they found a place for her to go. We were the only place that would take her and the baby.

Homelessness was the major problem then. It was not until about ten years later that domestic violence and child abuse became the major problem.

The number of calls for shelter continued to increase and we knew we had to have another home to meet the need. A large home was offered to us for lease and we took it.

The family unit in the American home had begun being pulled apart and fragmented at an alarming rate. So many changes contributed to this national disaster.

Social mores had begun a free-fall, financial pressure on families had begun to demand two salaries, women's liberation movement had begun demeaning a woman's role of housewife and mother, the government had begun its departure from Biblical principles, discipline became an infringement of human rights, and the fallout of it all had begun the tidal wave of domestic violence as pressures and stresses on the family erupted into rage and the use of drugs and alcohol, which only fueled the flames of violence and abuse.

The
TWELFTH
Chapter

A humorous thing happened when World Vision magazine called wanting to do an article about us in their March 1984 magazine. There was increasing public interest in homelessness, and at that time, we were unique. People had begun to realize there were very few shelters, and even fewer Christian ones.

An appointment was made for the reporter and the photographer to come a week later and gather information and photos for the article.

I explained to them the need to be sensitive to the fragile emotional state of the women and children due to their abuse and the trauma of homelessness.

To ease any fears or discomfort the residents and staff might feel, I went to the shelters and told them the reporter and photographers would be coming in a week to interview them and take pictures. Knowing they might be embarrassed about their appearance and may not want to talk about what caused them to need to come to a shelter, or to be photographed, they were given the option to participate or not, as they chose.

The day of the interview, I went to the shelter a little before the time the magazine crew was to arrive. There was a great deal of laughter and excitement going on upstairs. Waiting downstairs I was happy to hear their excitement, assuming it was because of the upcoming interview.

Then as I watched them all come trooping down the stairs; I saw the real reason for their excitement.

With the help of the house managers, they had spent the week going through donated clothing, jewelry, and makeup. They all helped each other style their hair, put on makeup, and pick out the sharpest looking tops, skirts, and dresses. Added to that were earrings of all shapes and sizes, some dangling to the shoulder, swinging in rhythm to the stiff, stilted walk of feet unaccustomed to high heels.

I looked more homeless than they did! What a dilemma, I could hardly tell them to go back upstairs and look bedraggled, like they used to. By then the magazine was there.

We are grateful to World Vision for doing the article, and to Gene Hart, the reporter who did the writing, for his sensitive portrayal of our lives and the purpose and goals of The Sheepfold.

He was a delightful young man, and seemed to enjoy his time with us. It took many long hours, and covered five pages in the magazine when it was printed.

He was tired, but by the end of the day he had captured the heart of the ministry and unfolded our story from the beginning. He sat and ate with the women and children and all the staff in order to get a better feel for the story. It has never been more graphically or realistically told, and the photographer caught the essence of our daily routine so well.

If you happen to read this, Gene, thank you again for the blessing of a job well done!

At the close of the article, Gene printed an invitation in it that opened a new area for me. He invited anyone who was interested in starting a shelter in their own community and would like to learn how to do it, to write to me and I would help them.

We began getting responses to the article within three weeks of the magazine's distribution. They were wonderful letters that came from all over America. So many hearts were touched—especially readers who had similar experiences of abuse and abandonment. Understanding the desperation of homelessness, they wanted to encourage us to keep going:

> "I've just read in World Vision Magazine about The Sheepfold and you and the women and children who have found a home there.
>
> "The stories are very familiar. Abandonment, divorce after long years of marriage, the sense of crushing disappointment and uselessness (or worthlessness).
>
> "There was no Sheepfold in '68 and only by the grace of God, and His infinite love for us, have I been able to surface after having been 'down there.'
>
> "I'm willing, yes, and desirous of giving a helping hand. Please write and tell me what I can do and how."
>
> A.M.

In addition to these kinds of letters, there were over one hundred requesting information and details on how to start and manage a shelter.

As I sought the Lord as to how to explain the complicated process of shelter start-up and orderly management, the plan began to develop in my mind. I wrote it down, and we still use it to this day.

It is a three-stage plan. Stage one was to be sent first with basic start-up procedures. When (*and if*) that was completed, or nearing completion, stage two was sent. This involved staff and resident management, schedules, rules, etc. When (*and if*) this was completed, stage three was sent. This involved the teachings for residents, including daily Bible studies, how to train house managers, legal matters, and exit procedures.

Unfortunately, not many stage twos were ever requested, and very few stage threes. I've often thought through the years, if everyone who has *ever* written me, or asked me personally for the information on starting a shelter, had really started one, there would be a lot fewer homeless people in the nation.

But I look back over the years and remember what it took. I could not have done it if I were married. And I could not have done it if there was not a clear call of God on my life to do it.

That's the first thing I ask those who tell me they want to start a shelter.

"Do you absolutely *know* that God has called you to do this? Because, if He hasn't, or you're not sure, you cannot do it.

"There is a giving of a part of yourself to every woman and child who comes to you. Without the spiritual renewal of God's hand in the work, burn-out and emptiness are sure to come."

Over the years many, many people have asked, "How can I know what my ministry is—what God wants me to do?"

I always tell them, "It will start with something that you already know how to do, and He will reveal the vision as you pursue it. Starting out will be something familiar, but as you begin by taking the first step, He will expand the knowledge and skills necessary for the ministry to grow."

People tend to look at their weaknesses as character flaws that would hold them back from ministry. But, in truth, those are what God will use and develop. Instead of stumbling stones, they will become stepping stones. The very things needed for your particular ministry, because it is in our weakness that God can be strong.

Paul, the apostle, admits his weakness:

*"And I was with you in weakness, and in fear, and in
much trembling.
And my speech, and my preaching was not with enticing
words of man's wisdom, but in demonstration of the Spirit
and of power.
That your faith should not stand in the wisdom of men,
but in the power of God."* 1 Corinthians 2:3-5

Paul asked the Lord three times to be set free from a debilitating attack of Satan which made him weak in his flesh. I have often clung to the Lord's response as my "overcoming" insurance:

*"My grace is sufficient for you: for my strength is made
perfect in weakness."* 2 Corinthians 12:9a

I was fifty-three when I started The Sheepfold. Weak, afraid, insecure, alone, with no college education, a little banking experience as a sorting machine operator and a teller, my only abilities were cooking, laundry, cleaning, being a mom, and organizing life for the seven people in my family.

God took those weaknesses and small accomplishments and made something beautiful for His glory, the living memorial of The Sheepfold. Standing today, it continues to heal thousands of broken lives and bring the lost into the fold.

I was strengthened and upheld by understanding the *righteousness* of God and I included it in training the house managers.

*"Fear not, for I am with you: be not afraid; for I am
your God: I will strengthen you; yes, I will help you; yes,
I will uphold you with the right hand of my righteousness."* Isaiah 41:10

God's righteousness is the one true standard by which we (and the world) can judge right from wrong. In dealing every day with the sin and degradation of wrong living experienced by the women who came to us from the streets, we desperately needed God's standard of righteousness to stand against it and restore their lives.

It is the one sure anchor for the soul that will keep us in a safe harbor while the storms of life rage around us.

Righteousness has a force to it—it has the strength to uphold us and give us the ability to stand strong in our faith to face unrighteousness in any form that would come to undo, weaken, and destroy the ministry.

Unrighteousness will attack our faith, our moral standards, our relationships, our business dealings, and if possible, distort and seek to destroy our view of God.

Righteousness is given a lot of space and attention in the Bible. There are shades and varieties of meanings and different words for its expression, but all are based on justice and God's standards of ethics and morality.

In the verse quoted, the meaning of the word used there for righteousness has seven powerful parts that make up the whole:

1. Equity—is equally right for everyone—never more right for some than others—God's righteousness is no respecter of persons—it is fair to all. *"For He has made Him [Jesus] to be sin for us, who knew no sin; that we might be made the righteousness of God in Him.* 2 Corinthians 5:21

2. Prosperity—God's righteousness will bring success in living a godly life. *"No weapon that is formed against you shall prosper; and every tongue that shall rise against you in judgement, you will condemn. This is the heritage of the servants of the Lord, and their righteousness is of Me, says the Lord."* Isaiah 54:17

3. Straightness—*"He restores my soul and leads me in paths of righteousness for His Name's sake."* Psalm 23:3

4. Rectitude—uprightness of character and conduct; strict honesty; make things right that were wrong; setting things straight. *"Who shall abide in your tabernacle? Who shall dwell in your holy hill? He that walks uprightly, and works righteousness, and speaks the truth in his heart."* Psalm 15:2

5. Justice—justness, honesty, integrity. *"You shall do no unrighteousness in judgment, you shall not be partial to the poor or show preference for the mighty, but in righteousness shall you judge your neighbor."* Leviticus 19:15

6. Liberation—righteous conduct issues from a new heart. *"Keep your heart with all diligence for out of it flow the issues of life."* Proverbs 4:23

7. Peace—*"Mercy and truth are met together; righteousness and peace have kissed each other."* Psalm 85:10

All of these issues come up in any ministry. They certainly are prevalent in shelter ministry. To remain faithful to the calling, to always be fair to each woman and child, to conduct leadership with integrity, to settle disputes, etc.

We share those truths with the residents as well as the staff.

We cannot obtain righteousness by being good, therefore, whether we are good or whether we sin and repent and are forgiven, it is the same, for all righteousness is from Jesus. He is our righteousness.

That's why we can't do ministry and still be dealing with guilt over our past mistakes and failures. Jesus placed a robe of righteousness on us when our spirit was born again. And no person, or sin, or circumstance can take it off our shoulders.

"If we confess our sins, He is faithful and just to forgive us our sins, and to cleanse us from all unrighteousness."
1 John 1:9

These truths had a powerful effect on Dee. We'll call her Dee for the sake of privacy, but her story could be that of hundreds of women. Her incredible story is one of survival in a violent world. Seeing her delicate beauty and quiet manner, it is hard to believe what she has lived through.

Hers is a sad story of innocence stolen at the tender age of five, when three uncles began molesting her. At age eight her brothers began, then three of their friends became involved.

She has been on her own since age twelve, and she joined gangs at that age to be part of a family. By 16 she was addicted to crack cocaine and she and her boyfriend would get high together. She became pregnant and had a son by him.

When she was pregnant her boyfriend would beat her up and chase her with a gun, intending to use it. Her violent lifestyle continued and so did her pregnancies until she had four children, which were taken away from her four times by Social Services because of abuse and neglect.

She went to a recovery home to try and get her life together. When she left that home she soon started using crack again and knew she was in desperate trouble. She had scars where she cut her arm thirteen times trying to kill herself, before coming to The Sheepfold.

The day she came to us she had slashed her hand again. She was high when she packed her children's clothes, but she heard an inner voice that said to get up and go.

She came to us with her four children. She did well in our program and at the end of six months she was able to start a new life on her own. She obtained her own apartment and a job. We provided a safety net of support for her and the children to be sure she did not become overwhelmed and return to drugs. Only the Holy Spirit of God can deliver a soul from such bondage.

Whenever she felt weak from raising four children by herself and trying to survive on a low paying job, she came and talked to our shelter supervisor and received strength and comfort from her and the Word of God. She knew He was with her and would not let her go, and she knew we would not abandon her. These two things gave her the courage to survive and have a future and a hope, free from drugs.

It was an exciting time when $5,000 was presented to The Sheepfold by The Register newspaper at their annual Community Service awards ceremony in 1984. That was the largest award we had received up to that time.

This was followed by a guest appearance on TV, and a filming crew from the 700 Club spent an entire day filming The Sheepfold story, to be aired on their television program.

It was fulfilling to have new carriers of the message of the plight of single mothers in poverty, raising the children of men who had abandoned their role of a father.

By the fifth year we had another shelter in operation—increasing our capacity to meet the ever growing need for shelter among homeless women and children.

Sandra, the first lady who came to the new shelter was living in half of a garage with no kitchen facilities and no bathroom, and having to pay $25 a week for the privilege of living there.

She and her three children had gone from relative to relative for help after they were evicted from their apartment. Sandra had one medical problem after another, including a hysterectomy that kept her from being able to hold a job. And, with no way to keep her clothes nice, and nowhere to leave the children, she could not go out and look for work. Sandra was 38, and many companies do not want to train someone that age.

She and the children were coming from the degradation of sharing a garage with a motorcycle gang who were addicted to drugs, seeing the smeared blood from a young addict's frenzied attempts to find a vein to inject heroin into, to the peaceful, loving atmosphere of The Sheepfold. It gave Sandra new hope for the future. She knew it was God's hand that led her here and that he would help her erase the ungodly sights and sounds that were etched in her children's memory.

A few months after Sandra completed her stay with us and had begun a new life, the kind she had been searching for, she wrote us a little note about how she felt when she came.

"I felt very alone and insecure, and then The Sheepfold opened its arms to me. I was greeted by the staff with love, warmth and genuine concern. People of all ages, color and backgrounds were living together and there was camaraderie and caring that only the Holy Spirit could bring about.

"The children were especially beautiful. Many of them had never had a home and had lived in cars or slept on the street or in parks. At a prayer meeting in the home one Friday night, a twelve-year-old boy was asked if he had a prayer request. His prayer was that his mother would always be as happy as she was that night.

"We're all making it. We have a much better life now thanks to God and The Sheepfold."

S. and kids

The

THIRTEENTH

Chapter

Mothers with children in need of shelter include the unedu-
cated and the highly educated, the unskilled and those with
a profession, the loving and the unlovable, the angry and the
gentle, the fearful and the brave, the victims of mental, verbal,
and physical abuse, and those in depression and hopelessness.

Some came from poverty, and some from wealth; some from
broken homes and some from solid two-parent families.

I have developed a deep respect for these mothers who have
taken responsibility for the well-being of their children by running from the treacherous situation, often at risk of personal
harm, with nowhere to go, trying to find shelter and survive while
struggling to give emotional support and love to their little ones.

Brenda was a mother like that. When she came to us she
had been living in the woods with her three sons. They were

badly bitten with mosquito bites, and told us about skunks coming up to them as they were sleeping on the ground.

Brenda came from a background of poverty, being one of twelve children. She went to live with a man at an early age in order to escape from home. Her dream of happiness soon turned into a nightmare as the man had a drinking problem and physically abused her when he was drunk. He and his brother would get drunk together and both would attack her.

She wanted to maintain a father for her three boys so she stayed with him until the situation became unbearable. During her last pregnancy doctors discovered she had cancer of the uterus. They wanted to abort her baby, but she wanted to keep it. Even though she was not a Christian, she believed God would take care of her and her baby. She gave birth to a healthy boy. Believing God had saved her and the baby, she accepted the Lord during her time with us, followed by her sons. They were all baptized at a local church.

The church took the family under their wing when her time at the shelter was completed. They helped establish the family in an apartment and assisted them in becoming self-sufficient and growing in their knowledge of the Bible and godly living.

This reinforced a dream of mine that another way churches could become involved in the lives of our women and children is by adopting a family that has completed our program; getting them involved in the church; helping them grow and be strengthened and watched over by loving Christians.

Church members working together to help furnish and equip an apartment and help supply food and clothing until the family can become self-supporting can be very exciting and satisfying. The ones who have done it really enjoy it. Just one family, loved and accepted, forever off the rolls of the homeless, may not seem like much of a ministry to some people. But, the Good Shepherd left the ninety and nine who did not go astray to seek after the one that was lost.

Although this particular aspect of help has not been undertaken on a large scale, there are many, many other ways churches and Sunday schools are deeply involved with us.

The teachers in a local church Sunday school saw the opportunity to teach their fourth, fifth, and sixth graders a practical application of the "parable of the talents" (Matthew 25:14).

When the teachers heard about The Sheepfold, they wanted their students to do something for the children we shelter. They chose to provide a basketball hoop and backstop, and money for the post and small court area as their project.

Using the parable as their basis, the teachers gave each student $5.00, instructing them each to earn as much from it as possible to go toward the project.

The students showed remarkable ingenuity. One bought ingredients and baked cookies to sell at her school's soccer games. Others held a sale at church selling handmade items and decorated candles they had created. Another collected donations to send cookies in baskets to shut-ins. One student had a party with a cover charge.

Because of the good use they made of their "talents" to serve others and not themselves, they raised $260.00, purchased the equipment, and presented it to the kids in the shelter.

They learned a valuable lesson and we were the recipients of their learning. In God, everyone wins.

Another instance of the immense value of church involvement with shelters was when Crystal came to us. In her own words: "When I came here, pink hair and all, everybody was good to me." She was a nineteen-year-old punk-rocker who had been deep in the maze of satanic lyrics and demonic rituals and was frightened and wanted to be free of it.

Earlier in the year, she took a job as a live-in housekeeper and soon found out she was hired for sexual favors by her employer as well as domestic duties. His meaning of "domestic duties" was very different from hers. Listening to the radio she heard about the ministry of The Sheepfold and believed it was a solution to her problem.

She had no family to turn to. Her father, a heroin addict, had died the summer before; her mother's whereabouts were unknown; and her brother was an on-the-road musician.

Because of Crystal's satanic background she needed deeper instruction and deliverance than our house managers had the time, or experience, to give her.

The pastor at a local church was instrumental in teaching her the Christian way of life and baptized her. The Bible studies in the shelter helped her get grounded in the Word of God.

She missed being able to go out at night to where her friends were. She wanted to witness to old friends in punk "gigs" (concerts). "They're just like I was," she said. "They are in a cult, they're into punk and Satan worship and heavy metal. I still look punk like them so they will listen when I tell them about all the wonders the Lord has worked in my life these last few months."

Crystal needed to gain more spiritual strength before returning to areas of demonic activity, and she needed to further her growth in her new-found faith. "We have daily Bible studies and prayer here," she said, gleaming. "It really lifts my spirits and helps me learn God's Word—the ultimate!"

We deeply appreciated the tremendous help this pastor gave to us and to Crystal. He led her by the hand into a new life. The members of his church remained a strong support group for her after she left the shelter and helped her move in and set up her own apartment.

It is impossible to tell all the wonderful things that churches and their members have done to help The Sheepfold and touch the lives of the women and children, but God knows.

The Lord loves these women and children and is ever watchful to keep them safe. One of the most dramatic proofs of this occurred in one of our shelters when a car suddenly crashed through the front wall of the house.

All of the women residents and the house manager had been sitting in the room just minutes before the accident. The children fortunately, were all asleep in the back bedrooms except for the house manager's son.

The house manager reported after the accident that she had suddenly had a strong impulse to tell all the women to go to their rooms immediately.

The women did not understand why, but they went directly to their rooms. This undoubtedly saved many injuries, for within minutes the room was filled with flying objects and shattered mirror and window glass.

The house manager was seated on the couch against the wall that the car came through. Her six-year-old son was sleeping at the end of the couch. She had been praying, asking God to stay very close to her during difficult or traumatic times that might lie ahead of her. And then the car hit!

The car hit the house like an explosion! There was a 4 x 4 beam in the wall directly behind the couch that the house manager and her little boy were on which saved their lives.

The force of the car against that beam pushed the couch ahead of it clear across the room. It threw the house manager to the floor and when the car stopped, she was on the floor looking up at the bumper directly over her head in front of the left tire.

In spite of the cut on her head, this courageous and dedicated house manager put the care of the women and children before her own needs.

It was as if God spoke simple, clear instruction to her in all of the noise and confusion that followed.

The car had hit a gas main. The house was filled with escaping gas. There was a great deal of steam from broken hoses on the car.

After making sure her little boy was all right, she obeyed that inner voice of instruction and went in to each of the bedrooms, opened the windows, punched out all the screens with her fists, and told the women and children to go out the windows as quickly as possible because the house was full of leaking gas.

Just a day or two before, the pilots had gone out on the stove and would not hold a flame. We praised God for this since there were then no open flames to ignite the escaping gas in the house, and the water heater was in an enclosure outside of the house.

Everyone was terribly frightened, and our house manager was badly bruised and shaken up, but no one was killed or seriously injured. Had the car entered the house even a foot or two higher, it would have been a much different story.

God once again proved His faithfulness to protect and care for those who minister to the needs of the widows and the fatherless.

I had been in the ministry for some time before I really began to realize the deeper spiritual meaning of the word "fatherless."

It was after I became aware of how badly these children needed a father that the word became a part of my vocabulary in describing the ministry.

Wanting to know more about the word in Scripture, I began researching its meaning through God's eyes. I quickly found that in order to really understand the word "fatherless," I had to gain a deeper understanding of the word "father."

There are many meanings inherent in the word "father." Guardian, provider, teacher, advisor, upholder, counselor, family head, nourisher, protector, and the one in authority, are just a few of the responsibilities embodied in the word.

The whole Bible is based on the respect and authority to be given a father—especially the fatherhood of God.

God was not called "Father" as one of His names in the Old Testament. He was addressed as the God of their fathers, but was never known as or called "our Father" by the Jewish people.

That was why the Jewish people were so offended at Jesus when He told them, "God is your Father," in Matthew 5:16, and called Him "My Father" in Matthew 7:21. They vehemently protested, saying, "Abraham is our father!"

Jesus had the right to call God "My Father." And it was God's will to become the spiritual Father of all who accepted Jesus Christ, His Son, as their Savior, so those who did so could become a member of His family and also call Him "My Father." Ephesians 1:5,6

"The Spirit itself bears witness with our spirit, that we are the children of God." Romans 8:16

Because of Jesus we all can have a Father—no believer can ever be "fatherless." The word "fatherless" only appears *once* in the New Testament in the Scripture verse:

"Pure religion and undefiled before God, the Father, is this; To visit the fatherless and widows in their affliction, and to keep himself unspotted from the world." James 1:27

David affirmed that God would take the place of an earthly father in the hearts and lives of the fatherless in Psalm 68:5 when he wrote, *"A father of the fatherless, and a judge for the widows, is God in His holy habitation."*

The definition for the word "fatherless" is "lonely, bereaved, an orphan." Basically, "Where has father gone?"

That is a question we hear often at The Sheepfold, and even if it isn't spoken out loud we see it in the eyes of the children, and read it in their written words in letters to their fathers that are never mailed because they don't know where their fathers are.

"Dear Daddy,

I am eight years old now and my sister is four years old. I didn't know if you remembered because we haven't seen you in a long time. I was crying today because I miss you so much. When we were at home you had a problem with drinking and you would get so angry and mean. I know you love us daddy so please get some help so we can all come home."

Melody (8 yrs)

"Dear Daddy,

One day I got up to go to school and mom was sitting at the table crying. I asked her what was wrong and she said you had left and you were not coming home ever again. I know you lost your job and things got hard when we didn't have enough money, but I still don't know why you never said good-by. I don't know everything that happened between you and mom but you are still my dad. I'm pretty tall now and I am getting good grades in school. Mom even says I'm handsome. I don't know where you are. Maybe someday I'll go back to where we used to live and maybe somebody there will know where you live now. I'm glad I wrote this letter because for a little while it made me feel like I was talking to you. I love you dad and I pray for you every night. Happy Father's Day!"

Your Son (10 yrs)

Every person, child or adult, has an image that comes to mind when the word "father" is heard, or read.

The fatherless children we care for have been abandoned by their father. Some have memories about him, some don't. But, born in each and every one of them is the intense need of a father's love.

Every human being has a certain place in their soul that can only be filled by a father's love.

As we introduce the women and children to the love of God the Father, and they begin to experience the tender love He has for them, that father void within them begins to be filled.

"Dear Daddy,

I am a grown woman and I have such a hard time telling you how I feel. After you left, Mom had a few boyfriends but she never married any of them. It's so hard for me to relate to men as a grown woman, because all my relationships have turned out for the worst. I am an intelligent woman yet this one area is such a nightmare for me. Since being here at The Sheepfold shelter I have accepted the Lord and I am learning about His love for me. I never knew Jesus could love people that have made so many mistakes. I haven't seen you since I was little and I don't know if you have a new family or not, but I hope you are happy. I still have some anger towards you but as I read my Bible more and more, my anger is less and less. All these years I have carried so much anger and now come to find

*out that I was only hurting myself! I don't know why letting go
of the anger is so hard even if it's something that is not good for
me. A few months ago I could have never wished you a Happy
Father's Day, but today I can say it from my heart. You might
not know me if you saw me walking down the street because
it's been so many years, but I will always remember you. I was
very young, but I will never forget you. Distance of time does
not change the fact that you are my Dad and once again I wish
you a very Happy Father's Day!"*

Sharon (35 yrs.)

God's original perfect plan for mankind was based on the family unit. A father and mother who loved, or at least cared for and respected each other, and their children. Many have been raised in that kind of family and cannot imagine what their life would be like if their parents had not been there for them. An ever-increasing number of children have not been raised in that kind of a family and can't imagine what it would be like.

When a parent neglects, abuses, or otherwise violates their parenting role, the effect on the child can last a lifetime, surfacing in the teen years, crippling the adult years.

The women we minister to are almost always adult children from dysfunctional families, and the children part of the next generation of abused, fatherless children who will become abusive, dysfunctional parents themselves without a direct intervention of the grace and mercy of God in their lives to rescue them and show them there is a better way they can live.

Many fathers have done their best but were abandoned or never felt close to their own fathers and therefore were unable to meet their children's needs. The father-wound is especially critical among boys. They will father the next generation and if they have had no role model of what a father should be, they will treat their children the way they were treated.

When a boy child is raised by a single mother who is homeless and destitute, without a father, grandfather, or someone who takes a father-role in his life, that child may grow up without being nourished and instructed in manliness, without a man's love and understanding. The child is vulnerable if he is without protection from mistreatment, injustice, distorted self-perception, and lacks knowledge about his own relationship with men.

This is devastatingly true for girls as well as boys. Without a father figure present in their growing years, girls often are uncomfortable in relationships with men, unable to trust men, or feel at ease with them, often feeling inadequate as a wife and mother after they are married.

God made woman to be a helpmate, to be honored, and loved. I realize I am in deep water here, but based on over twenty-three years of counseling and ministering to thousands of homeless, abused, abandoned, and bereaved women, I take my stand on the Word of God when I say a woman has an inborn desire to give and receive love, and for a husband who will care for her and need and respect her. When the pattern God set is distorted or perverted, women's lives, and those of her children, can only be healed by the love of God and His grace found in His written words, made alive by His Spirit.

Unfortunately, growing up without guidance and a relationship with a father, a woman usually will seek love in the wrong places, with the wrong people, giving herself sexually because she believed that it was love—only to find herself pregnant and alone. As a result, sometimes they become responsible for as many as four or five children, each from a different father.

These statements regarding fathers and their importance in a child's life are not quoted from a book. We learned them from listening to the heart rending life stories of hundreds of abused and forsaken women and children.

The

FOURTEENTH

Chapter

A s public awareness of the need for shelters grew, the government set apart funds for housing to be administered by the Federal Emergency Management Agency (FEMA). The funds were issued in the form of grants to shelter providers.

This was all very new and we had no idea what the receipt of government money entailed. It had always been our policy not to ask for state or federal funding because it would restrict our freedom to require that the residents participate in Bible studies during the term of the grant.

However, the way the FEMA grant program was presented, it seemed to us like an emergency one-time gift, without religious restrictions.

We filled out the necessary paperwork and were quickly granted $20,000, which we immediately put as a down payment on another shelter. The money did have strings attached that allowed Bible studies, but a woman could not be required to attend as a condition to remaining in the shelter.

We adhered to that stipulation, but it was never a problem because all the women *wanted* to participate in the Bible studies.

That was the first and last time we ever accepted government grant money. It did not hinder our freedom, but I don't believe it was God's plan for us to use tax dollars to fund His work.

About this time God sent a very special lady, Chris Williams, to come alongside me as a paid assistant. She was a tremendous help and became a friend as well as an efficient coworker. She stayed with me for eight years, and shouldered much of the heavy responsibilities of shelter operation, personnel management, and the administration of ministry business and finances.

An opportunity was given to us to purchase another shelter with no down payment required. A local church group had planned to use it for a home for girls in crisis pregnancies. The management of the home by volunteers proved too difficult, so they decided to sell. One of the members of the limited partnership that had first purchased it "just happened" to be a member of The Sheepfold board of directors and asked if we would like to buy it.

The staff of the city in which the shelter was located were excited and pleased that we were opening a shelter in their city.

The local newspaper ran the following article:

CENTER HELPS WOMEN, KIDS
By Brian Hall, Staff Writer

Joy White wandered the streets with her three children before finding the door of The Sheepfold, one of the few centers for battered or homeless women that accepts children for an extended period.

Motel bills were too high for the widow, who had been laid off from her waitress job. She was no longer able to pay apartment rent, was living on Social Security, had her car stolen, and faced mounting medical bills.

Other homeless shelters would take the family in for only 48 hours.

"You can't keep bouncing around when you have kids who are supposed to be in school," White said. "They had already missed too much." Like all The Sheepfold's school-age children, her 12-year-old son and her 7-year-old daughter now attend school regularly. To lend stability to their lives, friendships and education, White hopes to put her 3-year-old daughter into a child care program by June, while she returns to work and subsidizes a local apartment.

Doreen has three of her seven children currently at the shelter. Fearing for their lives, Doreen, 23, arrived at the center with a private investigator, following a month of homelessness. She said she was forced out of her boyfriend's house after having testified against his family during a murder trial.

A variety of ordinary and extraordinary circumstances bring families to The Sheepfold as a safe haven of last resort.

At that shelter we began a remarkable Primetime Friday Night reading program led by a compassionate teacher desiring to promote literacy among disadvantaged children. It was a sacrifice for him to give so generously of his time and the children's reading ability increased significantly. How I wish we would have such a program in all our shelters.

This same year The Sheepfold was given the free use of a four-unit apartment house. We were thrilled! This gave us the opportunity to offer extended housing to our residents who had completed our program, but were not yet able to be self-sufficient.

Mothers with three or four children, but few job skills or little education, would find it very difficult to leave the shelter and be able to provide for all the needs of her family—housing, food, clothing, medical, and day care, all take a lot of money. Another six months at The Sheepfold apartment made the difference between success and failure. Or a resident who may have successfully overcome a drug habit could easily fall prey to its vices again if she were to return to the neighborhood she came from, because she had nowhere else to go.

Through the following years this facility has proven to be a tremendous advantage in stabilizing a little family while they adjust to a new, self-sufficient life on their own.

We have a staff person on site to supervise the apartments, and there are certain rules they must still follow, but they are given much more independence. Each apartment is a complete little household, with complete kitchen, dining area, and one or two bedrooms.

The women and children love it and it is a healthy step to independent living that assures there will be no return to homelessness.

We deeply appreciate the kindness and generosity of the owner of this property. God will surely reward him according to His promise to bless those who help the widows and the fatherless.

According to the Bible, there are two kinds of widows: women whose husbands have died, or women who have been abandoned, forsaken, abused or bereaved by divorce.

God loves the widow and the fatherless. Over and over in the Bible, believers are commanded to take care of them. His commandments about them are very practical; feed them, clothe them, and see that their needs are met.

They are very important to God because traditionally they have been the disadvantaged.

"He executes justice for the fatherless and the widow, and loves the stranger in giving him food and clothing."
Deuteronomy 10:18

"You shall not afflict any widow or fatherless child. If you afflict them in any way, and they cry at all to me, I will surely hear their cry." Exodus 22:22,23

Women are becoming widowed by domestic violence at a faster rate than by the death of a husband or divorce. Discarded physically through the violation of moral decency and her right to dignity, the abuse and endangerment finally reach the point where she has to take the children and run from her home to escape.

I will never forget the phone call I received from a young woman who was terrified. She wanted to know if we had a room for her and her children if she could get out of the house without being caught. As I was telling her to be very careful, and we were arranging a place to pick her up, I suddenly heard a shout of rage—her abuser had heard her talking to me—he grabbed the receiver and threw it against the wall, but I could still hear the screams of the young woman, and crash of furniture. The enraged man was yelling and cursing—it was shocking and terrible to hear this uncontrolled violence. Shaking and trembling with helplessness I couldn't think what I should do. I didn't have her phone number or her address, or even her name. Then suddenly, the phone went dead. She never called again. I found out later perhaps the call could have been traced, but I didn't know it then.

It is difficult to describe the exhaustion, fears, and emotional stress experienced by a woman who has had to secretly plan her escape from her violent abuser so he will not suspect anything. Leaving is the most dangerous time.

When a mother leaves an abusive man, the enormity of what she is doing weighs heavily upon her because she knows that once her husband or boyfriend knows that she has left, she can never return without facing even greater abuse.

Leaving means she is taking on the full responsibility of providing food, shelter, clothing, schooling, and medical care for her children. In the eyes of the law, she will be considered an unfit parent and her children will be taken from her if she cannot provide these things.

One dear woman I interviewed was obviously suffering from self-neglect. Her teeth were very bad, and her mouth was infected. Her little six-year-old boy sat and listened as we talked, nervous and frightened, he was unwilling to play with the toys we provided; afraid to leave his mother's side for fear she might leave him. And she was clutching him as the only tangible thing she had left in this world.

It took courage for this woman to run from her husband. She knew if he found her, he would do her great physical harm. She had to protect her son. That gave her the courage to run away.

The boy's father was taking him along when he went to buy drugs and exposed him to other abuse and harm.

The women and children come from all walks of life, seeking safe refuge and a safety net from the free fall of homelessness into the streets.

Susan grew up with physical and verbal abuse, and all the neglect and broken promises that accompany life with an alcoholic father. She watched helplessly as her mother suffered. Searching for that missing love of a father, Susan had two relationships with men that ended in pregnancy, followed by desertion, leaving her with two children. Then she married a very abusive, controlling man, which is common for women who grow up in violence. Her obedience was forced by choking her. He kidnapped her baby and was found by police and jailed. That's when Susan came to The Sheepfold seeking safe refuge. She learned to trust in God, and her prayers of faith were answered with a wonderful job at a preschool where her two children can attend while she is working. Susan now has a future and a hope.

Melanie wrote to us to thank us for being there for her in her time of need:

> "I was living day to day with constant chaos. My husband was on drugs and it was very serious. I left so many times and went back for the little love and attention I received. I wanted my kids to have a father, but I knew I had to get out and stay out for me and my kids to get better.
>
> "Not one person in my family would help me. I felt alone and scared, but I had faith in God that He was going to pull me through this mess I made of my life.
>
> "I had stayed at strangers' houses for about six weeks when I called The Sheepfold. That call saved my life and my kids. They took me in, gave me a roof overhead, food and a loving environment that nourished me, and led me to Jesus.
>
> "God has blessed me so much. I've been able to save money, get a job, get day care, and, now—after six months, I'm waiting for an apartment that I'll be renting in a couple of weeks. Thank you, Sheepfold, and thank you, God!"

The widow and fatherless are two members of a foursome that God gives clear instruction for regarding the way they are to be treated. The other two members that are included are the poor and the stranger.

The Bible definition of a "stranger" is a "sojourner," a temporary resident; one from the streets; one who hides in fear; a guest in a strange place.

Those who come to The Sheepfold truly are the widow, the fatherless, the poor, and the stranger. God loves them so much because these have always been the abused, the forsaken, the downtrodden, and the homeless.

> "The Lord protects and preserves the strangers and temporary residents; He upholds the fatherless and the widow and sets them upright." Psalms 146:9

"And oppress not the widow, or the fatherless, the temporary resident [stranger], or the poor; and let none of you
imagine or think evil against his brother in your heart."
Zachariah 7:10 AMP

Their care is so important to the Lord that He made it the
basis of eternal judgment:

"When the Son of man shall come in His glory, and all
the Holy angels with Him, then shall He sit upon the
throne of His glory:
"And before Him shall be gathered all nations; and He
shall separate them one from another, as a shepherd
divides his sheep from the goats;
"And He shall set the sheep on His right hand, but the
goats on the left.
"Then shall the King say unto them on His right hand,
'Come, you blessed of My Father, inherit the kingdom
prepared for you from the foundation of the world;
"'For I was hungry, and you gave me food; I was thirsty
and you gave me drink; I was a stranger and you took
Me in;
"'Naked, and you clothed me; I was sick, and you visited
Me; I was in prison, and you came to Me.'
"Then shall the righteous answer Him saying, 'Lord,
when did we see you hungry, and fed you? Or thirsty and
gave you drink?
"'When did we see you naked, and clothed you?
"'Or, when did we see you sick, or in prison, and come
to you?'
"And the King shall answer and say unto them,
'Assuredly I say unto you, in as much as you have done
it unto one of the least of these my brethren, you have
done it unto Me.'" Matthew 25:31-40

This is our mission and calling at The Sheepfold. To reach out to the wounded by the side of the road of life—who cannot flow in the main stream—to soothe their wounds, give them a place of safety and refuge in our arms until they are healed and restored by the power of God.

Herein is perfected the love of God—that we love our neighbor as our self.

As the ministry grew, so did the need for transportation. Once again, God faithfully met our need in ways only He could.

God touched the heart of one of our donors who called and asked what we had a need for. I took a deep breath and said, "We need a big van!" He said, "What will it cost?" I knew the answer to that because we had already researched the cost.

I told him the price, and without a moment's hesitation, he said, "I'll cut you a check and put it in the mail this afternoon!" And he did!

For the first time our precious moms and little lambs could ride safely, in comfort with cool air in summer and cozy heat in winter. Of course, some house managers had quite a time learning to park this fifteen-passenger extended vehicle. But, they didn't mind. They used to have to make two trips in their cars to take the residents on an outing.

A second van was donated later by a large corporation, and eventually a van was donated for each shelter, making it possible for the first time to be able to take all the women and children from all the shelters on outings together. They loved it!

By now we were operating four shelters, an office, and a large thrift store.

We had begun to see a change in the type of problems that were forcing the women and children to seek safe shelter.

The

FIFTEENTH

Chapter

When I first started the ministry in 1979, the problem that brought women and children to us was homelessness, due to lack of a provider.

But, that began to change as we saw drugs and domestic violence emerge in ever-increasing numbers.

Drugs had been a chronic problem all along, but they had become increasingly linked with promoting violence. Especially after the Nicole Brown Simpson case, we saw a major shift of attention to victims of domestic violence.

Imagine living with parents and siblings who all use drugs. Imagine trying, in that environment, to stop using heroin and cocaine yourself, trying to clean up your life while those around you continue to use drugs and abuse each other.

That's how it was with Janet who, at age twenty-two, had been using heroin and coke for seven years. *"My parents were* cursing me," Janet recalls. "*Satan was in their hearts. They wanted to kill me. My boyfriend wanted to kill me. He came to get me one day and I cut his hand with a knife. I was very scared of him.*" Her family worshiped the devil and played music loudly throughout the house; her brother ripped toys apart; there was child abuse and pain everywhere around Janet. She sometimes hoped she would die of an overdose in order to escape the horror.

In the hope of breaking her addictive heroin habit, Janet took valium and methadone, but these drugs still kept her mind "blurred" enough so that she knew she wasn't seeing clearly what was happening around her. In spite of the drugs, however, Janet knew her situation was out of control and it was this realization that sent her to her closet where she prayed for help.

"*There was so much fear in my life that I knew I had to leave. The Lord would talk to me and I would tell Him everything, but the day came that I had to get out of there. I heard and saw what went on in that house for a long time, but was too afraid to face the fact that I had to leave there. The Lord gave me the strength to do it.*"

Janet weaned herself from drugs when she and her three-year-old daughter came into the loving environment of The Sheepfold.

The prayer meetings and Bible studies provide strength for today and new hope for tomorrow for the women and children staying at the shelters.

The women tell us that these times of sharing with others in their same situation, and the common bond of fellowship it produces, have encouraged them to face the future with new-found courage and determination.

Building their self-esteem and confidence through the Word of God, and teaching them their value in God's eyes, is one of the most important responsibilities that we have.

Denise wrote her story of deliverance in her own words:

"*I'm thirty years old with two-year-old twins. I had a cocaine habit before I had the twins, and during my pregnancy.*

I lived with my sister who also had a cocaine habit. Soon after I had the twins, I found God and went off the drugs for a little while, and everything was so great. I didn't think a snort here or there would hurt. Well, it did hurt. I soon wasn't paying rent, nor was my sister. So we were asked to move. All the time I was still doing coke and working. Finally, I had no place left to go but a motel. Soon after, I quit my job to go back on welfare. I used all of my money on cocaine. After about two months, I had to move out of the motel and started looking for shelters. I was trying to get off the coke, but couldn't. I called The Sheepfold and God allowed the perfect time to move in. The day I walked in, I quit smoking cigarettes, doing cocaine and drinking alcohol. God has put my life back together. I have a car, a job, and child care. And I thank God for it all."

Denise

Toni's story in her own words was especially poignant because of the tragedy she faced after she wrote it.

"I am thirty-five years old. I have five boys, but only three of them are with me. When I first walked into the welcoming doors of The Sheepfold home, I was 6 months pregnant.

"I didn't want to continue the pregnancy. I was tired, sick, hurt and run down—still filled with poison in my drug-abused body. I was confused mentally and had a lot of anger burning inside of me.

"I had been on the streets living a loose, rebellious, drug-controlled life. I didn't want to be in a shelter, but my sister, who was the only friend I had, said, 'No more! Either you take this chance at The Sheepfold to get your life together, or I am through with you!'

"At first, there was a lot of anger inside me because I didn't want to be in at 5:30 P.M. or follow any rules. I didn't know how good and beautiful it was for me and my kids.

"I desperately needed something or someone in my life. The Sheepfold introduced me to Jesus and when I accepted Him as my Savior, my whole attitude and life changed. I am a new Toni now, I love to pray, go to church and study the Bible.

"My fifteen-year-old son, who was ashamed of me and drew away when I was on drugs and living the street life, has now drawn close to me again. He came to church with me and is reaching out to the Lord. I had my baby, he is a beautiful 6 lb. 9 oz. boy named Isaiah for the Bible. I took alcohol and cocaine and did a lot of other things to try and get rid of this baby, but I stopped drugs three months before I had him. I praise God for letting him live through it. It is a miracle that there is nothing wrong with him. He is drug free and healthy.

"I have completed a Chiropractic Assistant course, I have saved my welfare money, so now I can move into my own place. HUD housing has a place for me.

"I'm not in darkness anymore. I am a saved Christian now and forever. Praise God for The Sheepfold and its House Managers, who loved and cared for me and my children and brought us into the family of God. We will never be homeless again.

Thank you Sheepfold for being there!"

Toni

Five months after Toni left us, she was released from the hospital burn unit, while two of her little boys were still there recovering from smoke inhalation. The day she left the hospital was the day of the funeral for her little two-year-old son, Aaron, who did not escape, but died from smoke inhalation in the apartment when fire broke out and went quickly out of control. No one was able to reach little Aaron in time. Even in her time of grief and loss, Toni knew Aaron was with Jesus because he joined God's family while he was at The Sheepfold.

Drugs play a major part in most acts of violence either civil or domestic. Whether alcohol or illegal drugs, the victim's suffering is just as painful, but the drugs seem to produce a more lethal threat to the victim.

Rudy was fourteen when he stayed at The Sheepfold. His father was an extremely abusive drug addict and alcoholic. He remembers always hiding in the bathroom, looking out the window, terrified, to see if his dad was coming. His mom would tell the boys to hide when his dad was coming home, and she took the brunt of his abuse for them. Rudy said in his own words:

> "When, in his rage, he violently attacked the boys too, she would put all the kids in the back of the station wagon and drive to a park, or behind buildings, to sleep all night. My mom did not know what else to do except hide the boys and take the brunt of the abuse. What does a mom do with five boys, with no income, and no one to help her…just stick it out, for the kids. She went to work every day, but dad used all the money she earned on drugs and alcohol."

There is a lot of talk today about "family planning." But, the kind of family planning the world is talking about is really planning the prevention of unwanted children.

God instituted a family plan when He first created man in His image, which much of the world now ignores—to their own destruction.

God's planned parenthood says there will be a father who provides and cares for his family; respects his wife as a helpmate to him, and the mother of his children; and nurtures and raises his children with love.

Domestic violence, infidelity, abandonment, unscriptural divorce, drug and alcohol addiction, sexual perversion, adultery, incest, and pornography have corroded and made a mockery of God's beautiful plan for marriage and family. The fallout is abused and forsaken mothers (or fathers), aborted babies, abused and unwanted fatherless (or motherless) children and unscriptural marriages.

The Bible is very clear in portraying God's marriage plan in Ephesians 5:25, "*Husbands love your wives, even as Christ also loved the church, and gave Himself for it.*" And again, regarding a man who is physically abusive and will not receive correction for it:

> "...*the Lord was witness [to the covenant made at your marriage] between you and the wife of your youth, against whom you have dealt treacherously and to whom you were faithless. Yet she is your companion and wife of your covenant [made by your marriage vows].*"

> "*For the Lord, the God of Israel says: I hate divorce and marital separation, and him who covers his garment [his wife] with violence...*" Malachi 2:14, 16 a. AMP

When people hear of a woman being battered over and over, they say, "Why doesn't she just leave?"

It takes great courage for an emotionally exhausted, mentally scarred, terrified woman with children to face the future as a single mother, the sole support of her children. The weight of the responsibility falls heavy on her shoulders the minute she leaves.

As the challenges of providing shelter, food, clothing, school, and medical costs begin to seem impossible for her to face alone, she becomes doubtful of her decision if she has no place to go for help. The fear of the future outweighs the fear of the punishment, even knowing if she returns she faces the worst beating of her life—and possible death. Sound too drastic? Statistics prove otherwise:

> "I did not leave my husband while he was enraged; I waited until the penitent "honeymoon" phase that always

followed. That was the safest time to escape. I knew it would be dangerous once my husband found out we were gone.

"I started calling shelters. The ones I called were full. The situation was bleak. I began to wonder if I made the right decision, or if I would end up back in an even worse situation.

"The morning I called The Sheepfold, I was almost out of hope, the emotional roller coaster had worn me out. Miraculously they had an opening. My sons and I were transported to their safe refuge, and the Christ-centered atmosphere, loving support, and teachings transformed our lives from utter chaos to stability and security."

-G.R.

One woman graphically described the drug related violence in her home, drawing a clear verbal picture of the horror of domestic violence. Never just a one-time incident, violence always escalates, and women live with it, sometimes for years.

"My children and I had to flee in the middle of the night. My husband of several years had become very abusive. It was no longer just mental abuse, but now it had become punching and shoving and he had purchased a gun. At first I thought that maybe I deserved what he was doing to me, after all I was the one that made him angry, at least that's what he always told me. Things were always my fault no matter what I did or how hard I tried to be 'good.'

"My friends had tried to tell me that this was not appropriate behavior and that no one should be treated the way he treated me. Not really wanting for anyone to know the truth, I always denied that anything was wrong. I was too ashamed to admit to anyone that there was a problem. After all, how could something like this happen to someone like me? I had a good job, a nice home and everything looked so nice on the outside. No one would have guessed by our material possessions that everything was so wrong.

"My children spent a lot of time in their rooms alone, because they did not want to 'rock the boat.' My husband's problem, like so many people nowadays, was with drugs. Even when he wasn't using he still had terrible problem with anger. So the drugs just made it worse. Because of his continued violence, I became terrified for the lives of my children and myself. I managed to escape with just what I could carry for us and found The Sheepfold.

"Living here at The Sheepfold has brought so much peace into my life. I had forgotten what it was like to live without fear and torment. It had become normal to me. Here at the shelter we have a beautiful room to sleep in. My children can now play in the family room and no longer have to stay in their room day in and day out. They don't have to hide in fear listening to all the yelling and fighting anymore.

"The Fourth of July will be a great day for us. We will be celebrating our freedom from fear and bondage. My children will never have everything that I wanted for them, because they don't have their father, and I will probably continue working through a lot of stuff in my life, but now at least I have hope for us. We are safe here and happy. The children and I will keep praying for their father that one day we can be a family again, living in peace and love with Jesus as the head of our home."

W.E.

Domestic violence was once considered a problem only among the economically and socially disadvantaged, but today it permeates every level of society.

"My abusive mate was upper middle class, handsome, charming, intelligent, and had been popular with girls in high school. He was also jealous, possessive and controlling in our dating years, which were signs of trouble ahead, but I didn't realize it at the time.

"Shortly after we were married, the verbal abuse began and eventually turned into physical abuse with my life being threatened. I was constantly being told that I was ugly, stupid, worthless, hopeless, and helpless. After awhile, I started to believe these things about myself as I already had a poor self-image when I entered the marriage.

"The physical abuse involved being pushed against walls, bouncing off of furniture, and being chased after with a knife. Once I forgot to buy bread and served dinner rolls instead which made him angry enough to take a plate full of hot beef stew and shove it in my face and then dump what was left in a pot over my head.

"In another incident I was kneeling in front of him, pleading for my life as he held a gun on the side of my head. I was scared to stay with him and scared to leave, but the day came that I knew I had to get away or he was going to take my life. He had moved me to another state and I was isolated from family and friends.

"It has been a long road to recovery, but by the grace and strength of God and the help of caring people, I've made it! Now, I am here to help and encourage other women to do the same—to be a comfort to others as I have been comforted."

M.A.

Batterers and victims are created, not born. As with every problem in our society, domestic violence occurs because God's laws are being broken. The breaking of His most basic laws occurs when violence becomes the means of communication between two people.

It occurs when "normal" communication breaks down. It, therefore, follows that most batterers **and** victims are people who are unskilled in being able to adequately express themselves through conversation.

A definition of conversation is "social intercourse." When most of us hear that word, we immediately put a sexual connotation on it. But, actually, the word is synonymous with "talking." There is *more* intimacy in talking to another person, where they really understand you, and you really understand them and share their emotions and innermost thoughts, than there is in sexual intercourse, in which body language does the talking.

Discourse is simply communication of a thought by words, but *inter*course is the interchange of thoughts verbally with deep understanding, with each person actively listening and giving appropriate responses.

When this element of communication—the unthreatened interchange of thoughts and opinions—is *missing* in a relationship, and one of the partners has a message he or she feels very intense about—that person will increasingly experience the frustration of being unable to express his or herself through "normal" conversation until the buildup of that inexpressible frustration finally explodes in uncontrolled anger and/or physical violence.

When we can't adequately express our deep feelings through words, because of lack of education or knowledge, or the inability to rightly define our strong emotions with descriptive words, our only other means of expression has to be physical. And, if *neither* partner is able to adequately express themselves, it compounds the problem.

We see this phenomenon in all forms of nature. The stronger, dominant participant will forcibly attack by sheer strength until the weaker one finally submits and stops resisting; acknowledging the stronger one is in control.

There we have the scenario for domestic violence.

There are not enough adjectives to describe "abuse." It has become such a commonly used word that its meaning has become watered down.

It is a covering word that protects public sensibilities and hides the morally disturbing truths about the true depths of violence in our homes and in our nation.

God's Word, taken from the Bible pages and applied to the lives of victims of violence, has a spiritual power within it to heal the body, mind, and soul of those victims, no matter how horrible and depraved their experience with "abuse" has been.

We do not tell the horror stories on radio, or in the newsletters, so that it will not appear that we are trying to capitalize on "shock value" to obtain funding for our ministry. We don't need to do that—God takes care of the funding, and every other area of provision needed by the "widows and fatherless" we care for.

I have decided to share in this book a sample of some of the shocking experiences our women have gone through—and recovered from—through the grace and mercy of God. His Word empowered by the Holy Spirit can bring restoration and new life where there were unshakable, tormenting memories of suffering and inhuman degradation.

One painfully burned woman told us her story of sadistic torture that was hard to even listen to. The only reason I tell it is to show the extremes that abused women are subjected to. She told of being beaten and tied to a bed and burned with a curling iron. Her screams were heard and neighbors called police and ambulance. She left him and came to The Sheepfold. God healed her physical and emotional wounds and after six months with us, she began a new life.

Lisa's drug-addicted boy friend plunged a kitchen knife into her body many times, then stole her car and dumped her in a ditch to die. Why? Because she told him to get out of the house and get his act together.

Another woman came to us from one of the worst possible backgrounds. She was raised by parents steeped in Satanism and evil occult sacrifices. Troubled by demonic spirits, hospitalized three times because of severe physical violence by her drug-addicted husband who slashed holes in the furniture and threatened to stab her and the children if she didn't obey him, she was forced into degrading prostitution in the motel and on the street to get money for his drug habit.

At one point I saw the actual manifestation of a demonic spirit taking over her mind and body. Her facial expression became hard, the pupils of her eyes expanded until her whole iris was black as pitch, her voice changed into a deep man's voice. It was when I asked her if she wanted to know Jesus that the spirit manifested. I looked her in the eye and commanded that spirit to leave her in the Name of Jesus Christ! And it did. It came back once or twice in the shelter, but again was subject to that powerful Name of Jesus, who said, *"Behold, I give you power to tread on serpents and scorpions* [satan and his demons], *and over all the power of the enemy, and nothing shall by any means hurt you."* Luke 10:19

Drugs don't put evil in the hearts of men (or women)—I say men because I have read statistics that have shown that 98 percent of battering and violence is men against women. Drugs and alcohol exacerbate an already existing problem. They don't put evil in the heart—they bring out what is already in there.

> *"...whatever thing from the outside enters into a man, it cannot defile him, because it does not enter into his heart. That which comes out of the man, that defiles the man. For from within, out of the heart of men, proceed evil thoughts, adulteries, fornications, murders, thefts, covetousness, wickedness, deceit, lasciviousness, an evil eye, blasphemy, pride, foolishness. All these evil things come from within and defile a man."* Mark 7:18-23

Education and legislation regarding the problem of domestic violence (and all violence) are good for treating the symptoms of it, but in the final analysis, violence is a matter of the soul—the soul in rebellion against God's commandment. This is an age-old problem from the beginning of time.

Rage, cruelty, jealousy, threats, yelling, blaming, criticizing, and the whole gamut of unleashed destructive human emotions are just the tip of the iceberg. Underneath the waterline, there is always a base in the life of the abuser, made up of fear of abandonment, shame, low self-esteem, insecurity, childhood abuse, molestation, or any other wrongs or abuses he suffered growing up.

All batterers were abused in some way as children. Because of the resulting insecurities, they have a desperate need to be in control, and if that takes violence, it's okay with them.

Even more heartwrenching and shameful is the violence done against innocent children who are unable to defend themselves when the terrible seed of violence and abuse is planted in their little souls, to bear the fruit of it in yet another generation.

It tears me up inside to hear it, and to tell it.

Yet, in all the suffering, there arises the light of restoration, salvation, forgiveness, and new life in Jesus.

Stories like Samantha's are what dispel the darkness and restore hope.

Parents divorced...dysfunctional family...youngest of eleven children...sent from one relative to another...from one state to another...drove mom to night clubs...picked her up drunk at 2:00 A.M....brother and sister on heroin...mom made her quit school at age twelve...took care of sister's baby...worked at Burger King on work permit—then one day the marshal came and locked up the apartment. Her mom had gotten kicked out because of drinking and not paying rent.

Samantha took her sister's baby and went to a motel where her brother and another sister were living. Others lived in the same room. Drugs and alcohol were used by everyone there. Samantha lost hope and started using pot and alcohol at age thirteen. Then her father came and took her nephew to New Mexico.

She ran away with a sixteen-year-old boy and got pregnant at fourteen. Still using drugs she was pregnant again at seventeen. Her husband had a $200 a day cocaine habit. They were constantly running from people they owed money to. At twenty she had her third child, who was born with skin cancer.

A friend took her to a Billy Graham crusade. She accepted Jesus as her Lord, and her baby was healed. After a few months, her husband lured her back into cocaine, then left her for her best friend. Left alone with three children to raise, hooked on drugs, with no work experience, she went to her husband and found him with a prostitute. Druggies felt sorry for her and gave her free drugs.

Her mother gave her an old Malibu car for her and the children to live in. When Samantha didn't call her, she reported the car stolen. An officer stopped her one day and told her to take all of her things out of the car. The car was returned to her mother.

Neither she nor the children had any shoes. Her eighteen-month-old baby was crying for a bottle. She put her few belongings behind a dumpster and started looking for help. As she was crying and praying to God, a woman walked up and put an envelope in the baby's hand. Inside was a list of shelters to call and $50. She got a room and called all the shelter numbers including Sheepfold, but they were full. Ready to give up her children the next day, she called The Sheepfold one more time and there was an opening.

Her life began a change that would affect her whole family. She rededicated her life to Jesus and studied the Bible. Her children were prayed for by The Sheepfold house managers and became very peaceful. When her stay was over, one of her brothers helped her get an apartment because of the change in her. After awhile, she began seeing a young man in the apartment complex. He was a deacon in a church. She told him of her past and about The Sheepfold and how she had changed. As time passed, they fell in love, were married, and he was ordained a minister. They are going as missionaries to Costa Rica.

Her mother has accepted the Lord and no longer drinks alcohol.

Her sister knows the Lord and is strengthened in her fight against AIDS.

One brother was delivered from heroin and accepted Jesus.

Another brother also is set free and runs a home for a prison ministry.

All this began because they saw a miraculous change in Samantha and wanted the peace and joy she has.

The

SIXTEENTH

Chapter

As a nation we are increasingly furthering the inability to communicate in our children. The TV set has become the strongest message communicator, instead of mom or dad, other children, or family members. Children spend hours, and often so do mom and dad, watching and listening, advertantly or inadvertently to violence, perversion, and wars, even in cartoons.

They see shows giving the right to children to make the decisions for themselves as to who they will live with—or if they will divorce themselves legally from their parents; whether or not to sue their parents if they are disciplined; whether they will get condoms at school and become "sexually active"; whether they will have their counselor take them to an abortion clinic during school hours and not tell their parents;

and even make their own decision whether they are really a boy or a girl, in spite of what their birth certificate says.

An even greater deterrent to interpersonal communication is the advent of computers. Teachers, parents, and libraries no longer have to express in words the instruction once considered of great value, namely reading, writing, arithmetic, and communication through the knowledge of words.

There is communication intercourse between the person and the computer. Talking is done through the fingers and reception is through the eyes. The human voice is never heard in this communication between child and computer; information is received, and believed. Solitary games further distance them from other human contact. Somehow the human voice has become of lesser value and is considered of less intelligence than that of the computer, yet it has to be a human being who programmed the computer in the first place.

If, in addition, these children are raised in a home where domestic violence and abuse occur, they are even further withdrawn. Violence and abuse take many forms. And, when it is actually occurring in the home, or whether children are watching it on TV or video games, as a survival strategy, children, out of fear of being hurt, will align themselves with the batterer by trying to please him so he won't hurt them.

There is a traumatic bonding in domestic violence that causes little girls to take on the message of becoming a passive victim when exposed to violence in order to survive, and for little boys to feel they want to be aggressive and controlling because the batterer doesn't get hurt.

The name for this syndrome is the Stockholm Syndrome. It occurs in adults as well as children. They begin to take on the thinking of the abuser so they can please him and avoid pain. Victims and children will do anything to survive.

We had a classic example of this in one of our shelters. The mother was a battered wife whose will was completely broken. Her son, twelve, and her daughter, ten, had both assumed the

Stockholm Syndrome role. They had been abused and had watched their mother be battered all of their young lives. The boy was like a grown man in his behaviors. He combed his mother's hair the way he wanted it. He told her what to do and how to do it. He told her what to read and chose where they would live. The little girl was his sister, but he was literally acting the role of her father. He spanked her when he thought she needed it, while mother watched and said nothing. As a result of all this, the girl had many behavior problems and emotional issues. She was very cruel to the little ones in the shelter and had to be watched all of the time by the staff.

I carry in my heart stories like the young twenty-year-old woman who telephoned, sobbing out her story of literally being held captive in her own house by her husband who would not let her leave the house for any reason unless he was with her. She was not allowed to drive a car or have a driver's license as she had before she was married.

She was being punched in her abdomen in his unreasonable anger against the unborn child she was carrying. The abuse was always on parts of her body that would not show in case anyone saw her.

Her young boys were beginning to hit her like they had seen their father do and she was afraid they were going to grow up and be like him. So, she knew she had to try to get out, for the children's sake as well as her own.

She thought she heard his footsteps and hurriedly hung up, promising to call back whenever she got another chance. She has never called.

Prenatal battering—punching, hitting, or even kicking the abdomen of their pregnant wives or girl friends—is a very common form of abuse. That baby represents loss of absolute control over the whereabouts and actions of the mother.

Watching and hearing violence against their mother has a devastating effect upon children. Children in the juvenile justice system in almost every case come from an abusive home.

And, I have read that 70 percent of juveniles in custody for homicide are there for killing their mother's abuser.

An abuser seldom stops with just hurting his wife. In time, as the abuse goes on, he will begin to abuse the children. This is usually the reason a battered mom can find the courage to leave.

After hearing thousands of stories of the ways children are abused, I have zero tolerance for a man or woman that will abuse a child in any way: physically, verbally, psychologically, sexually, spiritually, or by abandonment. My emotions instantly escalate to both great anger and intense sorrow for the destruction of the innocence of these precious children.

Untainted innocence is a divine quality unique to children, which can never be restored once it has been tainted, stained, defiled or fouled by selfish, self-centered, out-of-control men or women.

It's not possible to hear stories, year after year, about the cruelty of people to each other, and to their children, without breaking out with righteous anger.

Violence against a woman is bad enough! But violence against helpless, trusting children is intolerable:

"Whoever shall offend one of these little ones who believe in me, it would be better for him that a millstone were hung about his neck, and that he was drowned in the depth of the sea." Matthew 18:6

At The Sheepfold we love our little lambs and honor their heroic struggles to overcome fear and terror—fear that only a little child at the mercy of a drunken, drug-addicted father or mother can know. Fear that only a little child hiding in a corner, covering his ears, with tears running down his face as his father yells his rage while he viciously beats the child's mother—wondering if he will be next can know. Fear that only a little child can know when he is the victim of unspeakable abuse leaving his body with bruises, welts, broken bones, and a broken spirit. Fear that only a little child can know when he hears his bedroom door open quietly in the night, and knows he is going to be secretly violated again. Fear that only a little child can know who only has his mother, and she has no food, no money and no place for them to sleep.

Our Sheepfold children often walk a lonely, frightening road and our society has become so fast paced that these little ones are too often left as debris, scattered along the side of the road of life. God loves these children and their destitute mothers:

> *"For He delivers the needy when they call, the poor also and they who have no helper. He will have pity on the poor and weak and needy, and will save their lives.*
> *"He will redeem their lives from oppression and fraud and violence, and precious and costly shall their blood be in His sight."* Psalm 72:12-14 AMP

When asked why her little two-year-old sister always screamed when she was taken upstairs for a bath, Joyce replied,

> *"She screams because our dad tried to drown her one night when he was taking drugs. He took a dining room chair one time and broke it across my back. My brother tried to help me and my dad went out and got the hose and beat him with it."*

> Joyce (11 yrs.)

> *"When I was home I had to hide under the sink when my dad came home. Sometimes he was drunk and mad; he scared me because he said he would kill me and my mom. So I always hid under the sink so he couldn't find me."*

> Mark (8 yrs.)

It's almost too hard to even write about the darling three-month-old baby girl who will never bear children because she was sexually abused. Or the woman who stayed with us but who couldn't believe a person could be forgiven for their past sins, and would face a life in hell if they sinned. She wanted to spare her three children from hell before they could sin, so after she left us she shot and killed all three of them while they slept.

Or the father who got into the occult and mind-control and exerted severe psychological abuse, as well as physical against his family. He believed his wife should be in a mental hospital and tried to drive her out of her mind. He would put the kids on the kitchen counter, or high bar, or on top of the refrigerator and make them sit there for a long, long time, afraid to move, their eyes filled with fear, too frightened to cry, knowing what would happen if they did. He bit the little girl, and burned them with the toaster, and committed other unspeakable acts.

I rejoice to be able to tell that this story, incredibly, has a happy ending. In the mother's own words:

"After six and a half years I had all I could take. For weeks he kept talking about mental hospitals and that I should be in one. I believed he and Satan truly wanted me in a mental hospital. At around midnight he kept laughing these evil laughs and looking at me straight in the eyes. I told him he was strange and weird. I really thought 'something's going to happen to myself and the children if I don't get out quick.'

"I wasn't in denial anymore and he could tell. He became even more abusive.

"When I came to The Sheepfold shelter I learned that I wasn't alone, that there were many there that had come from the same or similar situation, just like I was in. I learned that I was wrong for allowing myself and my children to be in an abusive situation.

"I learned that God does care about how others treat me wrongly. I learned that God hates 'A man covering himself and his wife with violence.' Malachi 2:16

"Before, I felt I had to stay in the marriage because I knew God hates divorce, so I felt I had to stay married and living with him regardless 'til death do you part.'

"But now I learned I did the right thing by fleeing from my abusive husband. It's the best thing for both of us and the children.

"Thank you God, and the many others in The Sheepfold ministry."

J.S.

Clara and her two school-age sons were forced to go to her husband's workplace with him every day and sit in his truck because he found out she was seeking a shelter to escape from him. One day, the social worker from school made an appointment to come to the house because the boys were not attending school, so they didn't have to go to work with him that day. When she heard the situation, the social worker told her to call The Sheepfold. A call was made and we had an opening. She had no time to grab anything. He might return or drive by. We sent a cab. The eight-year-old boy had to be hospitalized for a nervous breakdown. His father had terrified him—telling him he would rip his heart out, put it in a box, and mail it to his mother, as he threatened him with a knife. The younger boy was terrified of rats. The dad got a rat mask and would jump out at the boy or come in his room at night and scare him. These were not just one-time incidents or the only ways he traumatized these boys.

Only God's love can ever heal this kind of destruction to these innocent children, and only prayer and seeking God, allowing the Holy Spirit to work in the heart of an abuser, can a person of violence be set free. He always feels his rage is caused by someone else—saying if only they would do what he tells them, he wouldn't hit them.

"A wise man fears and departs from evil, but the fool rages and is confident." Proverbs 14:16

"The heart of man is deceitful above all things, and desperately wicked: who can know it? I, the Lord, search the heart, I test the mind, even to give every man according to his ways, according to the fruit of his doings."
Jeremiah 17:9,10 NKJ

Separating the abuser from the victims by restraining orders, or jail, or by the women and children going to a shelter, sends a message to the abuser that his crime is no longer hidden behind locked doors, or his midnight visits to a terrified child's dark room are no longer secret, but that people are aware, and professionals are involved and the spotlight is on him.

Children are not just remnants of a relationship, although they are too often treated that way. They are tomorrow's parents. Battered and abused children are likely to become battering, abusive parents. I read a study done in San Quentin that showed 98 percent of the prisoners came from abusive homes, and *all* of the inmates of death row did.

Child abuse is now legally a crime, but only through intervention by adults can their little voices be heard. Knowing there are resources to call for victims and mothers of victims can be at least a slight deterrent to batterers. But once the rage is out of control the victims can still only run or hide until the rage has passed.

Abandonment is another form of abuse often perpetrated by a father—leaving the mother with the full responsibility for herself and the children.

One of the most touching and heartwarming times at The Sheepfold was when Ruthie was with us.

Ruthie was a twin. Her twin sister was a bright, healthy, active six-year-old. But Ruthie was born with cerebral palsy and her little body, no bigger than a two-year-old, had to be carried wherever she went. She showed no emotion except to cry.

Her mother was a lively, kind-hearted, gentle woman. She was unable to work because of her handicapped child and this made her homeless. The father walked away because of Ruthie's disability.

Because of her financial situation, the mother had never been able to have physical therapy for Ruthie. She had always wanted this so she could move Ruthie's arms and legs to strengthen them and make her child more comfortable, but because they had never grown normally, she didn't know how to do it.

All of us stand in awe at the goodness and compassion of God working in the lives of desperate women and children in situations like this that seem so hopeless. Once again He met the need.

The same day Ruthie came to the shelter, we also took in a young woman who turned out to be a physical therapist! She loved Ruthie and worked with her every day, explaining to her mom how to move and stimulate Ruthie's muscles.

Everyone at the shelter took turns holding Ruthie and loving her when she cried. Her mother's eyes filled with tears many times when she saw that others loved her suffering child so much.

There are always so many tender little things that happen in situations like this. For example, one of the ladies at the shelter gave Ruthie's mom her food grinder because Ruthie had no teeth and did not know how to chew. She could only eat finely ground food or baby food.

The day Ruthie laughed out loud for the first time in her life, everyone had tears in their eyes as they witnessed the mother's joy. Each person that held Ruthie in their arms, stroking her little cheek, gently brushing her hair back from her sweet face as they gazed into her vacant eyes, did not feel that their own life was so bad after all. This mother's faith and hope for the future was restored while she was here.

Janie was just two and a half when she experienced the shock of being taken from the peace and security of "grandma's" house into an overcrowded, noisy house where nineteen people lived in an environment of drugs, alcohol, and violence. Her momma and daddy lived there with other drug addicts, drug pushers, prostitutes, and alcoholics.

Her momma and daddy were acting like all the other people there. Janie began to change. Her shining brown eyes, which once had held the joy and eager excitement of life, became dull and listless, filled with fear and sadness because of what she was seeing.

After awhile, she began copying the bizarre behaviors of the other children there. Her little two-year-old cousin wanted her mother to do that to her arm like she did to hers and daddy's. The other children in the house all looked forward to the time their parents would give them drugs too because that was what the grown-ups did and they wanted to be like everyone else.

Janie lived in a barrio now. She heard strange, loud sounds in the night that frightened her, but there was no one to comfort her. She was afraid to go to sleep. She lay there in the dark, her tired little eyes wide open—fearful of the night sounds, but more fearful of the coming day spent at the mercy of her abusive, drug-addicted father. He acted so strange—either not paying any attention to her at all, or else yelling so loud it made her cry. He hit momma and made her cry. Janie was terrified he would hit her too.

Then momma told her she was soon going to have a baby brother or sister. When the baby came, no one had time for Janie any more. Nobody seemed to care if she was hungry or didn't feel good. Finally Janie began to refuse to do what she was asked to do. She was three and a half now and she had not worn diapers for awhile, but now she started needing them again. She had been a charming little chatterbox—but now she began to whine instead of talk. She didn't feel good inside and she wanted to be at "gramma's" house.

Then one day, momma went to church with a friend she had met. She gave her life to Jesus as her Savior at that service. She started taking Janie to church with her and began protecting her and her little brother from the foul-mouthed depraved people that they lived with. Now that momma was a Christian, she began seeing her terrible living conditions with new eyes.

While sitting and drinking at a girlfriend's house, it was as though scales suddenly fell from her eyes and she saw her children clearly for the first time in over a year. She realized what was happening to them. Their hair was dirty and tangled, their clothes were ragged and filthy, they both had runny noses and their eyes had dark circles under them.

She returned to the house where they lived and for the first time she could feel the spirit of lust, homosexuality, drugs, and violence so thick it was like a blanket smothering her. She knew she was facing another night of violent argument and abuse if she stayed there, and another night in that awful house was intolerable, so she turned around and walked out the door with her two children. She went to her Christian friend's house.

The next Sunday at church she told the pastor that she did not know what she was going to do, with two kids and no money. As God would have it, the pastor was a good friend of mine and he gave her The Sheepfold phone number.

When she came to the office for an interview, she was scared at first when she heard the rules, and at the thought of living with strangers—but once in the shelter she began to love being there.

In the process of time, she became a house manager at one of the shelters. Janie was once again a radiant, bouncy four-year-old, and this was just the beginning of a brand new life for them. When she shared Janie's story with us, it was hard to believe it was the same little girl.

Sometimes the children end up wards of the state because of the ungodly selfishness of the man and woman who conceived them and brought them into this world. Two people who cared more about the cravings of their flesh than they cared about the human products of that flesh.

The day I stood at my office window watching two young boys being driven away in a police car, I felt like my heart was breaking, and at the same time I felt an impotent rage at the parents of those boys.

They were being driven to the county home for orphans. The father had been arrested for child abuse and neglect and using drugs. The boy's birth mother had abandoned them eight years before. Their stepmother had two younger children of her own and was trying to save all the children from their father and his lifestyle.

She had called the Child Abuse Registry and they came to the house with the police. When they saw the unbelievably filthy living conditions, and learned of the drug abuse and neglect of the father, they made arrangements for the mother and children to come to the shelter.

Since the stepmother did not have custody of the two older boys, she could not legally keep them, and neither could we. They had to be taken to a county facility.

Seeing those two boys, obvious victims of gross neglect, hug their stepmother, and with tears in their eyes, say goodbye to us—trying to be brave, facing a strange place, an unknown future, and probable separation—is a picture I cannot erase from my mind or my heart.

In talking to the stepmother later, she told me the mother had deserted them because of the father's heavy drug addiction, which left him in a self-induced stupor most of the time. The boys had to take care of themselves from the time they were toddlers.

"My greatest concern," she said, "is that all their life they have seen drugs being used and know exactly how to use them and how to get them. I am afraid they will begin to use them too."

Negligent, unfit parents plant the seeds, and society reaps the harvest.

We shelter more children than we do women because every woman has to have at least one child to come in to our shelters, and most have between two and four, but it is not unusual to have a mother come with five or six children.

All of the children who come to us have been abused or neglected in some way, but in the shelters they have so much fun with the other children, playing with all the toys and games that they get a break from the fears and stress-filled situations that brought them here.

The children usually adjust quickly, and our greatest joy is to hear them laughing and playing together.

The

SEVENTEENTH

Chapter

Our shelter children write, say, and do the most precious things that come straight from their little hearts:

> "I will always remember the Sheepfold because they gave my mom, my brother and myself a home and food. And the most important reason is because they showed me how to be a Christian. You've showed me how to follow God! God is in the house and he will take care of you if you let him come into your life. Thank you so much Sheepfold!"
>
> Love, Kasandra (10 yrs.)

Terry, age seven, was forced into being the "man" of the family, comforting his mother when she was beaten, while he himself was often hurting from the bruises he had received. His first thoughts were never for himself, but always for his family. While waiting for his brother to have a tooth pulled, Terry and the volunteer driver went for a bite of lunch. Terry said, "I'm going to save my orange juice for my brother because he won't be able to eat anything, and I'm saving half my sandwich for my other brother, because he couldn't come with us." Driving home, they were talking about Christmas and Terry said, "I wish I could get my mom a guitar for Christmas, but I don't think I have enough money." He wanted to use the one dollar he had saved for his mother.

Frankie, Terry's little two-year-old brother, was given a good used jacket from our clothing supply. To him, it was "new." He refused to take off his "new" jacket and slept in it and kept it on day after day.

Four-year-old Justin walked out of the shoe store staring at his feet. He couldn't take his eyes off his gleaming new tennis shoes. All he had been wearing for weeks were loafers that were too small and full of holes.

The children take what they learn about God very seriously.

One day the house manager noticed all of the younger children sitting under the dining room table. Breesha, a little three-year-old, who loves Jesus, was having a prayer meeting under there. She had all the children bowing their heads, folding their hands, and praying.

Down the hall, seven-year-old Terry was teaching his version of the Ten Commandments to his peer group.

Later that day, the house manager heard Breesha out on the porch. Her little brother had accidentally stepped on a bug, and Breesha had laid her hand on it and was praying: "Jesus, this little bug is one of your creatures. It's hurt, Jesus, and I want you to heal it. Now, little bug, you be healed in the Name of Jesus!"

The little bug got up and flew away!

When five-year-old K.C. lived at one of the shelters, there were two other five-year-olds there. They all loved to watch the Christian videos and Bible stories, and learned the songs by heart.

There was a break-in at the shelter when everyone was at church and the VCR was stolen. The boys were so upset about not getting to watch their videos, the house manager told them to pray about it and ask God to send them another VCR. The boys entered into prayer with all the enthusiasm that three five-year-olds can muster for such things.

After a few days, K.C. planted himself firmly in front of the house manager. *"I'm tired of praying!"* he said. *"I've prayed a thousand times!"* The house manager instructed the children in the value of "praying without ceasing," and that "faith" means not giving up.

When she finished speaking, K.C. asked if he could say a prayer.

"God, I pray that the man who stole from us would get saved, and that he won't do this awful thing to anybody again. Thank you, God, for the VCR somebody's going to buy us today! Amen."

A man who had heard about the break-in "just happened" to buy a VCR for them, and it was delivered to the shelter that day. God hears and answers the prayers of children.

Children in the community do many kind and thoughtful things for our Sheepfold children. There are hundreds of beautiful examples to cite but a local teacher did something unique that expresses the caring hearts of the children in her class:

"Dear Fran,

Recently, the 4-6th graders at our church collected money and then went on what we called a Sheepfold Shopping Spree. They bought gifts to give to the children you minister to. It was such a blessing for me to see them *go down the aisles of a local toy store, looking for the best bargains, knowing they had $60.70 to spend. They did pretty well . . . they got to the cash register and found the total to be $60.71! It was great! We laughed about how close they came, and in their eyes I knew it was something like nothing else they had ever done. God Bless You."*

J.B.

Christmas takes on a deeper meaning in a shelter full of underprivileged children. They learn for the first time the meaning of Christ in Christmas, the best present they could receive. And how they love their gifts! It's a joy to watch the wonder on their faces.

Especially at Christmas, the children and their moms are remembered in ways that reveal the love and caring hearts of the people.

These letters accompanied special gifts given to three children in the shelter from two little sisters at Christmas. They didn't have the shelter children's names, just their ages:

"Dear Eleven Year Old,

"I am ten and live in South Orange County. My mom's small group adopted a family through The Sheepfold and your family is the one they gave us. I accepted Christ into my heart when I was 8 years old. I was baptized by the Children's Pastor. Christ has helped me with many hurts in my life. One of those hurts has been the abandonment of my father. We have one true Father in Christ. He is always our father and will never abandon us. I will pray for you, although I do not know your name.

"The Sheepfold wanted us to give only new gifts, but I am sending you "my Tigger" along with the new coat and purse I picked out. I wanted to give something of my heart. Something I cherished. So I picked out "my Tigger." I use to sleep with him. He is little, but big in comfort. Please take good care of him. I wanted you to have him!

"Have a Merry CHRISTmas and remember God is always there! He answers prayers and above all He never stops loving you for anything.

"I Love you in Christ! Jesus loves you so much."

Lindsey

"Dear Unknown Twins,

"I wanted to give you something from my heart...something that I cherish. The Sheepfold wanted us to give new gifts, but I am giving you something that was mine also. I am giving you my baby doll that I bought with my allowance. I am only five and do not get much allowance, but my daddy took me to the store a little while ago to pick her out. She is a wonderful baby and I love her very much. I wanted you both to have her and share her. Please take good care of her and remember my family when you play with her.

"We are praying for your whole family. God answers prayers."

Katherine

Christmas is such an exciting time for everyone—staff, volunteers, and residents—especially when a mother and her children didn't think they were going to have a Christmas when they were homeless and had to come to a shelter. But they all say their Christmas here was the best they ever had.

A woman and her little seven-year-old boy came to us in January from an agency in another city where they had stayed a few days. She never spoke a word of complaint about the place, but when she was being interviewed she needed to dispose of the contents of a plastic bag she had brought, and she expressed concern that she might be putting cockroaches into our waste basket. She had a similar concern that where she had been sitting might be getting roaches on it from her clothes.

When her little boy saw some of the remaining Christmas paper, ribbon, and decorations in our office from our Christmas gift wrapping for the shelters, he said, "They didn't have Christmas where we were."

Well, needless to say, a statement like that from a precious seven-year-old, who had obviously been left out of many of the good things of life, was all that our mercy-motivated staff needed to spring into action.

They loaded up the van that would transport the boy and his mother to the shelter with toys, games, new clothes, and some special gifts for mom. That little guy was so excited he couldn't stand still. He exclaimed, "Are we going to have Christmas?!" He couldn't believe those things were for him and his mom.

The mother rededicated her life to Jesus while being interviewed, and when they were getting ready to leave the office for the shelter, she was asked if she needed a Bible. She said she did need one and the little boy said, "I need one, too." When asked if he knew Jesus, he said, "Yes." And, when he was asked if he wanted to receive Jesus into his heart to be his Lord, he said, "Yes." Right there in the parking lot beside the van, he accepted Jesus as his Savior and was born again. They both left the office with the Word of God in their heart and in their hands.

We like to give the moms gifts to give to their children from them. This often brings tears to mom's eyes because that is one of the deepest hurts of being homeless—they can't buy gifts for their children's birthdays or Christmas.

"Holidays here are a dream come true. Since my mom abandoned me and my brother seven years ago, I have been an orphan. I've spent all of my holidays and birthdays alone. I got into gangs because I was alone and scared. But then I

wanted a different life. I stopped looking, and acting like a low-life gangster. But, I became pregnant and homeless. I gave myself to my heavenly Father, came to The Sheepfold, and it saved me."

Sonya and Baby Vanessa

Deborah and Amber were deeply touched by the quality and quantity of the gifts they received and by the love with which they were given.

"I would like to start off by thanking everyone from Sheepfold for a Christmas I will never forget. Only God could have moved them to do what they did.

"If my daughter and I weren't here, I would hate to think about how it could have been. All we have is each other. Instead, my daughter and I were given a reason to be joyful. First, we knew we would be celebrating Christ's birthday in a God blessed home. That was enough to be thankful for. But then we were blessed with presents. Not just any kind of presents. Ones that only God could have known we wanted. My daughter was so excited. You would never have believed that just three months ago our lives knew no happiness.

"The day doesn't end there. All the children got to play with their gifts while we moms got to help with preparing a feast. And did we have fun! We got to fellowship with one another while listening to praise songs. And what a feast we had.

"After dinner we relaxed and played with the children. What was Christmas to my daughter and I this year? It was a spiritual blessing, filled with love, straight from the heart. We will never be able to thank you all enough. Praise be to God!"

Deborah and Amber

Michele was a teenage mom who came from a broken home.

"Spending our Christmas here at Sheepfold set an example of what Christmas is truly all about. I recognized that Christmas isn't just presents, it's the day that our Lord and Savior was born, and how He died for us so that our sins will be forgiven, and that we might be saved.

"I never had a true Christmas like this one at Sheepfold; being around family members who are in the Lord and love the Lord so much."

Christmas was especially meaningful to Yvette who came to us from a drug rehabilitation center and had been separated from her children for two years. She had to establish residence at The Sheepfold before her children were returned to her.

"I'm writing this letter to thank you for such a beautiful Christmas. I didn't expect such a nice one. Christmas for us was enough just having a roof over our heads and such a nice house to live in.

"Christmas Eve was very nice. I've never had it like all that before. It was very beautiful and very loving. The whole two days (Christmas Eve and Christmas day) the way you people gave it really gave me a whole new outlook on what Christmas is really all about. It's about the birth of Jesus Christ. Not about just presents and Santa Claus. It's a very loving, thankful time.

"My kid's room is packed with nice toys and they have really nice outfits. I couldn't believe how nice the clothes were. And I also got a lot of beautiful gifts. Actually it was the nicest Christmas the three of us have ever had. I feel very fortunate and grateful to be here. I like hearing Jesus come out of my children's mouth and talking about Him the way they're learning to do. It really makes me feel good inside about how I'm raising them. Thank you for taking us in the way you have."

Yvette, Amanda, George

"This holiday season has been the most pleasant of my life. I was at peace and my kids were so happy and excited. The Sheepfold provided a wonderful holiday atmosphere full of love and caring we will always remember them for that, and so much more. Thank you, Sheepfold, for everything."

Lucy

"The holidays here have been great. A blessing that I've starved for so long. Loving people helping one another. Now I've got a real loving family who respect each other, and wonderfully always give hugs."

Patti and Kids

Little Joseph had prayed for a watch for Christmas, and when he opened his presents and found one, he raised both hands and exclaimed, "Praise the Lord!"

Joseph loved Jesus, and when one of the mothers at the shelter was sick in bed, Joseph went to her room and laid hands on her and prayed that she would be healed.

He wrote:

"I like the shelter and everything about it. I like the food. I like the people and the managers. I like the toys and I have accepted Jesus as my savior. I like going to church. I like school and math. I like playing games. I want to be a fireman. I like crismis trees. I like hot choklit. I like craphs. I like Jesus movies.

"Merry crismis from all the kids at the Sheepfold."

Joseph (7 yrs.)

"I never would have thought that at the age of 14 years I would be living in a shelter and sharing a room with my mother and younger brother. I never would have guessed I'd ever be living in a shelter.

"We have been here since before Christmas and sometimes the past seven months all comes back to me in one quick flash. It brings tears to my eyes, and a deep pain in my heart because it's time to leave. It's hard not knowing were I'll be in a month from now. But, I know whatever God has in store for me when I leave, well . . . I know it's gonna be good.

"I remember not to long before we left my father, I asked him to get me a certain pair of shoes I'd wanted for a long time. He took me to the mall and I thought I was getting them, but I never did. The very first day I came to the shelter I was given those shoes. They didn't even know I'd been wanting them.

"Ever since then, God has been giving me endless gifts and blessings. God sometimes gives to us even when we don't ask, but He knows it's in our hearts and in the silent prayers we never pray."

Danelle (14 yrs.)

Danelle left with wonderful memories of her life-changing stay with us. All of our teenagers whose moms have success in the program, and remain the entire six months, find hope for their future and opportunities for maturity.

It was seventeen years ago that Theresa's parents came to live in California from Tijuana, Mexico.

Four months ago, after years of physical and verbal abuse, Theresa and her mother could not endure it any longer. A senior in high school, Theresa went to stay with a school counselor while her mom looked for a place for them to go. The school nurse recommended The Sheepfold. Her mom made the arrangements and moved into the shelter.

When Theresa was dropped off at the shelter to join her mom, she says she was an emotional wreck. This was her senior year, and like most eighteen-year-olds about to graduate, she wanted to have fun with no rules and no curfews. She wanted to go live at her friend's house until after graduation, but her mom could not have stayed at the shelter without having a child with her. So, Theresa stayed so her mom would have a place to live.

But, even though she was there in body, her attitude was not cooperative. She constantly asked her mom, "Why do I have to do these dishes...water the lawns...clean my room?" etc. Resisting every inch of the way it became a very stressful time for her and everyone around her.

She was very involved in her school and resented not being able to go to all the functions whenever she wanted.

When her counselors at school realized she had no money, they used school resources and some of their own to help her financially. They bought two prom tickets for Theresa and a guest, and bought satin shoes for her to wear with her formal, not knowing she didn't have a formal.

It "just happened" that an unidentified donor dropped off a white satin, black-beaded formal that "just happened" to fit her as though it were tailor-made for her. Another Sheepfold donor had offered to do a free makeover on the day of the prom. When Theresa went to the prom she looked and felt like a princess.

A long time dream was realized when, with the help of her school counselors and teachers, she was accepted at Marymount College. Her bad attitude began to change as she came to realize that if The Sheepfold and the school system had not freely given her all these opportunities, she could be on the street instead of going to college.

This is a story that could only happen in America, where a young girl who was abused all of her life, who had no money and was not a citizen, could be helped by so many people to become a benefit to society instead of another statistic on the welfare rolls. Theresa applied for her citizenship papers and has become a citizen of the United States.

Shawn was fourteen and at a crossroads when he came. Homeless, without a father, he was bullied and ridiculed at school. The friendship of gangs seemed to be his inevitable destiny, but God had a different plan. Shawn tells it this way:

"On September 22 this year, I got baptized. At first I was scared, but after I was done saying, "I believe Jesus is the Christ, and He died to cover my sins," I stopped being scared and I was excited that I was getting baptized.

"So when the Pastor said, "Are you ready to be baptized?" I said, "Yeah." I was calm as I stepped into the warm water and I was already feeling touched by the Holy Spirit. By the time I was done getting baptized I felt like a new person, a better person and now I feel very good.

"Before we came to The Sheepfold we were living in a real bad neighborhood and my mom was being told by the Social Services that me and my sister were going to be taken away from her because she was not taking good enough care of us. So we went to Arizona and when my mom reported where we were, they said if she didn't bring us back in three days, we would be taken away and she would be put in jail.

"So we came back and went to court the next day. Our social worker wanted to take us away, but my mom's attorney said there was a Christian shelter he knew called The Sheepfold, and if we went there, we wouldn't get taken away.

"He dialed the number from the court room and my mom talked to the lady in charge of the shelters and she said there was room and we were welcome to come. I wondered on the way to the shelter what it was like. I expected a big room with a bunch of beds in it. But, instead we came to a big house. It was pretty, too, and we had our own room.

"We were there in time for dinner and they had a birthday party for one of the moms there. The House Manager asked us what we needed like shampoo, soap, toothbrushes, pajamas, stuff like that. Then she went and got it and we went upstairs to our room. We took our showers, got all cleaned up and went to bed.

"After awhile I started high school. They took me shopping and got me a bunch of clothes. I was excited because I wasn't all raggedy and the kids didn't tease me for the way I looked, like they used to do.

"I started going to church on Sundays and Wednesday nights. A couple of weeks later I accepted Jesus as my Savior, and that's when I was baptized. He has really changed my life. He helped me get into high school even though for the past two years in seventh and eighth grade I was only in school seven months altogether. He helps me get good grades, 3 A's, B, A-.

" I don't have as bad a temper, I don't criticize like I used to, I've only used one cuss word since He got me in my regular grade in school and now I'm doing good.

"Before, I was going to have to be in a gang big time, or get being beat up, but now I don't even go near them any more—because I have a different point of view about everything—about my life, the way I want to be. I didn't have any goals or anything—and now I have goals I want to achieve.

"I'm planning to go to college and I'm trying to get to where I can get a scholarship—what classes I should take to be a drafting engineer. It's called CAD, computer aided drafting.

"I thank God every day for The Sheepfold, I always say, "Thank you, God, for steering Fran to open this place. It's one of the best places I have ever seen or heard of."

Shawn (14 yrs.)

Eva was only eighteen but had already lived a life without the boundaries of morality.

"When I was a little girl I got beat and stabbed by my mom, she just hated me.

"My mom died when I was seven. I went to live with my step dad and mom. Well, my step mom loved me, but hated my older brother. She would bite him and I couldn't take it so we ran away.

"Then we went from group home to group home. Then my grandmom finally got us. But my bad luck was never ending, I started getting molested by two more of my uncles. I kept it inside until I was almost nine. Then I went from group homes to the streets and gangs and drugs.

"By this time I knew God just didn't like me. I was sworn to be a loser by my family, so that's what I believed. I did a robbery and found myself doing three to five years in the California Youth Authority.

"Well, I got out and still didn't know who I was or what I wanted, but what I did need was a baby. God sent me my little angel, Ariana.

"I didn't have a home, I didn't know how to love and I still had hate. Until one day I got on my knees and cried out for help from God.

"I called all kinds of shelters and they were either full or I didn't qualify, but at The Sheepfold, God qualifies you. Now that I am here I have accepted Jesus as my Savior. The best thing is, He forgave me for everything. Even things I find hard to forgive myself for. I never thought I would have God in my life.

"This past month I talked about Jesus and was not ashamed or embarrassed. I was water baptized and God has been the best thing I've found, thanks to The Sheepfold."

Our nation celebrates Mother's Day and Father's Day, why not a Children's Day, a day to honor our children? It may never become a national holiday, but how we love our Sheepfold children! The sweet and lovable ones and the not-so-sweet and lovable ones; and how much **more** God loves them. He knows and understands why they are the way they are, and why they behave the way they do, good or bad.

He loves the funny, noisy boys; the silly, sad, or thoughtless boys. He sees brave heroes in those boys, full of truth and purity; He sees the fathers they will be, and the trials they will endure. He sees Himself within each one, and therefore, so must we.

God loves the happy little girls, the sweet and loving, best of girls; He loves as much the sassy girls, the selfish and demanding girls. He sees the women they will be, givers of life and grace. He sees Himself within each one, and therefore, so must we.

The

EIGHTEENTH

Chapter

In January, 1998, God gave a gift to me, and to The Sheepfold. John Wildman came alongside of me to be assistant director and vice president in charge of operations. John is a man of integrity, honesty, and godliness. He was a member of our board of directors for six years before 1998, and served as treasurer of The Sheepfold Corporation. Even before he joined the board he was a marvelous, tireless volunteer.

He gave up a very profitable, well-known and respected business to take this job at less pay and further away from home. But, he knew God called him to do it, and so did I.

When John came on staff, we knew we would need a pickup truck for him because part of his work would be taking things back and forth between the shelters, thrift stores, and office. So we were faced with the necessity of getting a truck.

The same week that he signed his Sheepfold employment papers, a woman called the office and said she and her husband had a 1993 GMC pickup truck with an eight-foot bed with a camper shell on it and they would like to donate it to us.

We went to look at it and could not believe our eyes! It was all white and looked like new, with no dents or scratches on it. The upholstery was beautiful. It had air conditioning and a radio. The tires were like new. It was perfect!

The owners said they had tried to sell it but didn't get even one call, which confirmed what they had felt from the beginning that God wanted it to go to The Sheepfold. We could not stop praising God for His goodness and His perfect timing, but He was not through yet!

Two weeks later we phased out one of our thrift stores because our lease was up. We wondered *how* we were going to move all of the big long racks full of clothes, and the bins and furniture and books, etc. It would take a moving van.

Once again a phone call came. It was a man offering to donate to us a 1984 International diesel moving van, twenty feet long, with a lift on the back and a new motor in it.

John went to look at it and it too was all white like the pickup.

John and I both took this on-time miracle as a confirmation that he had made the right decision to come to work at The Sheepfold.

After becoming involved in the inner workings of the shelters, getting to know the house managers and the women and children personally for a few months, he wrote the following article that beautifully expressed his heart for the ministry:

"I came on staff here at The Sheepfold about seven months ago, and as the only man on staff I have had a lot of opportunity to see the need for men's help in this organization to provide safety, comfort and hope to abused women and children.

"There is a request I have on my heart to ask my Christian brothers. Since I have had opportunity to see this ministry from all aspects, I see and hear the suffering the women and children have gone through, and the valiant efforts of the House Managers and the Office Staff to ease their pain and to minister the love of Jesus to them to change their lives.

"My request is that as men of God, when you have your prayer time or family devotions, please remember to lift The Sheepfold to the Lord in prayer. Specifically for the moms and kids staying with us, but also the House Managers and the Office Staff. We all hear very disturbing and shocking stories, but we see the greater power of our Lord Jesus in changing lives and restoring a future and a hope to those who are abused and forsaken. That's why they need us to pray for them daily.

"The earnest, heartfelt and continued prayer of a righteous man makes tremendous power available—dynamic in its working." James 5:16 AMP

"The Lord has said, 'I will not leave you an orphan without a father, I will come to you. Though mother and father may leave you, I will never leave you.'" Hebrews 13:5, Psalm 27:10

J.W.

Men who were fatherless often write to us expressing their understanding of the pain children go through. Following is one man's touching letter:

"I've been hearing about The Sheepfold for some time now. I thank God upon every remembrance of you and I thank Him for the grace which is working in you and abounding in blessings to many.

"I grew up in Oklahoma with eight brothers and sisters. We all have different fathers and I grew up without the presence or influence of a father in the home. I love my mom, but she loved to party. We all more or less raised ourselves and we were unruly and undisciplined. Most of us dropped out of school and some of us bounced in and out of prison.

"When I think of the work that you're doing with these women and their children my heart rejoices. My heart is filled with compassion and a desire to help. More importantly, I want to support you in prayers and supplications and in the giving of thanks. Let me know how I can pray for you and what you want Jesus to do for you. I love asking Him because He'll do it. He said 'Whatever you ask the Father in my name, He'll do it.'

"Jesus Christ has more than made up to me those things that I lacked growing up as a child. God has been more to me than my dad could ever be. He heals the broken hearted and binds up their wounds."

Love, Your Brother in Christ.

As always, there are two sides to every situation. Although we see only women raising children alone and children without fathers, it is growing more and more common for fathers to be the single parent raising the children, and our hearts are touched by their plight.

"To The Sheepfold,

"I am a thirty-four-year-old single parent father of two, so I can relate to the struggles of today. May God take care of and multiply this love gift one-hundred-fold for your organization.

"If I can be of any assistance in any area, please let me know. God Bless."

Sincerely, Tim

This last Christmas, two of the Christmas cards we received particularly caught my attention, because they were from single fathers raising their children. One of the men shared his story. His wife abandoned them to live a life of partying and sin. He has raised his two boys alone. He said he could relate to the women in the shelters; the abandonment, the loneliness, the overwhelming responsibility of work, cooking, cleaning, homework and all the other family activities. His devotion to the Lord was evident.

Single parenting is an extremely difficult task for anyone. There's a tremendous opportunity for all of us to minister to single parents in our own churches. Please lift these men and women up in prayer. In my opinion, all single parents who raise their children in the love and admonition of the Lord are the heroes of today.

"Dear Fran,

"I'm touched as I hear you on the radio daily and as I read your newsletter. I know these problems exist because I was at one time an abusive husband and my ex-wife had to stay at a shelter such as yours with my two sons on several occasions. I've been a single dad for over two years now and God has really changed my heart in this past year as I've allowed God to be the Lord and protector of myself and my two sons.

"God has been speaking to me ever since I heard of your shelters. I know it's frightening for those who have to leave their homes, but also wonderful that God leads them to you. As God continues to bless me I will make The Sheepfold recipient of my offerings. I thank God for your ministry and pray that he blesses you tremendously. May those you shelter feel Gods hand and reach out and grab hold. Yours in Christ!"

We had been aware for a long time of single-parent families, especially mothers with children, living in the most deplorable state of poverty in local residential motels.

It was on my heart so much that in January 1999, The Sheepfold began an outreach program to these local motels. It is a mission field right in our own backyard—not only ours, but in every large city.

Women and children are living in those dark rooms, behind locked doors with tightly drawn curtains over their only window, through which not even the smallest ray of sunshine could enter. They have to live this way because the door and window are right on the walkway where drug addicts and predators of all kinds are looking for new victims.

These motels are run-down, drug-infested, and trash-filled. The rooms that were built for single occupancy now often hold a mom and as many as four or five children. Those children suffer neglect and often play in unsafe greasy parking lots and overflowing dumpsters. It is not unusual to see two- three- and four-year-olds playing outside after dark, alone and unprotected.

The rooms we entered reeked with the odor of unwashed clothes piled everywhere if a mother did not have quarters for the motel washer and dryer. There were no drawers to put any belongings in; they became scattered across the floor on a filthy carpet. Although it's called a motel, there was no room cleaning or service of any kind for the residents by the management. The roaches ran freely over unidentifiable food scraps left wherever the last bite was taken.

These conditions existed because the mother had given up to hopelessness and depression, with no way out. When it got to the worst, she would often turn to prostitution to get enough money to pay the rent, which was not cheap, or to buy drugs. Drugs are commonly offered to her and appear to be a way to get relief from the hopelessness of her situation.

Her addiction exposes the children to things no child should ever see or experience. There are not words to adequately describe the horrors of the way they are living. Drugs, alcohol, prostitution, sexual perversion, assaults, violence of all kinds, roaches, lice, foul language, neglect, hunger—even these words cannot convey the trauma and emotional scarring that is happening to little children living in rooms where ungodly activities are taking place.

In their innocence they begin acting out these activities, and if there is no intervention, they will be the next generation of residential motel dwellers on welfare.

I prepared a program called "Moms In Motels" that gave volunteers a way to minister to single moms and their children in the motels.

The reports made by our MIM volunteers tell the story of motel life in graphic terms:

K. went for her weekly motel visit to see Tracy, a mother with three children. Tracy was strung out on a high dose of her seizure medication. The children were eating their breakfast of cold, canned spaghetti out of a shared plastic bowl. Tracy later shared it also. One of the boys was just getting over the flu and the soiled laundry was piled in a corner. Tracy did not feel well enough to go to the laundry room.

T. and L. went to visit Cheryl in her motel. Cheryl met them at the door with tears in her eyes. Then she said that she had almost lost it this week. She and Aaron, her fourteen-year-old son, had gotten into a fight which shouldn't have happened. She began to throw things and say words she shouldn't have said. They asked her why and she said that Aaron is out of control, he won't listen to her, he comes and goes when he pleases, he won't go to school, the truant officer is out after him and she hopes he gets picked up and taken to jail, because she just doesn't care anymore. She said that she was ready to put a gun to her head and she was going to do it so that she could just get out of this situation. They talked a lot to her about how she needs to finally get right with the Lord and begin to lean on Him. She continued to tell us that she was just going to end her life and she wouldn't have to bother with it anymore.

They asked her if they could help and she said there was nothing for them to do. They told her they would call the truant officer, which they did. He said that Aaron's situation is really sad and that he was too far gone for any program such as "Scared Straight." He said Cheryl has never called the school to find out if Aaron was in school or not. If she would start doing it, and if he wasn't in school to call the police department right away, they would go and pick him up and lock him up overnight. He said she has made no effort whatsoever to contact the school and help Aaron's situation. She is by law obligated to take care of and discipline Aaron, and if she is unwilling to do that, then he will be put in a home, which is where he should be anyway in order to try to save him from the streets and save his life. He said that Aaron is very street wise and knows how to manipulate his mother and that's what he is doing. He recommends Aaron be put into a home.

We've put our MIM program in its entirety on our website, making it available to anyone, or any organization, that desires to start a ministry in this much-needed area of caring for the widows and the fatherless. The design of the program through step-by-step, week-by-week achievement goals leads ultimately to their salvation, and a Bible-based walk with the Lord.

Every form of poverty of spirit, mind, and body runs rampant in the dark, disheveled rooms. Volunteers taking the light of the gospel into this darkness, an atmosphere of faith, hope, and trust in the Word of God, and belief that His promises are true for all who believe, will produce supernatural results in their lives.

The kind of success and deliverance that can happen is best illustrated in a motel mom's own words. One that we took into our Sheepfold apartment shelter shared her story with us:

She said one day she was down to her last few dollars—not enough money to pay the rent. She was so depressed from motel living, unable to move, nowhere to go. She didn't know what to do, where to go, or how she was going to live.

Her husband was in jail; she was responsible for providing housing, food, clothing, schooling and medical care for her three children. Everything was a mess.

Feeling totally overwhelmed, her emotions opened the inner door of her soul to that clawing, craving, cry for alcohol that she had kept caged for the past two years. Hopelessness overcame faith and she made up her mind to spend her last few dollars on a bottle of rum and get really drunk in order to block out her pain at least as long as the alcohol numbed her brain.

In God's perfect timing, as she was preparing to leave to go to the liquor store, there was a knock at her door; when she opened it, there stood a "Moms in Motels" representative.

From that point on her life was changed. The light of the gospel of Jesus Christ entered that dark room, and through the Word of God, hope was restored to her. Her practical needs were attended to and in a short time she was placed in our apartment shelter.

From there, because all of her daily needs were met, she was able to finish her schooling and graduate. She got an excellent job as a surgical technician, and now has her own apartment. Her husband is out of jail and they are reunited and are both Christians. One of the best things she reported was that she loved the Bible studies the MIM volunteers taught, because learning about God's marvelous love changed all their lives.

It is a good program, but after the first two years or so, we realized the problem was so intense it would take another whole ministry to really sustain the degree of outreach required and give vital help to everyone we met with. These few life samples above do not adequately portray the multitudes of women and their children living and dying in this kind of squalor and poverty of hope.

In conjunction with the MIM program, several fine Christian men and women were mentoring young boys and girls in a specially designed mentoring program. Our desire to reach those fatherless, disadvantaged kids was so strong that we knew we did not want to stop the outreach; so instead, we modified the MIM program to make it an approach of reaching the moms through the children.

In June, 2001, The Sheepfold Kids Mentoring Program became an entity of its own within the ministry and was successful almost immediately. A man had come to us who already had begun a small mentoring program, and knew he was called of God to a mentoring ministry to fatherless children. We hired him as a staff member for this outreach.

He developed an excellent program that covered all the aspects of mentoring, including fingerprinting and background checks for the volunteers.

It is an exciting program and each step of the way it has grown with quality and care, providing Christian mentors who are committed to serving the Lord by serving the fatherless.

Many of our Sheepfold Kids have never seen their dads or even know who they are. Some have been abused by their fathers, who are restrained from seeing them. Other dads just will not make themselves available to spend time with their kids.

Whatever the case, these children have been left without a father figure and role model in their lives, which they desperately need. It is this need that our mentors are dedicated to fulfilling.

Using the mentors already working with the motel children, more were added to include all of our current shelter kids and those of former residents. In time, as more single moms heard about the program, they urgently requested us to include their fatherless children in it.

It was not just little children in need—we were also finding young men and young women living in dark, overcrowded motel rooms with their overwrought mother and younger brothers and sisters. These young people had not been able to go to school because they've had to move so often. They are embarrassed to go to school because they are so far behind their peers. Their clothes are dirty and ragged. And, usually their shoes are filthy and have holes in them.

What a difference a male mentor can make to a young man at the crossroads, giving him a hand up from the street; helping him get his GED, tutor him if needed, show God's love and teach it, help him learn a job-skill or a craft, teach responsibility, help with a job, give him emotional support and encouragement so he doesn't see himself as a loser and turn to drugs—adding one more statistic to a lost generation. But God does not call it a lost generation. He calls it a fatherless generation. These young men didn't fail—their fathers failed.

One day Tim, a volunteer in our mentoring program, stopped by the office to share his excitement about the new turnaround in the life of Aaron, the young man from the motel whose mother had given up on him.

Because of the hopelessness of living in the deprivation of the motel environment for years, Aaron (14) no longer cared what happened to him, his mother or his school work. But, because of the mentors, that had all changed and Aaron had a whole new joy about life.

When Tim was asked what made the difference, his reply was immediate and adamant! "Prayer." It turns out that Aaron wouldn't ever pray for himself. So Tim thought, "Hey, my life's got it's own problems, too." He shared his problems with Aaron and said, "If you promise to pray for me everyday, I promise to pray for you."

Aaron agreed to the plan and he kept his promise and so did Tim. What an answer they both got. Aaron had been getting Ds and Fs every report period before this, but in the next report period he received almost all Cs. But that's not all—he was voted Student Of The Month!

That honor was rewarded by a trip to the ice cream store. But his greatest reward is in knowing someone believes in him, and that he has the potential to succeed, no matter how difficult life can be.

God is faithful! He is a fatherless child's best friend!

My life has been totally enriched and blessed by the hundreds of volunteers who have come alongside in the work of The Sheepfold ministry and also in my personal life. A thousand thoughtful things are done that could only come from hearts that have been touched by God.

The Sheepfold could not exist without them. Not only do they serve on our board of directors, work at our thrift store, serve as mentors and tutors, and do projects at our shelters, in our food storage rooms, and at our offices, there are also hundreds working behind the scenes, sometimes sending us items they have made for us, or money they have raised by their projects on our behalf, or bringing gifts and meals and cakes on holidays and birthdays and outings, golf tournaments and special events, and garden tours with all proceeds for the benefit of The Sheepfold. Even the children get involved and do special projects they thought up.

The director of the children's ministry at a local church read about our motel children and wanted to be involved in some way. She told the kids, who are first grade through fourth grade, about the moms and children living in poverty in the motel rooms and the kids decided they wanted to help by letting the moms and children know they care about them.

They put together thirty-six great lunches with notes of encouragement inside and Scripture messages printed on the outside of the bag, with pictures and their names.

These lunches were so well received by the moms and children in the motel. Their hearts were touched to see how much the school kids cared about them—and for some, the lunches became their meal of the day.

Our volunteer doctors also add a dimension of assistance that is invaluable. One chiropractor wrote and told us it had been a dream of his for a long time to help abused and homeless women to learn a skill and become self-confident and self-supporting. He had overcome a background of abuse and abandonment and understood the devastation it causes.

He and his wife set up a classroom three nights a week in our office workroom. The women from our shelters who attended the classes and successfully completed the course were presented with a certificate which entitled them to work as a chiropractic assistant in a doctor's office.

Medical doctors and dentists have also generously offered services to our residents. Some of the women and children who have had problems that were neglected for years, have received excellent care that restored their dignity and self-image.

God seems to know where all the volunteers are and sends them at just the right moment of need, and the need is met. It happens over and over.

For example, Saturday, March 28 was the day the new carpet was to be installed in every room in a shelter both upstairs and downstairs. It was also the day we had to empty our rented storage unit at another location. We had contracted with the carpet installer to have all of the furniture out of the rooms and the pad already laid. We had no idea how we would manage to move all that furniture out of the house, then put it back in when they were through, as well as go to the storage unit and empty all the furniture from there into a huge semi trailer. As we pondered this situation on Friday, March 27, the very hour we discussed it the phone rang and a young man said, "This is Joe Florentine. There are about five guys in my Bible study who would like to help you. They are all ex-football players so if you need anything moved, we can do it. Can you use us?" You can imagine our joy. They came the next day and worked all day long. Their remark as they left was, "You have worn out five good men!" They had worked hard.

At Christmas the holiday volunteers are always excited. The presents are coming in to be wrapped, beribboned, and put in the appropriate child's bag. Boxes that hold the gifts of every kind line the office walls, full and overflowing.

When we try to thank any of our hundreds of volunteers they all say it is a labor of love, and that they receive far more than they give. One volunteer said it this way:

"As a volunteer with The Sheepfold, I have felt that I have been more the recipient, rather than the giver. It reminds me how very small my world is, and as I think of the other volunteers during the month, I pray for each of them. At The Sheepfold, there is a hidden support system behind the scenes. Not only do they extend warmth and security to hurting mothers, but they provide a nurturing base for the volunteers as well!"

Our residents all receive help and thoughtfulness from volunteers in some way, seen or unseen.

One mother was especially needy and grateful:

"I had just learned I was expecting my baby when my alcoholic husband quit his job to stay home and drink. He had already defaulted on three months rent and utilities, resulting in our being served a three-day eviction notice. With nowhere to go and armed only with my faith in God and a list of phone numbers for service organization, I located The Sheepfold. It became home for the five kids and me.

"Had The Sheepfold not been there for us with its gentle caring hands of the Lord, I'm not sure we could have made it. We had been cut off from our friends due to location changes and circumstances, and had no family in the area. The Sheepfold became more than a shelter in the time of storm.

"Later, when we found our apartment, The Sheepfold's role in our lives changed, but did not cease. Through the difficulties of high blood pressure, diabetes and tests after tests, I was supported emotionally, physically, and spiritually. Volunteer groups of young adults came once a week to clean my apartment and assist me with the other children, giving me much needed rest. Our apartment was fully furnished, largely in part through friends of The Sheepfold (we had lost nearly everything during the eviction and my husband's selling things for booze). Transportation to the hospital for tests was provided when my van conked out. Repairs for the van were also provided by volunteers of The Sheepfold. When I was finally hospitalized for the Caesarean birth, one of Sheepfold's employees stayed with my children at night, affording me great peace of mind.

"The Sheepfold has truly become our family. My children remember fondly their stay at the shelter, a time which could have been extremely traumatic for them. They speak lovingly of Sheepfold's people and regard them as aunts and uncles.

"My faith has been strengthened because of the obedience of the children of the Lord through The Sheepfold. I named my new baby Faith so I would always remember all they did for us."

Barbara S.

Through the years there have been thousands upon thousands of volunteer hours of labor, love, and sacrifice that have brought this ministry to where it is today. They have given of themselves and their material possessions to further God's work. It is wonderfully impossible to list all the volunteer work being done. But, whether listed or not, it does not go unnoticed by us or by God.

And, it has all been done, and is being done with no expectation of reward other than God's promise in Hebrews 6:10: *"For God is not unrighteous to forget your work and labour of love, which you have shown toward His Name, in that you have ministered to the saints and do minister."*

The

NINETEENTH

Chapter

The administration and leadership of this ministry is important, but the heartbeat that keeps it alive is the daily care of the women and children in the shelters, given by the house managers. Unique among women, they are called of God to serve the widows and the fatherless. They are the front line of this ministry.

Every shelter has three paid house managers. They alternate day, night, and relief shifts 24 hours a day, 7 days a week. They are the unsung heroines who transform lives and heal broken hearts by the power of love on a daily basis.

We receive notes and letters from grateful mothers and children who are staying in our shelters and are being loved by them through the season of despair and hopelessness that follows abuse and abandonment, and from those who have completed the program and moved on with their lives.

"The Sheepfold's house managers' support, and their faith in God, has changed my life and so many others. May God Bless them.

"My life was such a mess, and the mess just kept piling up. By the time I was fifteen and a half I had my first child. After losing custody, I didn't feel like anything mattered. I hated my life. I was introduced to a drug called crystal meth and for four years my life was on a roller coaster that wouldn't stop. Living from place to place where the drug was part of the life style.

"When I was twenty I got pregnant with my second child. After deciding to keep the baby I stopped using drugs. I had the desire to do good, but didn't know how! I started to work, but then I started getting high again. Struggling to make it on welfare, I was always having to depend on others.

"Getting high was my way of escaping the fact that I was not just letting down my little girls, but myself. For years my mom would tell me about God, but I seemed to think I could do O.K. without Him. I was partying, but not having any fun. I became depressed. My daughter at two and a half seemed to be out of control, or was it my life? I started to realize how much damage I was doing to her and it started to eat at me! But I didn't know any way out.

"One night after getting high and having nowhere to go I decided to talk to God. I asked Him, "Please Lord, no matter what happens, please don't let my daughters suffer from my mistakes." I wanted Him to protect my little ones from all the damage I was causing them in my life.

"The Lord heard and answered that prayer. In order to protect my daughters, He had to change me. The day I came to The Sheepfold, I asked Him into my heart. It's amazing what God can do once you allow Him to. He has blessed me from that day, cleansed me of my past sin, hurt and guilt, and has reunited me with my family.

"The Lord working through The Sheepfold has given me so much more in my life then I could have ever imagined. I now have a future; and excellent job with Bank of America; and money saved for my own apartment. Thank you Jesus!!"

M.E.L.

"Dear Ladies of the Sheepfold,

"Where do I begin? I just want to say thank you from my heart for letting me be so blessed to be in this home. I am in awe everyday at the meals I receive, the fellowship, the room I have and most of all my son being fed and provided for. I wish I could let the unfortunate women who don't know about The Sheepfold know of its ministry. When I came in to your office in the rain, I had no idea what God had in store for me. I was heart-broken, devastated from the loss of job and home, and the abusive relationship, and felt hopeless. But my life has already taken a new course. The ladies who work here are to be commended on their work. This isn't an easy task and they have been a great blessing and witness. I can't extend my gratitude in any words! God bless you!"

Kelly and Cameron

"When my mom died when I was ten, I said that if there was a God, I hated Him and blamed Him for my deep loss. I didn't want that kind of God around me. I had a hard heart and I trusted no one!

"I tried to replace my emptiness with relationships that either hurt me physically, emotionally—or both. I have made many decisions that hurt me and my children.

"But now God has put love in my heart, softened it and changed it. No one has ever touched me like Jesus. Thank you Lord and thank all the women that have subjected themselves to serving Jesus Christ at The Sheepfold shelters.

"I found hope, and new beginning here. I'll be employable and have a new fresh start; and a future life serving God."

Inez & daughters

The residents often write poems about a house manager from their hearts. Cindy was especially talented and grateful:

I am black but beautiful
Says the lovely Shunamite
Girl, in the Song of Solomon.
But there is one who knows
She is black and beautiful
For Jesus shines from her face.
She's loving, gentle, kind,
And I wish I was
More like her!
When she says to
My small son, 'Hello
Sir,' and hugs him,
It makes me warm
All over. She's a very
Bright light for our Lord.
She has a heartfelt
Compassion, and a
Sparkling, humorous soul.
"Her wit is quick, sharp
And alert. In her you
See her teacher Mom
Alight with fun and
Alert for trouble, she
Keeps us on our toes.
Ever aware that idle
Hands are the devil's toy

We all stay joyfully busy.
She dances even as
She walks, loving all
Who come her way.
She has much to give,
Correcting gently and
Prompting with smiles.
She asks no more of
Others than of herself
And so it's easy.
For you know it's because
She loves you so much.

Cindy

The children's notes to their house managers are especially touching:

"To my Sheepfold House Manager

"Thank you for praying for me. It really helped me and my mom. I think that Jesus gave you that message to ask me why I get so mad or sad. Before we get to the personal things, I want to say that you are pretty and have lots of faith in your heart. You're a really good friend and I will miss you when I'm gone and I'm sure you are going to miss me also.

"Now it's time for the personal stuff. Well, before she came here, my mom used to cuss a lot and lose her temper and I would get scared that she would spank me. At the Sheepfold she loses her temper sometimes when Brett and I fight and I get scared that she will spank me and I'm still scared to tell her some of the personal stuff because I would be scared.

"But, I'm really blest that you're at this house. Well, got to get running. If I write to you more I'll write too much and I don't have any more paper."

Girl (10 yrs.)

The house managers hear the children say the funniest things, like:

"Mom, there's so much food here, are you sure this is not one of those places where they fatten you up to eat you?"

Brandon (7 yrs.)

"Mom, please pray for me. I have a monster in my heart."

(After a tantrum, and a "time out") Jessica (4 yrs.)

"Can we eat all the vegetables in Veggie Tales for dinner?"

Valerie (3 yrs.)

"I pray for the world, for animals, all the hurt people, for food, and for cats who eat rats."

Blake (5 yrs.)

Even after they leave, the moms often write and tell us how they are doing:

"Now that we have our own apartment, I use the rules I learned to guide my children and keep organization on a daily basis, especially the meal time rules. Interesting how I could live my whole life and not have learned as much as I did in four months at The Sheepfold. Having positive enforcement and guidance through God's love is incredible and I hope to pass it on."

"Before I came to Sheepfold, I was trying to work, take care of five kids, do all the cleaning, pay all the bills and put up with yelling and mental abuse from my husband. My body started to react. I got short of breath, heart palpitations, pain in my chest, light headed. One night my husband got very violent with me in front of the kids, they were all scared and shaking. I hollered at them to call the police. The police came and took my husband to jail for four days. I called my Pastor, he told me to go to Sheepfold and I made the most important call in my life. The Sheepfold became a place of rest and restoration for me."

—⊸⌒⌣—

"The Sheepfold has brought me closer to the Lord and they helped me get in touch with my feelings and to find myself. I found out I can't do everything without the Lord. I found that special love that I have never experienced before. I feel appreciated and special."

—⊸⌒⌣—

"I thank the Lord every day for The Sheepfold. Being there gave me hope and built up my faith. They taught me that when one door closes, another will open. That encourages me to live God's way. And through God I can now be the mother He wants me to be and I want to be."

—⊸⌒⌣—

"After only eight days at the Sheepfold, I got a new job; I'm paying off my bills and saving money to get my own place. I thought it was impossible to pay my bills and never thought I could save any money."

—⊸⌒⌣—

"The word 'Sheepfold' is so beautiful because it is so true. We're like sheep that are lost and the Shepherd finds them and keeps them safe from harm. And He feeds them to make them strong, and when they are able to stand, He releases them to go out the door of the sheepfold. We are not afraid when we go out of this Sheepfold, because we know God is with us. We have learned to trust in God when the storms come."

The Lord is the Shepherd of the Sheepfold. *"He shall feed His flock like a shepherd: He shall gather the lambs with His arm, and carry them in His bosom, and shall gently lead those that are with young."* –Isaiah 40:10,11

Being a house manager requires so many skills. Every experience she has had in her lifetime will be used in her work. It is impossible to list the hundreds of little things that come up.

In the shelter her day begins at 7:00 A.M., cooking breakfast for ten to fifteen women and children, and making lunches for those who have to go to school, or to appointments. After supervising kitchen cleanup, she teaches the daily Bible study, being sensitive to the spiritual needs of the residents who come from all different backgrounds.

Then she oversees the housekeeping assignments given to the residents, while she is answering the phone, watering, reviewing schedules and going over rules with the residents, doing house laundry, and making lunch. After lunch she puts donations away in the food pantry and clothing room, folds laundry, keeps records of residents for the office, calls in her needs for supplies and food, settles disputes among children and sometimes among the moms, takes in new residents sent by the office, gets the new family settled, and fixes dinner.

A house manager has the unenviable task of blending mothers and children who are emotionally distraught over their lives, and are complete strangers to each other, into a group that respects each other, and still maintain an atmosphere of peace and joy in the house, while walking the fine line between exercising authority, and showing love.

She cannot be moved by her emotions to give more attention to those whose stories are more tragic than the others. She must always be fair and give equal attention, even though one or the other may have very severe circumstances and greater need for emotional support.

One house manager wrote this little glimpse of a shelter morning:

"It's a new day, and a new family will arrive within the hour. Everyone is busy getting ready for their day. One mom is doing her laundry; another mom is learning to discipline her child by putting him in a "time out." Another is busy feeding a crying baby that won't wait any longer for his bottle, and the other moms are cleaning. Then the new family arrives!

"They are scared and the children ask their mom why she is crying and they want to know if they are going to live here, or if it's just for the night. They have not eaten lunch, so soup and sandwiches sound really good, especially if you add chips!

"Mom eats, but is very emotional, asking how could she have made so many bad choices that have affected herself and her children. She tried so hard but it wasn't enough to make things work. She tells the house manager that if she had listened to her husband and had done everything he wanted he wouldn't have had to hit her. Her thoughts are so distorted that she really thinks that it's OK to be hit.

"Now her little three-year-old gets upset and slaps mommy in the face. This child has witnessed daddy hit her several times and has learned that this is what you do to mommy. Mommy doesn't know what to do about what has just happened so she does nothing. She thinks that because they have lived in a bad environment she owes it to her children to not discipline them.

"We find out her definition of discipline is to scream and yell at the child and use words that hurt or degrade. Words like 'You are bad,' or, 'I don't love you, so I'm going to give you away' until the child is crying, 'Please love me mommy, don't send me away.'

"Slowly this new mom will learn that this is not the way that God intended for her and her children to live. She will attend Bible studies every day and come to realize that she is valuable. She will no longer use the same destructive words to speak to her children, and she will learn that discipline with love is a good thing.

"She has a lot to learn, so Lord, I am very glad that You are the one who undoes all the damage. Thank you, Lord, that as a house manager I get the fun part, I get to love them!"

Another wrote a few of her first experiences as a house manager:

"When I started working at The Sheepfold, I asked myself what it would be like to work with the women and children who come here. Now God has shown me what The Sheepfold is all about.

"It's providing a home for a diabetic who hasn't eaten in two days and is so weak that she can't carry her six-month-old son into the house.

"It's going through donated clothing to find something for a woman and her two children to wear because they fled from their home in terror of an alcoholic husband.

"It's watching a mother and her four children hungrily eating three helpings because all they've had in two weeks is what they have stolen or picked off fruit trees.

"It's going to UCI hospital to pick up a 51-year-old woman from Hawaii whose scheduled twelve-hour cancer surgery has been postponed and she has nowhere to go, no money and no family, so the hospital called us.

"It's watching an eleven-year-old mature too quickly because she's had to be a parent to her five younger sisters as mother helplessly fought the loneliness and fear of no one wanting a 31 year old woman with six children.

"What's The Sheepfold? It's the joy of introducing abused and discouraged women and children to Jesus Christ, and knowing that at last they have found real love.

"It's baking a cake for a seven-year-old who's celebrating her birthday for the very first time.

"It's falling into bed at night, weary, but joyful that you've helped in some way to alleviate suffering.

"Everyone approaches their job in a different manner. Mine was organization. I embarked on my new career much like a ship captain taking command of his vessel—fully anticipating cooperation and understanding from my little crew of homeless women. I imagined they'd all be neat and tidy, on time, interested and awake during Bible studies, excited about going to go to church and totally enamored with my cooking. I also assumed they'd know how to make their beds, do the dishes properly and be capable of sorting their own clothes on their laundry day. But, frequently they were unable to perform these simple functions.

"As I became acquainted with the women and began to delve into their past, I discovered the key to some of the apathy and hopelessness they frequently displayed. If you've been kicked around and put down your entire life, it is very difficult to grasp the concept of a loving Father in Heaven who knows when even a tiny sparrow falls to the ground.

"Many of the ladies have lived in parks, or similar places; staying there until the police moved them on. How could an individual be expected to make a bed appropriately when possibly they'd never had one of their own. Others had suffered severe abuse—both physically and verbally and were reduced to feelings of total inadequacy.

"Stories were shared with me as to what it was like to sleep in a laundromat, bus station or underground parking structure—huddled together with their few possessions in an endeavor to stay warm. Taking turns keeping vigil throughout the night to prevent being raped or arrested for child negligence. My tolerance level increased significantly as I looked into the faces of children deprived of the joys of

childhood and forced to assume responsibilities way beyond
their years."

It is one thing to talk to homeless people and give them
referrals, or bus passes, or money, but it's quite another thing to
actually live with them and have the job of trying to blend a
house full of strangers from all different ethnic, educational, religious, and environmental backgrounds, with different customs,
and cultural differences into a smooth-running household.

It is difficult to be the one person in the house in authority over women and children who are often resentful because
at first they don't understand the need for rules and authority.
A house manager must always be adjusting to, and learning,
the personalities and habits of each new person.

It is an extremely difficult job, and we are very proud of all
of our house managers. It is difficult to find women who can
fulfill all of these requirements and who love God so much that
they are willing to be servants to the suffering. It's letters like
Sandy's that keep them going:

> "I was totally exhausted and scared when I came to The
> Sheepfold. I had been running away from God, my life had
> no real meaning...I was ready to quit. The house manager
> took me under her wing and brought me to know the Lord.
> He healed me from drugs, He took away the desire. He gave
> me His love, He reached out His hand and picked me up.
> The Sheepfold taught me the meaning of God's Love and
> what God is all about!"
>
> Sandy

To sum it up, a shelter manager has to have the unusual
ability to live with strangers, serve them, administer authority
with love, manage house cleaning, food preparation and storage, laundry and yard, teaching daily Bible studies, giving wise

counsel, comfort and encouragement to emotionally wounded women and children.

In order to help the house managers I was able to write a manual, by the grace of God, which includes detailed instruction on all phases of shelter management and resident care. The manual is entitled "The Shepherd's Staff" and it encompasses every phase of Christian-based shelter management and operation.

The Holy Spirit gave me the way to write the manual so that it could have universal use and understanding, not just for our organization but for any person, group, or organization that wants to operate a shelter or shelters. The manual is adaptable to any size facility, and to any target population of residents: women and children or homeless two-parent families, single men, single women, teenagers, unwed mothers, etc.

Used as a base, it can be easily adapted to any type of homeless ministry whether the cause be domestic violence, loss of employment, abandonment, or any other cause. Alcoholism and drug abuse require specialized treatment, which is not covered. However, the manual can be used for the operation of a facility for them.

"The Shepherd's Staff" is a compilation of our twenty-three years of shelter organization, administration, staffing, and program services for the residents, including all the printed forms we have developed. We are eagar to share this treasury of knowledge to give a jump start to people wanting to start new shelters, and stability to existing ones. We pray it will encourage more and more shelter agencies to open for homeless and hurting people who need them.

The manual came into being as I sought the Lord one day for new and more powerful ways to accomplish the restoration and daily care of our homeless mothers and children, and Mark 4:8 came into my mind, *"And some seed* [Word of God] *fell on good ground and bore fruit, some thirtyfold, some sixtyfold, and some hundredfold."*

That made three perfect phases—thirty days, sixty days, and one hundred days, adding up to a six-month stay, which was a perfect length of time.

Our residents begin the thirtyfold phase when they enter the shelter. This is basically a time of learning the household routine, doing assigned chores and beginning to learn or renew their relationship to the Lord, doing Bible studies, and seeking employment and child care if she is able to work.

Part of our recovery program for the women is learning accountability and responsibility for themselves, and teaching them parenting skills and how to discipline their children with love.

We give every woman a checklist of the papers she needs to have to demonstrate this accountability and responsibility. She is helped to obtain any necessary legal papers, medical and government cards, immunization and school records, job history, financial papers, birth certificates, and housing information, if she does not have them.

During the sixtyfold phase, the resident will apply the Word of God to her daily life, in order to take responsibility for her situation, seek practical solutions to her needs, and plan obtainable ways to reach her goals. She will be helped in every area of her need to learn any life skills that she lacks, establish sensible goals for herself, set priorities, find employment or attend job training, and get her GED if she doesn't have one.

She will be taught to tithe, keep a savings account, stick to a budget, apply new single-parenting skills, discipline her children with love, handle money, and build her self-confidence one step at a time.

The hundredfold phase is the victory phase. This phase prepares the resident to obtain her own place to live and be able to keep it. She will follow a customized budget plan to save money before and after she has left the shelter. She will be helped to find transportation. Cars are often donated and given to moms. She will be helped to find and move into an apartment and find a church near her new home. Our "exit" program will take her through the final steps and stay in close contact as she makes the transition to independence.

When she completes the Mark IV program successfully, our goal is that she will have gained the ability to apply the Word of God to problems that arise, be able to handle money in a scriptural way, have learned parenting skills, have forgiven but will avoid the abusers in her life, be able to discipline her children firmly with love, to love God and believe that God loves her, be once and for all off the rolls of the homeless, and will no longer be a statistic, but a vital Christian woman proclaiming victory in Jesus!

This complete manual is available on The Sheepfold website and can be downloaded, ready to use or adapt. It is copyrighted, and cannot be reprinted for sale, but it is free to anyone.

Printed Bible studies complete with questions and answers that we use in our shelters are also available on the website or from the office. They are Christian and Bible-based, but they are non-denominational. I geared them to the need for practical application to the wounded lives of abused and homeless women and children dealing with the issues they face and their painful experiences in light of the Word of God and the love of Jesus.

They are designed for women's shelters to be taught in individual or group setting with each woman having her own copy to keep. There are over eighty studies keyed to abused women and they have proven to be very effective. They are a way for the house manager to lead a daily Bible study, with a new topic of study each morning, without having to prepare one every day. She has enough to do.

They can be easily adapted for any shelter population and type of housing offered.

We offer everything free of charge because Jesus said, *"Freely you have received, freely give."* Matthew 10:8

The

TWENTIETH

Chapter

The mothers who come to The Sheepfold are among the bravest and most courageous women I know.

Knowing some of the issues they face, I question if I would have the strength that they do to go through them. A woman alone, without money, without a job, with children, pregnant, and facing the prospect of having another child to provide for could understandably look for ways to free herself of that added responsibility. It is too overwhelming to face.

There is much talk about "pro-choice" being a woman's choice to choose abortion, but pro-choice is also a destitute and homeless woman's choice to keep her baby, against all odds, and trust in the Lord to help her.

We received a phone call from a lady with a five-year-old daughter. She lost her home and had been bouncing from friend to friend's houses and motel to motel. She was calling at her check-out time from the last motel and didn't know where else she was going to go. She had called a referral line and they gave her The Sheepfold number.

After being accepted she just started to cry. She told us that she was five months pregnant and had an appointment to terminate her pregnancy. She felt so pressured by all her friends to get an abortion. The baby's father had deserted her. She was told she had no right raising another child in her condition of homelessness. She didn't want an abortion deep down in her heart, but felt like she didn't have any other options.

The Bible studies showed her the value of human life in God's eyes and four months later a newborn little lamb came into the fold. When she read Psalm 139 she realized how wrong it is to say that an unformed baby is just a blob of tissue. The Word of God saved the life of the child.

"Your eyes saw my substance, yet being unformed, and in your book all my members were written, when as yet there were none of them." Psalm 139:16

When Sylvia came to us she was barely eighteen years old. She had a little girl already and was pregnant with another child. She had little education and no one to turn to.

She rejoices and praises God now for opening the door at The Sheepfold. She came into the shelter on a Friday, and had an appointment to have an abortion on Sunday. In her distress she knew no other way out.

As the house managers began to minister to her, they restored her hope and began to show her in Scripture the reality that her unborn child was created in the image of God. Now, as she looks in the face of her beautiful son, who came so close to not being born, she understands the reality of life and is forever thankful she did not do something she would regret.

So many people gathered around to be supportive of her because she was so alone. The shelter had a baby shower for her, and she received all the baby's needs. She named him Roman because that became her favorite book in the Bible.

She kept her son and would not give him up for adoption. She went to special classes during her stay with us to get her GED (high school diploma).

She put her faith and trust in God, knowing He would make a way for her to support her little family as she was faithful to seek Him first in her life.

Lisa came to us with her four-year-old daughter. She had had four abortions and was considering the fifth when she came to us. She started drinking and taking drugs when she was sixteen years old. Her parents were divorced. Lisa and her brother lived with their mother, but mother was never home. There was no one to tell them what to do or what not to do. In her own words she said, "I have lived in the drug world over half of my life."

Before she came to us she had been struggling to find places to live, going from motel to motel, staying until her welfare check ran out, panhandling on the streets to pay her rent.

She did not want to go to a shelter because pride got in her way, and also because she was so scared, not knowing what to expect or how she would be treated.

But finally, the day came when she was homeless, on the streets, and tired of it, messed up on drugs and so sick from them that she wanted to give up. But concern for her little daughter caused her to set her pride aside and call a shelter. She expected living in a shelter to be something awful, but in her own words,

"It turned out to be very beautiful. The house managers are very sweet and the food is delicious. I have received Jesus into my heart and I am continuing to study His Word.

"I feel more contented and secure. I can think more clearly now that I am off drugs. Having Jesus in my heart makes me feel brand new. I no longer feel alone and empty. I have a brand new Father in my life now.

"The house managers and Jesus showed me what a wonderful person I am. That I thought I never could be. They read to me Psalm 139. It helped to make my mind up on keeping my baby."

Lisa

The whole shelter got involved when Marti had her baby. She wrote:

"God has granted me peace and a precious baby boy. Which is why The Sheepfold is such a God-send. My relationship with God needed healing, and this was just the place to do it, after having two abortions.

"I thank The Sheepfold for the clarity of God's Word revealed to me by your wonderful Bible studies, by your Sunday church services, by your example, and most of all by Jesus Christ—who lives in the house.

"The joy within my soul which I had so longed for has been restored through the grace of God. I'm so happy God brought me there. You have no idea how much the spiritual gifts and the material gifts mean to me.

"What more could somebody ask except for a clean heart and a clean soul and now I have that. Praise God!"

Everything went like clockwork because the whole shelter had gotten together three days earlier and made a schedule of what each person would do when Marti's big moment came.

They wrote out a check list containing the doctor's name and phone number, and the hospital name and number.

One resident, who goes to work very early, was to take her to the hospital if it happened during the night or early morning. And the day house manager was to take her if it happened after 7:00 A.M.

When the baby started coming at 11:30 P.M., the designated driver got dressed, came downstairs, got the check list, called the doctor and the hospital.

They arrived at the hospital at 12:15 A.M. and little Jesse was born at 3:00 A.M.

He had lots of Sheepfold aunts and cousins taking turns holding him and loving him when he came home to us.

There are strong emotions and much controversy regarding a woman's right to have an abortion. I get criticized by some women for my position on the issue, but I am a Christian and believe that abortion is totally against the will of God. Some would argue that the fetus is just a blob of tissue, but if that were true, where does the DNA kick in, and how does it develop from nothing, when the Bible clearly says God sees the moment of conception and writes all the days of that person's life before his outside body parts even grow.

I received a call from a young girl who wanted counseling about having an abortion. I thought she was undecided about whether to have one or not. But, as we talked, she said she thought the baby might have a weak heart, so she didn't want it. I encouraged her to have the baby, and then if she still did not want it, to consider adopting it to a couple who would give the baby a home.

"I don't want to talk to you! You're anti-abortion! I want to talk to someone who will tell me *how* to get *rid* of this baby!" and with that, she hung up.

I put the receiver down, knowing that the precious child she carried in her womb was soon to become a statistic to be added to the million plus babies that will be victims of abortion this year. Also I knew that there would be emotional scars in the mother that she's not even aware of yet.

It is a frightening thing for a woman to be homeless. It is even more frightening if she is homeless with children to provide for; and it is almost unbearable if she is homeless, with children and is pregnant.

This is the point where many women feel forced to give up their unborn child. But, when they find a safe refuge where the Lord restores their future and their hope, mothers keep their babies and there is rejoicing.

Unfortunately, not all mothers receive help in time. The emotional devastation that follows those who wanted to keep their babies remains locked away in their heart all of their life as expressed in the following words written from a mother to her aborted baby:

If I knew then
What I know now,
You never would have died.
I'd have held you close
And nurtured you
And kept you by my side.
I'd have sung you songs
And treasured you
More than silver,
More than gold;
But this song is all I have to give
To the Baby I'll never hold.
I've never written poetry
That hasn't been a praise
To the Lord Who wept with me
And held me through those days.
Jesus, now I'm asking,
I know You hear my plea,
Won't You take my child
In Your Hands,
And hold my Baby for me.

Author Unknown

God said: "*Before I formed you in the womb I knew you; and before you came forth out of the womb, I sanctified you, and I ordained you a prophet unto the nations.*" Jeremiah 1:5

Because God created human beings in His image (Genesis 1:27), and places eternal value on them from the time of conception, it is often difficult for mothers who have had an abortion to forgive themselves. Some feel shame and guilt compounded by low self-esteem that is often already present in their hearts. Most of them were wounded in childhood or grew up with shame.

The forgiveness of herself is what determines a woman's quality of life. She will never really be free until she has forgiven not only herself, but those who neglected, abused, or abandoned her as well.

To forgive is like taking the stinger out after being stung by a bee. You have the ability and the choice to pull it out. If you leave it in, the pain will continue and the wound won't heal.

Unforgiveness is a barrier that keeps the victim within it. It will keep them bound to the past, making the future unattainable.

"I was so lost and unhappy before I came. Since I've been here, God has shown Himself as a loving God, one that understands my loneliness and brokenness and can comfort my pain and renew my joy.

"My husband abused me in every way possible. Sometimes the verbal abuse was so bad and degrading it was worse than the physical abuse because it would last for hours and I would find myself praying to just die.

"As the physical abuse increased, my husband felt less and less remorse about it. This led to rape and that is when I left my husband for the last time. My own husband that I loved so much that I had given my hand in marriage degraded me to the point that I now hated him and myself.

"My two-and-a-half-year-old son was becoming angry and mean because he was so confused and hurt at everything he had seen and heard. I knew I could never go back. And, being pregnant again gave me all the more reason to get out. This is what brought me to The Sheepfold, and thank God this is where I came.

"I have been able to forgive my husband and be healed. God bless The Sheepfold and the vessels He works through to bring hope back to people like me who were broken and lost."

Cathy

"I came from an abusive home life so when I met my husband at seventeen, I felt right at home around his alcohol and drug abuse and the physical abuse.

"My husband brought me clothes he found in dumpsters. Those, and his brother's old clothes, were all I ever had to wear. I was eighteen when my first daughter was born. I frequented churches for food assistance. They ministered to me as they gave me food. That's when I learned about God.

"As the abuse grew worse, six months into my pregnancy, I cried out to God, 'Get me out of here alive and I'll change my life!' Six hours later I slipped out of the house with just the clothes on my back. I was running to my brothers in California to ask how to change my life. They had become Christians. When I got there I accepted Jesus Christ into my life.

"They helped me get my five-year-old girl from her school bus back in Las Vegas, and we returned to California, but my two-year-old was still in Vegas. My emotions were on overload and finances were minus. Into all of this my third child was born. The day after I got out of the hospital, I had to move. My baby was one week old and I was ready to give up and go back to the abuse, even though it would be worse than ever if I went back. I decided to try shelters one more time.

"There was one last name on my list...The Sheepfold. As soon as I started talking to who answered the phone, I felt God's love pouring through her to me. She really listened to me!

"When I came, the staff started teaching me about Jesus and how to have faith and forgiveness. I contacted several resources for information about how to get my two-year-old girl back. I had not seen her for five months.

"Doors began to open as I prayed. My husband and his brothers were illegal aliens and had broken some laws. Immigration Service told me to be in Vegas in three days and when they picked them up they would hand me my daughter. The house managers said they would watch my children. The office paid for my bus ticket and all the phone calls.

"The night I got there they were going to my husband's house. They said that someone just had to open the door and they would have the right to arrest them and take Monika to me. This was a one shot thing. NO room for error or they would take off. When I got to the hotel I called the detective that was going to arrest him. There was no answer. I had to wait and pray and trust God. Two hours later the phone rang. I said, "Hello" and I heard, "I've got Monika." It was the detective. I thanked God profusely.

"Being a new Christian, this was a whole new way of life for me, to see prayer and faith in action. God is awesome! Without The Sheepfold all this could not have happened."

In His Love,

Brenda, Chrystal, Monika and Austin

Another woman found forgiveness and a new beginning:

"I had given up on life. I asked God to take my life because I was tired of living the shame, the disappointment and stress of anger.

"My family had abused me mentally and physically, but most of all my father that I had looked up to and thought was God sent.

"My father, two uncles, and grandfather had sexually molested me. They told me that this is right in God's eyes, that if I don't, then God won't love me anymore. Through all of the shame and the guilt they felt, my grandfather and one uncle got saved by God.

"I had went to the doctor, and he had told me I had a tumor growing in my ovary and needed surgery or I would die. But in my mind and soul I was dead already. I had already gave up on life. I was waiting for the end of my life. Even when I knew Brittany that is ten months needed me, my daughter, my sweet daughter.

"I prayed to God to send someone to help me. I was given the number to The Sheepfold by a sister in Christ.

"Through all the tears and the heartaches, the Sheepfold have gave me an entire new attitude about myself and a new beginning in Jesus Christ.

"He has healed me of my tumor, and now my daughter and I have a wonderful relationship like never before. And every morning when she wakes up she wakes me up with a smile. With that I can make it through anything in Jesus name.

"I bless Fran and what The Sheepfold is about. Healing the soul and giving you a new beginning.

"And for the ones that's been in this situation or are going through it, GOD LOVES YOU. And don't feel ashamed because it is not your fault. Be strong in the Lord for you are a diamond in God's eyes."

A grateful resident

Dolores experienced mental, spiritual, and physical healing:

"Before coming to the Sheepfold, I was merely existing. Everything went wrong for me. My life was out of control. Just when I thought things couldn't get worse they did. I found myself out on the street with three children and one who was ill. I called many shelters only to hear 'I'm sorry, we're full and others are ahead of you.' I was living in the car going from gas station to gas station, or restaurant, to plug in my youngest son's breathing machine every three hours. He had severe asthma. I was very discouraged, thinking I would have to give my children up so they could be cared for and have a warm bed to sleep in.

"I had one number left. It was late in the day but I was desperate. I picked up the phone and a friendly voice said, 'Sheepfold.' I explained my situation and was asked, 'If we can't see you today, will you have to sleep in your car?' I said yes and she told me to come on in. That night we had a full stomach and a warm bed to sleep in. So many wonderful things have happened since then. I finally started seeing my life turn around. Everything started looking up. Everyone prayed over my son that he might be healed from his asthma and since being at the Sheepfold he has not had one asthma attack. In fact, the breathing machine he used to use every three hours has been packed away.

"I myself have received a healing. I was diagnosed with cervical cancer. I told my doctor I wanted a second opinion. He made me an appointment with a specialist who ordered more tests. After all the tests I had five days to wait for the results. I was prayed for and the day I was getting my results, the doctor came in and said, "I don't understand this but all your tests returned normal." I told him I understood. I said that I had received a healing. He just looked at me and smiled.

"I know now why every other shelter was full. I was supposed to come to The Sheepfold so all these wonderful things could happen.

"Without Jesus I couldn't live a happy life. After all, He gave me life twice. How many people get that chance? Without The Sheepfold I wouldn't be what and where I am today. Thank you!"

Dolores and family

It is only by the grace of God that we all have a second chance. Grace is the divine influence on our heart, and its reflection in our life. Forgiveness is possible because of God's grace.

Jesus set the standard when He said on the cross, *"Father, forgive them, they know not what they do."* The innocent have to pay the price of forgiveness. True forgiveness mentally tears up the evidence of what was said or done to us and is silent. It does not accuse the person who caused the hurt by telling them we have forgiven them. They don't know how much they hurt you and telling them only causes more hurt.

Victims of abuse have much to forgive others for; things that most of us will never endure. Fear of that abusive person's ability to hurt them, or seeking to somehow win that person's approval will keep them in bondage until they are able to accept the all-encompassing forgiveness of Jesus Christ. Applying His forgiveness will cover every painful memory that lives in our thoughts.

Applying forgiveness will soothe, cover, and protect us from anything that irritates, aggravates, or puts us in subjection. No matter how long the problem has existed, or how deeply embedded it is in our personality or engrained in our mind, the spiritual "mother of pearl" of forgiveness will cover it if we deal with it as a spiritual matter and not keep trying to deal with it by ourselves.

That irritating memory or painful thought can become a pearl of great value if we will coat it with forgiveness every time it presents itself in our mind. There is no painful memory, no matter how disturbing, that forgiveness cannot cover.

The only way to recover is to re-cover the memories by accepting them and internalizing them as part of our lives. They happened. That cannot be changed—every time they resurface, choose to cover them with forgiveness.

It's our choice. A memory can remain an ugly, painful grain of sand, or it can become a pearl.

I know because I have a string of those pearls myself.

"Let all bitterness, wrath, anger, clamor and evil speaking be put away from you with all malice. And be kind to one another, tenderhearted, forgiving one another, even as God in Christ forgave you." Ephesians 4:31

"Bearing with one another, and forgiving one another, if anyone has a complaint against another; even as Christ forgave you, so you also must do." Colossians 3:13

The
TWENTY-FIRST
Chapter

Our twenty-third anniversary has just passed at the time of this writing. During those years over sixteen thousand women and children have come through our doors.

There are hundreds and hundreds of incidents and stories to choose from for inclusion in this book. Every story and incident that I have included was either told, or written, to us by the mother or child themselves. They wrote and spoke from their hearts.

The stories may sound similar because their backgrounds and the results of their stay with us are often similar. I tried to let them convey in their own words the reality of their experiences and suffering. It's hard to put into words the reality of someone who is stronger than you, screaming at you while choking you, punching you, and kicking you; or to describe the destruction to your human dignity and self-worth.

The stories and incidents run the gamut of human emotions; some tragic, some irritating, some humorous, some painful, some tender, and some miraculous. I tried to choose those stories and incidents that best portray what they go through, what issues they face and have dealt with, how we helped them, and how God has changed their lives.

I wish I could tell you all the miraculous changes in the personalities of these moms and their children. I use the word miraculous because they weren't able to change themselves and we couldn't do it on our own. Only when they accepted Jesus as their Savior did they begin to change their old ways of wrong thinking and handling life's problems the world's way.

Not until they learn that they have received total forgiveness, and get a glimpse of the love God has for them that will be theirs forever, which **no one**—no abuser, no molester, no rapist—can take away from them, will they begin to heal and blossom.

Most of the mothers who come to us have no happy memories of their childhood and the mother or father who raised them. It is a contributing factor to a woman being victimized, or suffering the painful consequences of poor life choices, made from a broken heart that searched for love in the wrong way and finally had to reach out for help.

That is why it is so beautiful to watch as their faith and trust in the reality of God's love fills that empty void and they are able to move on in their lives—making faith-based decisions, not emotion-based.

They learn that when a child does not receive the love and nurture of a mother and father it leaves a void that no other human being can ever fill. This helps them understand that only God's love can replace what was lost and it is the lack of reconciliation with Him, the one who created them and loves them, that causes them to be victims of domestic violence, to fail in love relationships, to make poor choices for their life, and to stay in abusive situations.

If we had only been there for one mother like J.B., and her children, it would have been worth it all.

"I was brought up in a family that had problems. My mom drank to try to hide from her own problems, but I never knew whatever they were. We all helped my mom when she was drunk.

"I had my oldest son out of wedlock. When he was one and a half, I met a man and I moved in with him, not knowing about his violent temper.

"The only thing I can say as to why I let abuse happen was I didn't know how to handle the situation. I had fear so instilled in me and I wanted to be a submissive wife. It wasn't in my nature to fight, so I just let things happen to me and I just ducked, cried or ran.

"I used to get hit driving down the street if I happened to look at the person in the next car. I either got slapped or when we got home I got picked up by the throat, thrown down, kicked, punched or whatever.

"Insulting things were said to me about what girls that had children out of wedlock were. He called me obscene names for this. Three abuse-filled months into our marriage, I left. I never had any help, so after three weeks I went back because I was pregnant.

"Things got even worse. Now threats for my life were added and wilder accusations about me with other men. He believed I left him to be with other men.

"During the years that followed, I remained a submissive wife. I would get up at 12 midnight to cook a dinner meal for him and be there so whenever he was in the mood for sexual relations, I had to be willing and ready, no matter what time of day or night.

"During the years, I would leave but always go back, because I thought I couldn't make it on my own.

"I was not allowed to go anywhere because he thought I would meet someone. I could not have conversation with any man, even young boys, because the accusations would start flying from his mouth.

"I could never go to the store by myself or go to a friend's. I was not allowed to have any contact with my family.

"We started going to a church. I began getting closer to the Lord, but my husband got worse and became more physically violent.

"After I was baptized, something was happening to him. It was like Satan was taking him over. I had an eight-inch knife at my throat while I was backed against the washer and dryer. The last time my eyes were blacked something inside me snapped. I knew I would leave and not return.

"The Sheepfold gave me a room in a shelter far away from my husband. My husband has given me the children and moved. I have a good job and can support my kids.

"I have learned the power of prayer. I have regained my strength, my self-worth, happiness and—I'm learning to forgive.

"There's so much joy in waking up knowing that the Lord is ready to take my hand and lead me, and dry my eyes when they're filled with tears.

"God bless The Sheepfold and the ministry that The Sheepfold staff has put upon my heart."

J.B.

"Dear Fran,

"I just wanted to write you to tell you how grateful I am to you for starting this program for people like me. I pray blessing upon blessing for you everyday because you deserve it for starting this ministry for single mothers in difficult situations.

"We truly have been blessed here. And I praise God for opening this door to The Sheepfold for us when every other door shut. I really believe God put me [us] here to find Him again and show me the purpose of my life, and that is to serve the Lord with all my heart, soul, and mind.

"I was finally broken and humble enough to see that Jesus is the way, the truth and the life, and through Him I can do all things. He healed my heart so I don't feel hopeless anymore, or any despair.

"It's the first time in a long time I'm actually happy and feel peace in my heart. I know we'll be O.K. because God is taking care of us."

With all my love and gratefulness,

A.P.

"Dear Sheepfold,

"All those dark memories and fear of being alone were with me yesterday when I came to The Sheepfold. But, this morning I woke up feeling as though a great weight had been lifted; blinders were gone from my eyes and the pain in my heart had been eased by the Lord.

"In just one night with The Sheepfold I have found the feelings of love, kindness and compassion I have been searching for, for eight long and painful years. After just one Bible study I feel differently. Women who yesterday were perfect strangers have become perfect companions.

"I now realize I am not alone; there are others who have the same fears, and once my relationship is true and complete with the Lord, I will never be alone again. I would like to leave you with a thought He has just given me as I write this:

"I cannot fret about yesterday, for it is the past

"I cannot fear about tomorrow, for it is the future

"I can, and will, live in the presence of God today,

"For it is a gift, and that is why we call it 'the Present!'
"Every day is new!"

K.L.

"To The Sheepfold,

"You have given so many women and children a gift that some will never know. You have given my family something we never knew. A chance to be with Christ Jesus. All my tears have turned to joy. All my fears, I now rejoice.

"Where others turned their backs, you've reached out and saved lives through Christ that would of ended up shattered. I cannot tell you in words how grateful and happy your walk has made me and the peace I feel knowing someone loves me. Really loves me.

"Praise the Lord, God bless you and your great ministry."

J.M.

"Dear Sheepfold Ministries,

"I would like to thank you for all the help I received at the shelter.

"It was a great testimony to my father who thinks Christian organizations and churches are only there to get rich. He was astounded that you didn't ask for one cent. He commented on how nicely my children were dressed.

"I am so touched and often cry just thinking about what you guys have done for us. I was completely shattered back in October. I was very deep in despair. I cried out to God—how will I get through this, where will we go, what will happen to us!

"Well here I am ten months later renting a beautiful three-bedroom home. And in between that time I was befriended by the house managers—loved, supported, nurtured in the Word of God, cried with, laughed with and prayed for.

"What was done for me and my two girls will affect us our whole life. Not only now, but will be for eternity, and when the fire tests your works, I'm sure there will be gold."

L. and girls

What a witness to the power of God to change lives and restore hope and joy! Their defeating circumstances brought them to the place of victory—the foot of the cross of Jesus. These lives and hundreds like them will never be the same. Even if they can carry all of their earthly possessions in one plastic bag, they can never be defeated again because they have found something far greater than material possessions. They have found that place of abiding love that we all seek— our eternal home in the heart of God the Father.

The gospel of Jesus is based on the principle of seed and harvest:

"Most assuredly I say to you, unless a grain of wheat falls into the ground and dies, it remains alone; but if it dies, it produces much grain." John 12:24 NKJ

Seeds have potential. Potential is the power of God in seed form. An acorn has in it all the potential it needs to become a mighty oak tree. Every seed bears fruit of its own kind. An acorn cannot choose to be an apple seed.

Only God knows how many apples are in an apple seed, and only He knows how much our seeds of potential will produce. He always plants seeds—not full-grown plants. It's our job to feed them, water them, and cultivate them.

God made the laws of nature and the sum total of the physical forces at work throughout the universe. He has never changed those laws. When they are followed, there is peace and harmony. When they are broken, there is chaos.

Just as He set the laws of nature and physics, He also set spiritual laws for man to follow—commandments that have been in place ever since man was created.

They govern the spirit world as surely as the natural laws and physical laws regulate their worlds. And, just as He has never changed His natural and physical laws, neither has He ever changed His spiritual laws.

It follows, then, that if the breaking of those natural laws brings chaos and disharmony, the breaking of spiritual laws will produce the same chaotic results in our lives.

If we break them, or others break them, there will always be consequences. God does not stop the consequences.

Dealing with those consequences can cultivate the seeds of our potential if we make the right decisions about how to handle them. The decisions we make about those consequences will be the determining factor in our lives. They can either get us into trouble or keep us out of it. They are the rudder that determines the direction our lives will take.

An uncontrolled will results in unintended circumstances, but a deliberate choice to do what we know is wrong, is sin. That's why He sent Jesus—to forgive our sins and see us through the wrong choices made by ourselves, or others, that affect us.

He alone can provide spiritual healing and restoration that removes the power of those consequences to make us stumble. We cannot remove every obstacle, but we we can, by the grace of Jesus, go around it so that it does not become a stumbling block to us. We don't have to spend all of our energy trying to move an immovable object.

If a farmer is plowing his field and he comes to a boulder that cannot be moved, he must plow around it so he can finish planting his field. If he stopped there and spent all his time trying to move one stone, believing he could not go on with his work until it was moved, he would miss out on the potential harvest he would have had from successfully planting his seeds in the rest of his field.

The very effort to get free of the bondages of the past that hold us back from serving God—the struggle to overcome fear of failure, inadequacy, lack of resources, insecurity, and lack of self confidence - brings forth physical and spiritual resources in us which would have remained forever unused, or perhaps undiscovered.

After we have gained a glimpse of the higher and better life God calls us to, we must break the bonds that bind us and hold us back—and reach out to obtain that higher life—or the desire to reach out will soon die if no effort is made to satisfy it.

One small talent with freedom is better for serving God than one genius that is in bondage. As your vision is, so will your life be. All bondage is in one place only—in the mind.

Colossians 2:3,9 says, "*In Christ are hid all the treasures of wisdom and knowledge. For in Him dwells all the fullness of the God head bodily.*"

When we receive Him as our Savior, the Bible says we become one spirit with Him. So we have access to that godly wisdom and knowledge.

Being involved in the lives of suffering women and children has been a journey to my own maturity. There is no doubt that God called me to this ministry. He did not cause the losses and painful circumstances and consequences in my life, but by His grace they became stepping stones into a fulfilling new life.

Of all the people this ministry has helped, I have been the one it has helped the most. I count it an honor to be entrusted with it by God. I have been privileged to be admitted entrance into the souls of wounded women. Their healing contributed to my own.

This is the final chapter of my book, but it is not the final chapter of my life.

There is an eternal chapter that is written when our life on earth is over.

It will be written in heaven or in hell.

Eternal life in heaven can only be obtained by accepting Jesus, God's Son, as our Savior while we are here on earth.

This book would never have happened if I hadn't done that.

I want to end my book with a prayer that something written in it would cause anyone who has not asked Jesus into their heart as Lord and Savior to do it now.

If you will do it, He will be your eternal companion in this chapter of your life and the next.

He has already forgiven your sins when you receive Him, and He will never leave or forsake you, so you can boldly say, "The Lord is my helper, and I will not fear what man shall do unto me." Hebrews 13:6

EPILOGUE

In writing this book I relived all of the things that I wrote. I obtained closure of the painful memories, and found renewed joy in remembering the multiplied thousands of good things, great and small, that only God could have done.

He has been my constant companion in this ministry. He called me to it, He sustained me in it, He comforted me through it, He gave me wisdom beyond my own ability, strength beyond my own endurance, mercy without restraint, faith that is unshakable, and a love that I did not know was possible.

Each time I came to the end of myself, He was there. When I was forsaken and there was no one who could help me, He was there. Whenever fear clutched my heart, He was there. When there was a problem I thought I couldn't face, He was there. When I was sick and felt helpless, He was there.

My sole purpose in writing this book is to give God glory by revealing to others how He can take a woman that is alone, bereaved by divorce, forsaken by family, tired, afraid and unprepared, and use that unpromising material, by the power of His Word and His Holy Spirit, to start a soul-saving, life-changing ministry to thousands of homeless, abused, and desperate mothers and their children.

The choices and decisions I had to make were not always easy. Some of them were misunderstood and criticized, but everyone of them was, to the best of my ability, made in the best interest of the ministry.

Insecurity had an inconvenient way of popping up at those times, but the words of God proved themselves true for me: *"My grace is sufficient for you, for my strength is made perfect in weakness."*

I have mentioned only a few names of staff, board of directors, donors, organizations, churches, friends, or volunteers because there are simply too many, and I know they would rather receive their reward from the Lord instead of public recognition anyway.

I have been blessed to know them all. They made the vision come to pass. Any reward that I may receive on earth, or in heaven, is their reward also. God will not forget their labor of love which they have shown toward His name, in that they have ministered, and do minister, to the lost and hurting.

Through the years I am very grateful that I have had, and do have, godly men and women to serve on our board of directors. They see this ministry as theirs, and guide it with wisdom and prudence in the sphere of influence of their position as board members. They faithfully pray for the ministry and volunteer their services without pay.

Our donors are remarkable. They don't just give, they give from the heart with expressions of love and blessing and encouragement for us and the women and children who are the recipients of their giving.

We do not ask for money. We trust God to touch the hearts of His people. We have never lacked for anything that was needed. Every time we expand, the finances increase to meet the expenses, because He is faithful, and His people are faithful. They care about the widows and the fatherless.

There are five people that I want to especially honor because of their investment of time and counsel in this book and in my life: My son, John Lundquist, who steadfastly encouraged me, kept me on track with his insightful comments, and loved me through it. John Wildman, operations director, who saw the value of the book for the women in the shelter, for the ministry, and for the public. Mrs. K. C. Riley, who faithfully typed and retyped all of the chapters and corrections in manuscript form for the publisher. The whole book was handwritten, so you can understand the magnitude of her work, done with a willing heart because she believes in the message of it. Mrs. Andrea Springer, of The Sheepfold office staff, who typed many of the original chapters, skillfully deciphering my scrawls, arrows, and interjections. And, finally, the person who started me on the "book path" a long time ago, a good friend of mine and of The Sheepfold, Lee DeVore, Chief of Police, Twin Falls, Idaho.

I can testify by my life that the written Word of God is alive and powerful, and that Jesus is the living Word. Because of Him, today I walk in peace, and when my tomorrow comes, and I walk into the heavenly Kingdom of God, I pray that I will hear Him say, *"Well done, thou good and faithful servant."*

Amen

May He bless you, and keep you, and give you peace.

With love in my heart,

Fran Lundquist

To contact
The Sheepfold
P.O. Box 4487
Orange, CA 92863

Telephone: (714) 237-1444

E-mail: mail@TheSheepfold.org

To order

ACW Press
85334 Lorane Hwy
Eugene, OR 97405

(800) 931-BOOK

or contact your local bookstore